"Beautiful."

Something in his tone told her that he wasn't talking about the squirrel, and she turned to look at him. Her breath caught at the expression in his eyes. There was desire there, but there was also love.

"Do you think they have a rule about kissing in front of the animals?"

"I don't know."

The kiss was warm. They drew apart slowly.

"I think I'm falling in love with you," he said. Gwenn's eyes widened in shock, and Chase laughed self-consciously. "Maybe that sounds foolish. We're married. I *should* be in love with you."

Gwenn said nothing, and he went on. "I know there was something wrong with our marriage, even before the kidnapping. I'm not asking what it was. Right now I don't want to know. Let's just enjoy today and not think about the future or the past. Let's have today for us."

Dear Reader,

When two people fall in love, the world is suddenly new and exciting, and it's that same excitement we bring to you in Silhouette Intimate Moments. These are stories with scope, with grandeur. These characters lead the lives we all dream of, and everything they do reflects the wonder of being in love.

Longer and more sensuous than most romances, Silhouette Intimate Moments novels take you away from everyday life and let you share the magic of love. Adventure, glamour, drama, even suspense—these are the passwords that let you into a world where love has a power beyond the ordinary, where the best authors in the field today create stories of love and commitment that will stay with you always.

In coming months look for novels by your favorite authors: Maura Seger, Parris Afton Bonds, Elizabeth Lowell and Erin St. Claire, to name just a few. And whenever you buy books, look for all the Silhouette Intimate Moments, love stories *for* today's women *by* today's women.

Leslie J. Wainger
Senior Editor
Silhouette Books

IMRL-7/85

Dallas Schulze

Moment to Moment

Silhouette Intimate Moments
Published by Silhouette Books New York
America's Publisher of Contemporary Romance

SILHOUETTE BOOKS
300 East 42nd St., New York, N.Y. 10017

ISBN: 0-373-07170-1

First Silhouette Books printing December 1986

America's Publisher of Contemporary Romance

Printed in the U.S.A.

DALLAS SCHULZE

loves books, old movies, her husband and her cat, not necessarily in that order. She's a sucker for a happy ending who's writing has given her an outlet for her imagination and hopes that readers have half as much fun with her books as she does! Dallas has more hobbies than there is space to list them, but is currently working on a doll collection.

For my agent, Pat Teal, who opens doors and quickly shoves my foot in before I can chicken out.
Thanks.

Prologue

Cold. Bitter cold. He felt colder than seemed humanly possible. It was the first thing he was aware of, and for a long time the cold was so pervasive that it was all he could think of. The only clear thought in his mind was that he couldn't possibly be this cold and still be alive.

But if he was dead, he wouldn't know that he was cold, would he? Surely dead people didn't know if they were cold. Of course, he hadn't talked to very many dead people, he argued to himself.

Gradually other thoughts filtered into his mind. He became aware of more than just the cold. There was pain. A great deal of pain. He couldn't feel it now, but he knew it was waiting for him. When he moved, that was when the pain would strike.

The pain waited just beyond the edge of sensation like some great hulking beast, its jaws open and slavering, eager to seize him and drag him down into that pit where he had spent such a long time. He could fool the pain, he thought slyly. If he didn't move, it would think that he was dead and go away.

Remembering the pain made him realize that he must be still alive. Dead people might feel cold, but he was sure that they didn't fear pain. And he feared this pain, feared it as he had never feared anything before.

He could beat the pain by not moving, but if he didn't move, the cold would kill him. He couldn't stay where he was and survive. And he wanted to survive. He had to survive. He had a reason to survive, though he couldn't remember what it was now. Maybe the only reason was a need to beat the monster. If he let the pain take him, it would win, and there was a core of will inside that balked at that.

With a massive effort he managed to lift his eyelids slightly. It was the merest flicker of movement but also a triumph of will. Gradually he opened them farther. The pain surged forward triumphantly, but he fought it back. He would not let it win. He would fight it off, cage it, force it to respond to his determination. He would bend it into a tool to use for survival.

For long moments he was blind to his surroundings as he fought his inner battle. Slowly the creature was subdued. Struggling for control, he forced it back into a corner, and iron bars slammed around it until it could only rage impotently at its confinement.

Only then did he dare to focus on his surroundings. Walls. Dark walls, stained by trickles of moisture. He turned his head cautiously to the side, but there was nothing else. Just the walls. He struggled to sit up, finally bracing one elbow against the hard surface on which he lay and forcing his body more or less upright.

The creature screamed and rattled at the bars of its cage, demanding to be let out, but he forced it back. Someone was whimpering, he realized. The soft sound barely reached his ears. He turned his head, searching for the source of the sound, but there was no one in the room but him. He must be the one who was whimpering. He really should stop, he thought vaguely.

His head fell forward, more by accident than design, but he lacked the energy to raise it again. He sat on a rusted metal cot. The steel bar at the edge bit into the backs of his legs. There was a thin mattress that did an inadequate job of covering the metal springs providing its support.

He was naked from the waist up. A pair of slacks covered his legs. They had once been a pale blue, but now the fabric was a dirty gray, torn and stained with streaks of some dull rusty-looking substance that he vaguely identified as blood. His blood, he thought without interest.

He needed to get up. There was a touch of sluggish urgency in the thought. He needed to get up now, while he was alone. While there was no one to try to stop him. He braced his hands against the edge of the cot and started to rise.

The monster roared in triumph and surged out of confinement. Pain lanced up his arms, and the whimpering became a silent scream of agony. Cold sweat broke out on his body, running down his naked back and chest. His teeth bit into his lower lip until he tasted blood as he fought to swallow the scream that rose in his throat. It was not pride that urged him to silence. It was an unformed but insistent knowledge of the need for secrecy. *They* must not know that he was conscious. So he fought his battle in silence, pounding the pain down to a bearable level.

When he could finally lift his arm to look at his hand, he realized he was shaking—not fine tremors but hard shudders that racked his body. He had to blink several times until his vision cleared enough for him to focus on his hand. When he did, he felt a surge of rage that burned away the shaking and left him still. His left hand wavered in front of his face. One of the fingers was obviously broken, and the palm was covered with raw, red patches that marked recent burns.

He knew without looking that the right hand was much the same, and the knowledge served to clear his mind as nothing else could have done. Someone had done this to him. He didn't know who, but he had to get away from here before they came back.

He turned his head, searching the room. He briefly looked at the door, but it was shut tight, and he didn't have to push against it to know that it was locked. Perhaps he had tried that exit in some dim and forgotten past. The room was bare with gray concrete walls and floor. A naked bulb hung from the ceiling, suspended on fraying wire. Besides the cot, there was only one other item of furniture. His gaze settled on the small stool. Its sturdy homeliness was incongruous in a room that had the aspect of a jail cell.

His eyes narrowed into bloodshot slits of animal cunning. Yes. That would do nicely. But he had to be prepared. He didn't know when they would be coming to check on him, and he had to take them by surprise when they showed up.

He didn't trust his legs to support him, so he slid off the edge of the cot and crawled over to the stool, using it as a brace to pull himself partially upright, and then replaced it with the wall. He came close to passing out several times during the interminable minutes it took him to reach his goal. Each time, he ground his scorched palms mercilessly against the nearest hard surface, using the raging monster of agony to retain consciousness.

Finally he leaned against the wall near the door, the stool gripped in one hand, with his good fingers curled around a thick leg. There was a pleasingly solid heft to his chosen weapon, and he felt a primitive pleasure in having it.

It was fortunate that he had not long to wait. Not even the pain in his hands would have served to keep him conscious for longer. The chill of the room seemed to have seeped into his bones, weakening them and leaving him exhausted.

He was aware that his head was beginning to droop, and his grip on the stool loosened no matter how hard he fought it. The sound of footsteps outside the wooden door revitalized him, snapping him out of the stupor that was creeping over him.

A key rattled in the lock, and he raised the stool over his head, his face set in lines of determination. The door began to open, and he pressed back against the wall. Waiting. He would only get one chance. He had to make it work. Pray there was only one of them.

Moments later, he stood looking down at his victim. He felt a surge of savage triumph. He had won. He had proved himself superior in the most primitive way possible. He had physically beaten his enemy. He stared down at the unconscious man for a moment before turning and staggering out the door. His wavering footsteps carried him up a flight of narrow stairs to a door that yielded to his touch, spilling him out into fresh air. He staggered a few feet, then came up against a pole, and for the time being, he couldn't summon the energy to go any farther. He could only lean against the rough wood and breathe in great gulps of clean air.

It was night. A warm summer night, filled with the diffused brilliance of street lamps. The thought that there might be someone with the man whom he had left in his cell finally gave him the impetus to push himself away from the pole and move down the street.

After that, time had no meaning. It seemed as if he had staggered along forever, though it couldn't have been more than a few minutes. The adrenaline that had surged through him at the thought of getting away was beginning to fade, and it was all he could do to put one foot in front of the other. And he wouldn't be able to do that for long.

The whimpering had begun again. The sound irritated him, and he wished it would go away. Keep moving. One foot and then the other. He had to stay alive. He had to get back to... To what? He couldn't remember, but it didn't matter. All that mattered was that he keep moving.

He staggered around a corner, and suddenly there were lights and people. People all around, moving in, surrounding him. Talking. Shouting. Reaching out. He threw up his arms to shield his eyes from the sudden brilliance of light and color, and he heard someone scream. The noise echoed over and over again in his mind, tumbling through the blackness that swallowed him. The blackness was broken only by the eye-searching flash of red lights and the scream that seemed to follow him down into the pit where the monster waited to swallow him.

He fell helplessly into its hungry jaws, and the agony rolled over him.

Chapter 1

He was once again in a small room where walls filled most of his vision, but that was the only resemblance between this awakening and the first one. These walls were an expanse of creamy white, broken by one window. Venetian blinds closed out the bright daylight outside.

He lay still for a long moment, mentally exploring his body. His head ached slightly, and his hands felt stiff and heavy. They were weighted down with bandages, and he knew that it was uncomfortable to move them, but it was nothing compared to the pain he remembered from his first awakening.

Satisfied with his physical well-being, he turned his attention inward, exploring his mind. The headache immediately intensified until the pain forced him to abandon the attempt. He became aware of a thin film of sweat coating his body. It was always the same. He was all right until he tried to remember, and then the pain would surge forward as if in defense of the barrier in his mind.

The doctor had said that he should give it time, not try to force his memory. But then the doctor wasn't the one who was lying in this bed with no identity. Oh, they had told him who he was, given him the bare outlines of his life, but it was not enough.

Chase Buchanon. He rolled the name around in his mind, waiting for some feeling of recognition, but it meant nothing beyond the fact that they had told him it was his. He ran through the facts he had been given, turning them in his thoughts as if he were reading them off a scroll.

His name was Chase Buchanon. He was thirty-nine years old, an executive at Johnson Industries, a large electronics firm in Los Angeles. A month ago he had disappeared without a trace, and no one had seen anything of him until he turned up on a busy street in Hollywood, looking like a reject from a horror movie. Rope burns on his wrists and ankles made it clear that he had been tied, and the burn marks that covered his hands, along with the bruises and cuts that marked his body, were an indication of what he had suffered during the time he had been missing.

He sat up slowly, swung his legs out of bed and slid gingerly to the floor. He was never quite sure that his legs were going to support him.

The blue silk pajamas he wore had been sent by his wife. His wife. He had a wife he couldn't remember. Somehow that was even more difficult to deal with than the fact that he couldn't remember his own name.

He crossed to the small bathroom and leaned against the sink, studying his reflection as he had done so often during the past week. He still found it difficult to connect the face he saw in the mirror with himself.

Maybe if the face had been unusual in some way, he would have been able to believe that it was really his. But there was nothing to set it apart from a thousand other faces. He was, he supposed, a handsome man. His features were regular. His nose was a little too large, and the thrust of his chin a little too bold, but overall it was a handsome face, in a clean-cut all-American way. Thick reddish-brown hair cut to a conservative length and hazel eyes kept his features from being completely mundane.

He turned away with a faint grimace of frustration. It didn't matter how long he looked at his reflection: he simply couldn't connect it to himself. But then, he couldn't connect anything to himself. He leaned one bandaged hand against the wall and deliberately pressed on it until he could feel pain. It was only a faint echo of the agony he had known when he had awakened in the basement, but it proved that he was real, that he existed.

He moved over to the window and raised the blinds. His view was limited to the hospital parking lot, but he didn't mind. The world beyond this room was a mystery to him, one he was not entirely sure he was ready to explore.

Who was he really? Who was the man that went with the name Chase Buchanon? What had he known that someone had felt was worth kidnapping him for? What had they been after, and—most important—had he given it to them?

He shut his eyes as the pain in his head intensified. He had to stop pressing his mind for answers it couldn't provide. He couldn't force his memory. According to the doctor, there was no physical reason for his amnesia. It had apparently been caused by some emotional stress that was beyond his capacity to handle. His mind had essentially retreated from something it couldn't bear to face, and when he could deal with the stress, his memory would return.

Until then, he was just going to have to learn to cope with the situation. He'd have to take things one day at a time and hope for the best. The first thing to be dealt with was his return home today. The thought of leaving the hospital left him with mixed emotions. He had no desire to stay in this room until his memory returned, but the hospital represented security, safety.

His mouth turned up in a rueful smile. He might as well admit it: he was terrified by the thought of trying to resume a life he didn't remember. He had a wife. How was she going to feel about accepting him back into their home when he was, to all intents and purposes, a total stranger?

He turned his head as the door to his room opened and a man came in. He was short, not much above five feet seven inches, but there was an air of confidence and authority about him that made it easy to forget his size.

His expression had been serious, his dark brows drawn into a frown, but when he glanced up and saw Chase, his handsome features were split by a grin. A grin that the other man had already learned could conceal Robert's thoughts as easily as it revealed his zest for living.

This was his brother-in-law. And, from what he had been told, they were close friends. It had been Robert Lawford who had been the one to give him what information the doctor felt Chase was ready to handle. He'd been the one to explain that the doctor had asked Chase's wife not see him until he was released. He wanted his patient to have some time to adjust to the idea of a wife before he was confronted with the reality. There was also the chance that seeing his wife in the familiar setting of their home might be a key to unlock his memory.

"Chase! Dr. Maguire wasn't sure you would be awake yet. How are you feeling?"

The man he had addressed hesitated a moment before answering. "I'm doing all right. My hands are healing, and the headaches are becoming more bearable. The doctor tells me I can go home today."

"I know. He caught me on the way up. I thought I'd wait to call Gwenn until after I found out how you felt about it."

Chase shrugged and moved over to the bed, seating himself on the edge of it. "I don't know how I feel. I don't have any desire to stay here, but I can't really say that I'm looking forward to leaving."

Robert settled himself into the room's one chair and studied the other man. "Gwenn is really excited about having you home. She spent the first two days after they brought you here camped out on a sofa in the waiting room."

"I hope she won't be too disappointed if I don't remember her. It's a little difficult to picture myself with a wife. In fact, it's a little difficult to picture myself at all, wife or not."

"Give it some time, Chase. Gwenn doesn't expect you to greet her with open arms. She understands the situation.

"Have you remembered anything about the men who kidnapped you?"

Chase glanced up, catching Robert's dark eyes on him. Their intensity belied the casual tone of the question. "Is this my brother-in-law or Detective Lawford asking?"

Robert grinned. "A little of both. The police are stumped on your case so far. No clues, and a victim who can't remember anything. You've got to admit that it makes it a difficult case for us."

"It's not exactly a picnic for me. If I remember anything, I'll let you know. Have you found the basement where they held me?"

"Nope. Your description wasn't enough for us to pinpoint anything. And since you can't remember how far you traveled or in what direction, it doesn't give us much to go on. It would have been nice if you could have left a trail of blood or something," he added wistfully.

After giving him a startled look, Chase reluctantly smiled. There was no resisting the mischievous look on the other man's face. "Next time, I'll see what I can do."

They shared a moment's amusement before Robert got to his feet. "I'd better go call Gwenn and let her know you're coming home. I don't think she'll really believe you're alive and well until she sees you for herself. She was not too happy with the doctor when he suggested that it might be better if she didn't see you right away."

"Let's hope she doesn't regret seeing me when I get there."

With an effort, Gwenn Buchanon pulled her hand away from her mouth. She stared down at her fingernails with a faint rueful smile on her lips. A month ago her hands could have been used as models in a dish soap commercial. Even two days ago, the nails had been short but neat. But when the doctor had told her that Chase was going to be allowed home today, he had signed the death warrant for her manicure.

She hadn't chewed her nails in years. It was a habit that she had thought was buried so deep it would never resurface. It formed part of what Chase had laughingly called her grubby youth. She leaned her head back against the nubbly linen of her chair. Funny, in the weeks since his disappearance, she had found herself calling up every silly little memory of him, things she had forgotten she knew.

It had been even worse since he had been found. The doctor had let her in to see him before he regained consciousness, and Robert had all but carried her out of the room. Seeing Chase lying so still and cold in that hospital bed had been like the realization of all her nightmares. He had looked more dead than alive. She had remembered another hospital, another time, and the still figure that had lain there.

Her eyes snapped open. She was not going to think about that. This time she was not losing someone. She got up and paced to the front window to stare out into the empty street. An anticipatory shiver ran up her spine. Chase. He was alive, alive and coming home to her. She could not suppress the thrill that thought gave her. He wasn't lost to her forever. She would have another chance.

Of course, the doctor had warned her not to expect too much too soon. Chase was weakened, both physically and mentally. It would be months before he was restored to full health, but it didn't matter. He was coming home. She had thought she'd never see him again, but he was coming home.

She had to remember that he might not even recognize her. Amnesia was unpredictable. There was a chance that seeing her would trigger the hidden blockage in Chase's mind, but Dr. Maguire had told her not to expect any miracles. There was no way of knowing exactly what had caused the condition in the first place. It was impossible to predict what might release it.

She put her hands on her upper arms, hugging herself against the inner chill that defied the bright August sunshine outside. Torture. It was hard to really believe that it had happened. Not in this country, in this day and age. Oh, everyone read the horror stories about the terrible things that happened in other nations, but they didn't have any relevance to the world Gwenn had always lived in. Now she was faced with the horrible reality that her own husband had actually been tortured.

She bit her lip to stem the nausea surging over her. Someone had hurt Chase. Why? That was the question that kept haunting her. Chase had never deliberately harmed anyone in his entire life. He didn't work for the CIA or the

FBI. She knew that his company did work for the government and had guessed that it was sometimes very high-level, hush-hush stuff.

She had certainly never thought her husband was involved with something that might get him killed. Chase had never hinted at anything like that. Of course, the lines of communication had not been very good for the past two years. Perhaps there'd been hints, and she had been too blind to see them.

Gwenn turned away from the window and crossed to the mirror hanging between the French doors that opened onto the patio. The mirror had belonged to Chase's great grandmother, and the silver backing was beginning to peel. Chase had suggested that they have it refinished, but Gwenn had insisted that the slightly worn look added to its charm. He had laughed, but he had also put his arms around her and told her that he loved her despite her passion for worn-out furniture.

She blinked to banish the memories and focused her attention on the faded reflection in the old mirror. What would Chase think when he saw her? What must he be thinking, knowing that he was coming home to a wife he couldn't remember? Would he be drawing mental pictures of her? Would she be a disappointment when he actually saw her? She leaned closer, studying her face.

She was still a pretty woman, she decided with satisfaction. Her skin was creamy smooth. The tiny lines that had begun to form at the corners of her eyes were invisible to everyone but her. Her eyes might have lost some of the innocent enjoyment of life that had filled them ten years ago, but they were still a clear smoky gray, fringed by heavy lashes. Her mouth was a little too wide for her oval face, but Chase had always said that it gave her character and saved her from being too perfect.

She put up her hand to the silky fall of hair that framed her features. The color hovered between brown and blond, seeming to reflect the smoky gray of her eyes. She usually wore it pinned up in a simple chignon, but Chase had always loved it down, so today she had brushed it until it crackled around the brush and left it to fall in a straight wave to her waist. Chase might not consciously remember that he had loved it that way, but perhaps he would somehow know that she had done it to please him.

At almost thirty years of age, she still had a very respectable figure. The rose silk of her blouse clung gently to her full breasts, and the soft linen skirt that fell around her too full hips hinted at the curves with admirable tact. Creamy pumps matched the skirt, adding an extra two inches to her five-foot-four-inch frame.

The sound of a car pulling into the driveway made her spin away from the mirror. Her body went rigid. He was here! What was she going to say to him? How was she supposed to react? Car doors slammed, and each concussion echoed in her paralyzed mind.

She moved forward, her steps stiff and forced. Now that the moment was here, she found that uncertainty was her reigning emotion. These first moments were so important. She was essentially meeting Chase for the first time. She had to make a good impression.

She made it as far as the archway that faced out on the foyer. There her courage failed, and she could only wait, one hand clinging to the molding around the door, her nails digging into the wood. The footsteps coming up the path seemed unnaturally loud, like echoes in a dream.

Her pulse quickened, and she could feel her heart pounding against her breastbone as if she'd just run a mile. She wanted them to hurry, and she wanted them to slow down. She could hardly stand to wait another second to see

Chase, and she could hardly bear the strain of seeing him again.

Her heart stopped and then picked up speed as the door opened and her brother stepped into the hallway. His dark brown eyes met the panicked gray of hers. He had time to give her a strained but reassuring smile before his companion stepped in behind him.

Chase did not see her immediately, and Gwenn was grateful for the few seconds this gave her to control her shock. The brief time she had seen him in the hospital had not prepared her for his changed appearance. The pants and jacket she had sent for him to go home in looked three sizes too large. They hung on his frame, giving him the frail appearance of an old man. Both his hands were bandaged, though the bandages on the right were light. One finger on his left hand was broken, and the bandaging was correspondingly heavier there. The doctor had promised her that his physical wounds would heal with time, but seeing him like this, Gwenn wondered if the doctor had lied to her. This man bore little resemblance to her husband.

Then he turned to look at her, and her uncertainty vanished. No one but Chase had ever been able to make her bones melt with even the most casual of glances. The eyes that stared at her were the same green she remembered.

She was barely aware of moving until she found herself halfway across the hall. She came to an abrupt halt in front Chase, rocking up on her toes as she controlled the need to throw herself into his arms.

"Gwenn?" The hesitation in the way he spoke her name told her that he was only guessing at her identity. There was no recognition on his face. Uncertainty. Wariness. But no recognition.

She swallowed the aching disappointment. Until that moment she hadn't realized just how much she had been counting on him knowing her. It didn't matter that the doctor had told her she couldn't expect miracles. She had been sure that he wouldn't have forgotten her, no matter what else had been lost.

She nodded in answer to his questioning tone and put up one hand to touch him on the cheek, contenting herself with that simple gesture when she longed to put her arms around him. He half raised his arms as if to put them around her and then let them fall to his side.

"I don't remember you." The frustration revealed in his flat statement told her that she wasn't the only one who had been hoping for a miracle.

She forced herself to smile, swallowing the lump in her throat that wanted to dissolve in tears. "That's okay. The doctor said it might take some time."

He nodded, his face closed. "So he told me." His gaze left her and moved restlessly around the hall, as if searching for something he could recognize, something to prove that he really was the Chase Buchanon who lived in this house and was married to this woman.

Gwenn felt helpless in the face of his obvious frustration. She threw an appealing glance at her brother. He responded immediately, just as he always had when she needed him.

"Why don't we move into the living room? There's no sense in standing around like we don't mean to stay."

When Chase didn't respond, Robert touched him lightly on the arm. Chase flinched as if the gentle touch had startled him and then looked down at the shorter man. Robert repeated his suggestion, and Chase followed him into the living room where Gwenn had spent the afternoon awaiting his arrival.

Gwenn followed more slowly. She rubbed her palms nervously up and down her soft cream colored skirt. This was going to be even more difficult than she had imagined. On the surface, she had accepted the diagnosis, but there had been no inner acceptance of the fact that her husband had completely and totally forgotten her. He had no memory at all of the years they had spent together.

She watched the two men disappear into the living room, but it was a moment before she could join them. She needed time to regain her emotional balance. The pain of having Chase look at her as if she were a stranger had struck deep. It didn't matter how many times she told herself that it was not his fault and that it was nothing personally directed at her. She still felt as if he had rejected her, as if he had deliberately buried her memory because it offered more pain than pleasure.

Gwenn drew a deep breath and forced herself to move forward again. She couldn't afford to be selfish and she had to remember that Chase needed her help now more than ever, even if he didn't know it. She had failed him once before by pushing him away when she should have reached out. She wasn't going to make the same mistake this time.

When she entered the room, she found that the two men had seated themselves. Robert was on the couch, his compact frame slouched comfortably into a corner, and Chase sat in a chair opposite him. The contrast between the two men was painful. This was Chase's home; he was sitting in a chair that had been his favorite. Gwenn couldn't count the times she had seen him comfortably relaxed in that same place, his long legs stuck out in front of him, his nose buried in a paper. Now he sat stiffly upright, his feet together, his hands held tensely on the broad armrests.

She smiled when he looked up, catching her eyes with his. She walked across the room and took a seat on the sofa near her brother. There was a moment of uncomfortable silence while all three of them searched for something to say. Chase spoke first.

"I'm sorry, but I don't even know how long we've been married."

She smiled at him, trying to ease his embarrassment. "Five years."

He nodded and looked away from her. His discomfort was almost a visible presence in the room.

"Have we lived in this house long? Hell, I don't even know how long we've lived in this state, let alone the house."

"We're both native Californians, and you owned this house when we met. It originally belonged to your grandparents, and you inherited it when they died. We modernized it a bit after we got married."

She felt some of the tension leave her muscles. It wasn't the homecoming she had hoped for, but it wasn't as bad as it might have been. He seemed willing to accept her at face value and just wanted to fill in some of the missing background.

"Nobody mentioned children, so I assume we don't have any." Robert stiffened and threw a quick glance at his sister. Gwenn felt the color drain out of her face, and she clenched her hands into fists until the nails bit into her palms. The faint smile on her face became a ghastly stretching of the facial muscles, without meaning.

If Chase had been looking at her, he would surely have guessed that something was wrong, but his eyes were busy roaming the room in their unending search for something to tell him that he belonged here.

"No children." It was Robert who answered the question, giving Gwenn a few precious seconds to control her emotions.

She couldn't sit here a moment longer, she thought frantically. "I think I'll get us something to drink." If her voice was pitched slightly higher than normal, then only her brother noticed, and the look he threw her told her that he understood. She got to her feet without waiting for Chase to answer and walked quickly out of the room, barely able to control the urge to run.

Once in the kitchen, she leaned against the counter, fighting for control. How could he ask her if they had children! How could he do that to her! Her fingers clutched at the edge of the counter. He couldn't have forgotten Livvie. But as incredible as it seemed, he had forgotten. The doctor had warned her, had even told her that it could be detrimental to his recovery if Chase found out too much too soon. Wasn't that why she had taken the pictures of their daughter and hidden them? So that Chase wouldn't be forced to come to terms with everything all at once?

Her hands were shaking as she eased away from the counter and opened the cupboard to get out glasses. Her movements were automatic, her thoughts in turmoil. It wasn't fair to blame Chase for something he couldn't help. He had no way of knowing how hard that question would hit her. He was just trying to find his way through the confusing circumstances he found himself in. Maybe it was best that he didn't remember Livvie. God knows, there had been enough times when Gwenn had wished that she could forget.

By the time she carried the small tray into the living room she had herself under control, and she was able to smile reassurance in answer to her brother's concerned look. She set the tray down on the coffee table and handed one of the glasses of iced tea to Chase.

"I don't even know if I like iced tea." There was frustration in his comment, but it was laced with rueful amusement.

Robert took a sip of the cool liquid. "Don't worry about it. The only things you won't eat are things that bite back. You've always had the appetite of an undernourished anaconda. Actually, come to think of it, I left my hamster with you when we roomed together in college, and it disappeared. You claimed that it escaped from the cage, but I suspected you might have roasted it for a midnight snack. It seemed a distinct possibility." He gave Chase a friendly grin and swallowed more of his tea.

Chase stared at him for a moment in silence, and then his mouth slowly tilted up at the corners. It was the first real smile Gwenn had seen. "You know, they told me at the hospital that you were a friend of mine, but I'm beginning to think they lied. I couldn't possibly have such awful taste."

Gwenn stifled a surge of envy as the two men exchanged smiles. Obviously, memory or not, Chase was getting back on his old footing with Robert. It didn't seem fair that he could fall so easily into the old patterns with her brother and yet be so awkward with her.

She got to her feet, trying not to feel unwanted. "I'm going to go finish dinner." She smiled shyly at Chase. "I made a stew. I thought you might welcome a change from hospital food."

"Thank you. I would." The smile he gave her was as strained as her own. They stared at each other in uneasy silence, each wanting to find something familiar in the other but turning away with the need unfulfilled. Gwenn turned to her brother with a hint of desperation in the depths of her eyes.

"You'll stay for dinner, won't you? I have plenty of food."

"Sure, I'll stay. I never miss a chance at a good meal. You ought to know that."

When she had gone, the two men sat in silence until Chase spoke abruptly. "She's upset. I didn't want to upset her. Maybe it would have been better if I'd stayed at a hotel or something."

"Don't be ridiculous. If you think she's upset now, imagine how she'd be if you went to a hotel."

"I can't imagine how she'd be. That's just the problem. *I don't know her.*" The tension in his lean body was almost visible.

Robert's eyes narrowed in concern as he watched the other man, but his stocky frame didn't shift from its relaxed position. "You were both expecting miracles, and you were almost certain to be disappointed. Gwenn knows it and you know it. Both of you need to come to terms with the fact that this isn't going to disappear overnight. Give your mind a chance to heal, Chase."

"Who the hell nominated you as resident psychiatrist?" Chase snarled, his frustration boiling over. "If I wanted psychoanalysis, I'd go to a shrink, not a cop."

"I'm a lot cheaper."

Chase sat rigidly for another moment, his furious gaze locked with Robert's. With a muffled expletive he sat back in the chair, closing his eyes. "Don't you ever get angry?" he muttered.

"Not very often."

"It must make you a very frustrating guy to have around."

Robert nodded as Chase opened his eyes. "So I've been told. It's not that I don't occasionally get mad, it's just that I'm too lazy to do anything about it. Besides, it drives other people nuts when they can't get a rise out of me."

Despite Robert's best efforts, dinner was awkward. Gwenn and Chase were trying so hard to act naturally that it was impossible for either of them to relax. Robert managed to keep enough of a conversation going to provide a surface normalcy. Gwenn had prepared a stew, both because it had always been one of Chase's favorite meals and because it didn't require a lot of dexterity to eat. With his hands bandaged, it was difficult for him to wield a knife and fork with any confidence.

Stealing looks at him from under her lashes, Gwenn had to resist the desire to urge him to eat more. He had lost so much weight that he hardly looked like the same man. But then, in a way, he wasn't the same, she reminded herself. He had no memory, and, when he would regain his memory, he would be changed by the experience of the kidnapping.

After the meal, Chase excused himself, asking directions to the bathroom. Gwenn watched him leave the room, sniffing to hold back the threatening deluge.

"Hey, kid. There's no reason to cry just because he wants to use the bathroom." She turned and buried her face against her brother's chest, taking comfort in the feel of his arms around her.

"It's so awful. He shouldn't have to ask directions in his own home."

"You could make a map," he suggested lightly. She shook her head without lifting her face from its secure resting place.

"You know what I mean. How could anybody do that to Chase? It breaks my heart to see his hands bandaged up, and he's lost so much weight. He's so polite. It's like he was a stranger."

He set her away from him, dabbing at her damp cheeks with a napkin. "He *is* a stranger, kid. He's a stranger to himself as much as you. You both need to give him some time. It's not going to be easy for either of you, but you're going to have to be strong. He's worried that it upsets you to have him here. Memory or not, he hasn't changed that much. If he thinks this is too hard on you, he'll move out. So dry your face and blow your nose and try and look at least semicheerful."

By the time Chase joined them, all traces of Gwenn's emotional outburst had disappeared. Robert left soon after dinner, and it was all she could do to stifle a panicked plea for him to stay. She wasn't ready to be left alone with this man who looked like her husband but wasn't. Chase stayed in the living room while she locked the door after her brother, and she entered the room reluctantly, wishing she had a valid excuse to go someplace else.

Her wary expression instantly changed to concern when she saw Chase. He was sitting in the same chair he had chosen earlier, but this time, he was not seated tensely on its edge. It was not comfort, however, that made him sink back into the soft leather surface. His face was etched in lines of pain and exhaustion. The way he held his hands gently along the tops of his thighs told her the source of the pain. The stiffly bandaged finger on his left hand was a rigid contrast to the boneless slump of his body.

Her heart twisted with compassion. She had loved and lived with this man for five years. All that love was in her eyes as she crossed the room and touched him lightly on the shoulder. His lids opened slowly, and he stared at her for a moment out of eyes darkened to muddy green with stress.

"Let me help you up to bed. You can take one of the pills the doctor gave you and get some sleep."

"I don't like to take pills," he muttered as he struggled to his feet.

She didn't try to help him, sensing that he was as uncomfortable about their relationship as she was. She was going to have to pretend that they weren't married, and to try to act as if they were just friends.

He made it up the stairs on his own, slowly but steadily. She opened his bedroom door for him and then hesitated, feeling her cheeks grow warm.

"My room is across the hall. I...I thought you might be more comfortable in here for a while."

He stared at her enigmatically, and she wondered what he was thinking. "Thank you. I'm still pretty restless at night. I'm glad I won't have to worry about disturbing you."

She nodded, sliding him a glance from under her lashes. "Do you need help getting undressed?" She gestured awkwardly at his bandaged hands. "I know it must hurt you to use them. If you want, I could help with buttons and things." She trailed off awkwardly, irritated that she felt so clumsy. It was a perfectly normal offer. Even if they hadn't been married, it wouldn't be out of line for her to suggest helping him. But she was relieved when he shook his head.

"My hands are stiff, but I can manage my clothes. My right hand still works reasonably well. Thanks for the offer, though."

She hovered in the doorway a moment longer before taking a step across the hall. "Well...I guess I'll say goodnight. If you need anything, don't hesitate to call me."

"Thanks."

They stared at each other, hearing the stilted tone of their conversation but not knowing how to change things. With a sigh, Gwenn opened the door to her room and gave him a strained smile.

"Good night." She shut the door and then leaned against it until she heard his door close. "Damn." It was hardly more than a whisper. She repeated it several times with emphasis. The whole afternoon and evening had been a disaster. She'd had such high hopes of this homecoming. It was going to be a new beginning for them. She hadn't expected to feel as though her own husband was a total stranger.

She got ready for bed absentmindedly, her thoughts on the man across the hall. She had to keep in mind that no matter how difficult this was for her, it was a hundred times worse for him. Robert had said that they just needed to give it some time. Everything would work out. She was just going to have to put her faith in that thought and hope he was right. But it was poor consolation at the moment.

Chapter 2

Sleep did not come easily for Chase. The bed was as unfamiliar as everything else in his life. His hands ached, not badly enough to justify taking a pain pill, just enough to make it difficult to relax. His mind was spinning with a kaleidoscope of new impressions and, despite the doctor's advice, he couldn't help but try to fit them into some pattern that he might recognize. The pain in his head made him give up the attempt almost as soon as he started.

If sleep came slowly, waking was just as difficult. He had to fight his way to consciousness through layers of dreams that seemed to cling like demons trying to draw him back down into hell. When he dragged his eyes open, he was trembling and almost as tired as he had been the night before. His lean frame was clammy with cold sweat.

Chase sat up, his eyes skimming his surroundings, reassuring himself that he was not back in the gray cement chamber that imprisoned him in his nightmares. The soft blue and gold of the room bore no resemblance to a dark basement, and the tension gradually eased out of his shoulders. He let his head fall forward, cradling it gently in his hands, forcing his breathing to slow to a steady rhythm.

He could remember very little of his nightmares except that in them he couldn't talk. He'd had the dreams before, while in the hospital. The doctor had told him that they were a manifestation of his disturbed mental condition. He was going to have to live with them until his mind had learned to deal with what had happened. The fact that in his dreams he couldn't speak, although he felt an urgent need to communicate, might be a sign that his memory was struggling to return.

Chase let his mind go blank until the pressure in his skull eased, and he was left with only a minor headache. He swung his legs off the edge of the bed, glancing at the clock that sat on the bureau. Nine o'clock. This was a Wednesday. Did Gwenn have a job? Why hadn't he thought to ask Robert for more details about his home life? He felt so blind, made helpless by a lack of the most basic knowledge about his life.

He got to his feet, crossed to the bureau, and leaned his hands on the top of it. He felt the warmth of the old mahogany surface beneath his fingers. The tiny nicks and gouges of many years etched the dark wood, giving it a feeling of permanence. This was a feeling that he needed to find in himself.

He had no past and, without a past, how could he believe in the future? He lifted his head and stared into the mirror above the bureau, searching, as always, for some clue to himself. Who was he? What was he really like? He shook his head and turned away. There were no answers there.

He searched through the drawers of the bureau, finding underwear and socks. His movements were automatic, and his thoughts turned toward the woman who, he had been told, was his wife. Gwenn. Gwendolyn? Guinevere? He didn't even know her full name. What must she be feeling right now? Her husband had disappeared a month ago, but the man who returned didn't remember her.

He crossed to the bathroom that adjoined his bedroom, oblivious to the soft gold warmth of the tile and carpeting as he began to unwrap the bandages from his right hand. The doctor had told him that he could take the bandages off whenever he felt ready to do so. Chase tossed the gauze in the waste basket and examined his hand carefully. His hands were large, the fingers long and heavy. It looked like a hand that belonged to a football player, not an executive. There were pink patches of new skin where the burns were healing. They looked raw and vulnerable next to the darker skin that surrounded them. He flexed his fingers, his brows drawing together in an unconscious grimace of pain. But the pain was bearable. He might not be ready to play the piano, but his right hand worked reasonably well.

He unwrapped the left one more slowly, careful not to disturb the splint on his broken finger. This hand had taken the worst punishment. The skin on his palm was still bright red, and the cool air burned when it hit the tender surface. Awkwardly he spread salve over the injured area and wrapped a fresh bandage around his hand. Maybe later in the day he could ask Gwenn to do a neater job on the bandaging. It was going to be a while before he could leave the protection off that hand. He supposed he should be grateful that it was his left hand that had taken the worst punishment. At least he could still function with the other. He'd have to be sure and thank his captors for their consideration if they ever met again.

He washed and shaved, finding everything he needed within easy reach. In fact, once or twice it was almost as if he knew where something was before he reached for it. As he dressed in the bedroom, his eyes narrowed in thought. There was something wrong with the setup here. Last night his wife had told him that she had just moved his things into this room. No, that wasn't exactly right. She had *implied* that this was a recent move.

But the longer he was in this room, the more obvious it became that his things had been here for quite a while. There was a feeling of permanence to the placement of his clothing. The toilet articles were all arranged in the most convenient way. That kind of order developed as a person lived in one place and gradually shifted things to suit himself. If Gwenn had just moved everything in here last week, she wouldn't have set things up the way they were.

He tugged the zipper up on a pair of dark slacks, noticing absently that the waist was loose. There had been no mention of any estrangement between him and his wife. Of course, who would have brought it up? Maybe they just had separate rooms. Some married couples didn't share a room. But then why would Gwenn have implied that this was a recent move?

He sat on the edge of the bed and slipped his feet into a pair of well-worn loafers. He had to keep in mind that he was, to all intents and purposes, a stranger here. He was going to have to feel his way along until he figured out exactly what the relationships were or until his memory returned.

Chase left his room and inhaled deeply. Bacon. His stomach rumbled hungrily, and he felt a sudden upsurge of optimism. Things could certainly be a lot worse. He was out of the hospital, his health was still reasonably intact, and someone was cooking bacon. Something about the sweet scent made him feel at home. As if he belonged here, after all.

Gwenn stirred the pancake batter carefully. She hadn't made pancakes for Chase in more than a year. Would he still like them? She set the bowl of batter on the counter and picked up a fork to turn the bacon.

The radio at the end of the counter played the soft strains of Debussy's "La Mer," but Gwenn was too tense to be soothed by the flowing melody. She felt as nervous as a young girl on her first date. It had taken her almost half an hour to decide on something to wear. Her first urge had been to wear a dress and heels, but she eventually settled on a pair of faded jeans and a bright yellow T-shirt. She wanted Chase to feel at home, not as if she had dressed up for a guest.

What was she going to say to him when he came down? Her mouth twisted in a rueful smile. She supposed she could start out with good morning. That ought to be reasonably safe.

She felt a tingling sensation at the base of her neck, and her spine stiffened. She had been so busy wondering what to say to Chase that she hadn't heard him enter the room, but she didn't need to turn around to know that he was watching her. Not even the distance that had grown between them in the past two years could erase the effect his eyes had on her.

She set the fork down slowly and wiped her suddenly damp fingers on the front of her jeans as she turned around. Her heart was beating with slow heavy thuds, and she had to make a conscious effort to appear calm. He was standing in the doorway, and the uncertainty in his eyes helped to ease some of her own hesitation. She had to remember how much more difficult this was for him than it was for her.

She smiled at him. "Good morning." She hoped the faint tremor in her voice was inaudible, and that he wouldn't think that she was afraid of him.

"Good morning." He cleared his throat huskily and moved forward into the room. "I couldn't resist the smell of bacon. I hope there's enough for two."

She wiped her hands on her jeans again, forcing another smile to her lips. "Of course. I heard you moving around upstairs, so I made enough for both of us. I'm making pancakes, too. I haven't made them in a while, and I thought you might like a special breakfast. Sort of a welcome home."

Their eyes met in a long look, filled with uncertainty and a tentative warmth. "Thank you." The words were quiet, but his sincerity was unmistakable.

He pulled his eyes away from hers and looked around the kitchen. "This room looks like it belongs in an old farmhouse." He nodded to the oak cabinets and the warm tile floor.

"We had the kitchen redone about a year after we got married. The house was built around 1920, and the kitchen was hideous. It was the first project we tackled together. You built these cabinets yourself."

She poured pancake batter onto the griddle, glad to have something to do with her hands. He seated himself at the oak table in the center of the room, his gaze moving about restlessly. "Did I . . . do I do a lot of woodworking?"

Nodding, she poured him a glass of orange juice, aware of the fact that they both had a tendency to refer to him in the past tense. It sounded as if he were dead. "You haven't done too much in the past couple of years, but you used to spend a lot of time out in the shop. You built quite a few of the things in the house."

Gwenn set a plate in front of him and then seated herself opposite from him, picking up her fork without much interest. She was too nervous to be really hungry, but she didn't want him to feel awkward about eating alone.

He took a bite of the pancake and chewed it before glancing across the table at her. She felt her heart bump painfully when he smiled at her, the first real smile she had seen in more months than she cared to remember.

"It's a good thing you know what I like to eat. I'd hate to try and guess at it myself."

She shrugged, her eyes dropping to her own plate to hide the shimmer of tears. "Robert exaggerated a bit about your appetite, but you're definitely not a finicky eater."

The rest of the meal was almost silent. Once or twice, Gwenn glanced up and caught Chase's eyes on her, but she avoided holding his gaze. She felt so awkward. What should she say to him? She wanted him to know that she was glad he was home, but the distance that had grown between them in the past two years was still a very real obstacle to her. It didn't matter that he didn't remember what their relationship had been like. She remembered.

"Am I a wife beater?"

Gwenn choked on her orange juice, set the glass down with a thump and coughed into her napkin until she regained her breath. A stunned "What!" was all she managed to gasp out, her eyes finally meeting his incredulously.

"I said, 'Am I a wife beater?' "

"Good Lord, no! Whatever made you think that?"

He shrugged. "Well, you jump whenever I move. I wasn't sure if it was because of the odd situation or if it was something else."

She blushed, but she also laughed a little. "You are definitely *not* a wife beater. I guess I am a little jumpy. I'm not quite sure what I should say to you. I mean, you're not a stranger, but you're not exactly the man I know, either."

He smiled ruefully, a twist of his mouth that held no humor. "It *is* an awkward situation. I guess maybe it's going to be even harder for both of us than I had thought."

Reaching across the table, Gwenn touched the back of his hand, waiting until his eyes met hers before speaking. "The only really important thing is that you're home and you're safe. Nothing else matters next to that."

His hand turned and clasped her fingers lightly. "Thank you." His eyes searched hers, noting the brilliance of suppressed tears that told him just how much she meant her words. Warmth eased into his mind, lifting some of the pain away. He didn't remember their marriage, but with each passing moment, his desire to remember grew stronger.

To break the emotional intensity of the moment, he laughed. "You know, it sounds ridiculous, but I don't even know your full name. What is Gwenn short for? Gwendolyn?"

She pulled her hand away from his and gave him the first completely natural smile he'd seen. "Guinevere. Mom was a romantic, and she couldn't resist the name. I put up with a lot of teasing when I was in school, and I used to wish my name was something nice and plain like Sally or Jane. Then, when I met you, you said that you thought Guinevere was a beautiful name. It made all the jokes about waiting for Lancelot worthwhile."

She felt a light flush come up in her cheeks as she remembered that he had always called her Guinevere when they made love. Standing up abruptly, she picked up the plates and carried them to the sink. She swallowed hard to get rid of the ache in her throat. It had been so long since she had lain in his arms.

And whose choice had that been, she asked herself while stacking the breakfast dishes in the dishwasher. Chase remained silent, but she was aware of him with an intensity that frightened her. She wanted to turn and throw her arms around him and soothe away all the pain he had suffered. She wanted to tell him that she loved him and that she regretted the distance that had grown between them the past two years. That she was sorry it had taken his being kidnapped to make her realize just what she was losing. She wanted to beg him to let them start again.

But he didn't have any choice about starting again, did he? He had no way of knowing that everything had not been perfect with their marriage. Even if Robert knew how badly it had suffered since Livvie's death, he would never have mentioned it to Chase now. The doctor had specifically warned them to give Chase time to heal, both physically and mentally, before telling him anything that might upset him.

She was getting her fresh start. The only problem was that Chase didn't know it. What was going to happen when he regained his memory? Was he going to feel that she had taken unfair advantage of his condition? Would he resent her, or would he be thankful that they had a chance to try again?

"Do you have a job?"

Gwenn jumped and spun away from the counter, hoping that she didn't look as guilty as she felt. One of Chase's brows went up slightly, and she forced a shaky smile to cover the turmoil of her thoughts.

"I guess I'm a little tense." She dismissed her startled reaction to his words. "What was it you said?"

He apparently took her explanation at face value. "I asked if you had a job. I hope I'm not keeping you from a job or school or something."

"I don't have a *job*, exactly. I own a lingerie shop in Glendale. You don't have to worry about keeping me away from it, though. I have a really excellent manager. In some ways I guess it's more of a hobby than a career. We certainly don't need the money. Which is a good thing," she admitted ruefully. "We're just now beginning to show a profit. Still, we made it past the worst stage, which is the first two years or so."

"It sounds like an interesting kind of a store to handle." He didn't tell her that in his mind's eye he was picturing her in a filmy black negligee. He blinked to clear the image, wondering if the vision was a memory or a figment of his imagination.

It wasn't easy, but as the day progressed, some of the tensions eased. Chase began to feel a little less like an alien visitor to a strange culture. He couldn't remember living in the big old house or being Gwenn's husband, but it no longer seemed quite so impossible. He could almost imagine what it would be like to be the person everyone told him he was.

He made a conscious effort to forget about the bizarre circumstances of his homecoming. He was physically, mentally and emotionally exhausted, and the serenity of his surroundings and Gwenn's undemanding presence soothed his battered mind. For just this one day, he didn't want to think about a past he couldn't remember or the future he couldn't even begin to predict. If Gwenn was surprised that he asked very few questions about himself or their life together, she concealed it. She offered him the supreme gift of complete acceptance, making no demands of her own.

As the day eased into evening he realized that, while she had been careful to avoid making him feel watched, there had been hardly a moment when he was out of her sight. He let his head rest against the back of his chair, feeling the soft leather mold to his frame as if it had been made for him. Outside the French doors the summer sun lingered, softened by the lateness of the hour and the huge live oak trees that surrounded the house.

The hills that made up Flintridge, California, had once been covered with native oak forests and, when homes had been built there, the builders had seen the advantage of preserving as much of the old forest as possible. The result was a carefully nurtured privacy for each homeowner, and a price range that discouraged anyone with an income that could be listed in less than six figures.

Chase let his eyes shift from the soft twilight outside to the woman who sat across from him. She had switched on a lamp next to the sofa, and her head was bent over the needlepoint frame that stood on the floor in front of her. Lamplight caught in her hair, highlighting the golden streaks that hid in the silky fall of brown. His wife. He rolled the word around in his head. He was married to the serenely lovely woman who sat only a few feet away.

Gwenn slid the needle in and out of the delicate canvas she was working, letting the familiar rhythm ease all the tension out of her body. Chase was home. She could reach out and touch him and prove that he was there. His presence had been felt during the past month, too. In her mind's eye she had seen him everywhere, but each time she reached out, his image had vanished, leaving her heart empty.

She had thought that nothing could hurt her as Livvie's death had done, that never again would she feel as if her world had been completely shattered. Chase's disappearance had dispelled that thought.

Through the veil of her lashes, Gwenn stole a glance at her husband. His eyes were closed, and the soft tempo of his breathing told her that he was half-asleep. She let her gaze dwell on him more openly, the needlepoint forgotten. He was home. She had to keep repeating the phrase to convince herself of its reality. And another phrase ran through her thoughts. *I love you.* The words were whispered in her mind. Now was not the time to say them out loud, but that time would come. It had been too long since she had said those words to him. Two years too long.

She dragged her gaze away from him and glanced at the Seth Thomas clock on the mantel. If they were going to eat dinner tonight, she was going to have to do something about cooking it. Moving quietly, she set her needlework aside and tiptoed out of the room. She would let Chase sleep as long as possible. He needed all the rest he could get.

Chase came awake suddenly, his eyes snapping open in an abrupt transition from sleep to wakefulness. Gwenn was no longer sitting on the sofa. Her needlepoint frame had been set aside, and the lamp had been turned down so that it barely illuminated the room. The curtains were still open, and the day had made the transition from soft daylight to almost dark.

A sound had pulled him awake, but he couldn't place it. The noise came again, and he got to his feet. Someone was ringing the doorbell. He waited for Gwenn to answer it, but there was no sound of footsteps in the hall, and the bell rang again. He moved into the hallway and hesitated by the door. He could hear the faint roar of some appliance from the direction of the kitchen. Gwenn probably hadn't heard the bell.

This time the visitor knocked, and Chase reached for the knob. He paused with his fingers around the heavy brass. What was he supposed to say to whoever it was on the other side? *Hello, am I supposed to know you?*

With an irritated jerk he turned the knob and pulled the door open. He didn't know when—or if—his memory was going to return. He couldn't spend the time until then jumping every time the doorbell rang and expecting Gwenn to shield him from the rest of the world.

He swung open the door, aware of—and resenting—the defensiveness of his posture as be braced himself to meet the visitor.

Chase was a comfortable two inches over six feet, but the man who stood on the wide porch was at least two inches taller than that. His shoulders were massive, tapering to a slim waist and hips. Weight lifter, Chase categorized him immediately, while sparing a fleeting thought for the irritation of being able to remember what would give a man that body type when he couldn't remember his own name.

"Chase!" The name was more an exclamation than a greeting. Silver-blue eyes widened in surprised pleasure. The porch light glinted off a shaggy mass of pale blond hair, casting shadows onto the almost too perfect face beneath.

Chase hesitated, wondering if a miracle was going to occur and he was going to know the man's name. His mind remained a total blank, and he shook his head slightly.

"I'm sorry. I'm afraid I..." But the other man was shaking his head, his mouth set in a self-derisive smile.

"Don't apologize. I'm Doug Johnson. We've known each other since we were kids. I should have called and asked if this was a good time, but I've always just dropped by when the mood struck. I guess everything is different now. I should have thought." His mouth curved engagingly. "I could leave if you're not up to seeing anyone yet."

As he spoke, he stepped into the hall. Chase automatically shut the door behind him and turned to face him. Tension gripped the muscles in his neck, sliding upward to lodge in a painful knot behind his eyes.

"I'm sorry I don't recognize you." He could hear the formal tone in his voice, and he sensed that this was not his normal response to this man. However, he couldn't erase the uncertainty that caused it. He didn't recognize Doug Johnson and there was anger in that realization. With each new face he kept hoping that something would turn the key that locked away his memory, and every disappointment was harder to deal with than the one before.

The sound of Gwenn's footsteps offered a welcome relief from the awkward situation. Chase turned as she entered the hall, unaware of the plea for help that was written in his eyes.

Gwenn paused when she saw that he was not alone, then her face lit up with pleasure as she recognized their guest.

"Doug!" She crossed the hall, and Chase found it difficult to put a name to his feelings as the other man put his arms around her and gave her a gentle hug, dropping a kiss on her forehead before releasing her. Chase watched the two of them and remembered his too-orderly bedroom. He wondered just how close a friend Doug was and whom he really came to visit. Angrily, Chase shook the thought away. He had no reason to think that Gwenn was having an affair. There could be any number of reasons why they slept in separate bedrooms.

He roused himself from his unpleasant thoughts as Gwenn turned to him, her face alight with pleasure. "You don't mind if Doug stays for dinner, do you Chase? You might welcome a change after all day with no one to talk to but me."

Her smile was coaxing and perhaps just a touch wistful. He hesitated a moment and then nodded. "Fine. As long as you don't mind dealing with my less than perfect memory." He could hardly tell the man that he had no desire to tax his brain by renewing old acquaintances.

But Chase's irritation lasted only a few minutes. Doug, Gwenn explained, was not only a friend of theirs, but he worked with Chase at Johnson Industries. Doug's grandfather had founded the firm, and his father was still president of the company, as well as a major shareholder. Anyone who offered Chase a tie to his former life was not to be ignored. And Doug was a personal *and* professional tie.

Doug Johnson was an undemanding and amusing guest. Dinner was enlivened by his anecdotes. Chase listened carefully as Doug talked, picking out names and filing them. He wondered if Doug was deliberately giving him an informal rundown of people they both knew, but there was no hint of calculation to be found in his open face.

There was only one awkward moment during the meal. Doug had just finished an amusing account of the breakup of his latest "serious" relationship, and all three of them were chuckling. Chase felt relaxed in a way he hadn't known since the waking in the cellar that marked the beginning of his life.

He reached across the table and picked up the saltshaker, and Doug's laughter stopped suddenly, chopped in the middle as if cut with an ax. Chase glanced at him, wondering at his sudden silence. The other man's face was still, a frozen expression of horror twisting his even features. Chase followed his eyes, wondering what could have brought on that expression. Then he realized he'd used his left hand to reach for the salt, and Doug was staring at the bandaging and the stiffly held little finger as if the sight of it made him sick.

Chase pulled his hand back, dropping it self-consciously beneath the cover of the table. Doug's eyes followed the movement and then lifted slowly to his friend's still face.

"What happened to your hand, Chase?" The question came out starkly, with none of the light-hearted warmth that had characterized his previous speech.

Chase's eyes flickered across the table to Gwenn, noticing the pallor of her features. He knew she was thinking about what the bandages concealed. He had been forced to ask her help in changing them earlier in the day and he had thought that she might faint when the puckered burns were exposed to her.

He shrugged, hoping to pass the incident off lightly. "Just a little souvenir of my time away."

Doug's face turned ashen, and his eyes had a stricken look in them. "They tortured you?" The words were hardly more than a whisper, but they expressed absolute horror.

Chase, aware of Gwenn's rigid figure across the table, managed a smile, though his stomach was clenched with tension. "Nothing that won't heal, given a little time."

"My God. I didn't know. Nobody told me." Doug shook his head dazedly, seemingly unable to absorb this new information.

"Like I said, it's nothing that won't heal. Now, I don't know about the rest of you, but I'm ready for a piece of that cake Gwenn baked this afternoon." He hoped his smile didn't look as brittle as it felt. He wanted the subject of his hands closed. Gwenn's pale features were haunted, and he was discovering that he felt very protective toward this wife he couldn't remember. Dessert was the last thing he was in the mood for, but it served to distract her.

By the time she had cut neat squares of the dark chocolate confection and set them on plates, some of the color had returned to her features. Chase picked up his fork as she put his plate in front of him, trying to convince his churning stomach that cake was a good idea. Doug hadn't said a word since his final muttered comment that he hadn't known about Chase's hands.

"Gwenn tells me this is my favorite kind of cake," Chase said lightly, trying to lift the suddenly heavy atmosphere. "I don't really have much choice but to take her word for it. Amnesia must be every mother's dream. Think of the things they could get their kids to eat, just by telling them it was their favorite food."

Doug finally came out of his shock and joined in the conversation, bantering with Chase about the possibilities of using amnesia as a nutritional therapy until Gwenn was laughing with them. Satisfied that she was going to be okay, Chase allowed her to talk him out of helping her load the dishwasher when they finished dessert.

If he was honest with himself, he had to admit that the strain of his first full day out of the hospital was beginning to catch up with him. He let her bully him into following Doug into the living room, accepting her offer to bring the men some coffee as soon as she was done in the kitchen. It would give him a few minutes alone with Doug.

"I'm sorry about making a scene at dinner," Doug said as Chase eased himself into the big leather chair and let his eyes skim over the other man. Doug stood next to the patio doors, staring out into the night, his figure rigid.

"That's okay. I suppose it is a shock when you first hear about it. I've gotten used to the idea now, but one of the first things I remember is my anger that anyone could have done this to me. I just didn't want to upset Gwenn any more than she already is." Funny how easily her name came to his lips.

Doug stirred restlessly, but he didn't turn away from the door. "She was devastated when you disappeared. We all were. One day you were at work, and the next morning no one knew where you'd gone."

"What kind of work did I do?"

Doug shrugged. "You were always the wonder boy of the firm. You could do just about anything. Your dad bought a goodly percentage of the stock when the firm went public back in the fifties. After you graduated with an engineering degree, it was only natural that you went to work there. Hell, your family owned almost as much stock as mine did, by that time.

"You started out in the engineering department and you've worked all over the firm. The past couple of years, you've been a vice president, in charge of marketing."

"Marketing? How did I get from engineering to marketing?"

Doug shrugged his massive shoulders, turning to face Chase. "Turned out you had a real flair for it. Things have been in an uproar since you disappeared. Especially since the plans disappeared with you. Things sort of came to a grinding halt."

"Plans?" Chase heard his own voice as if it were coming from a great distance. His heart began to beat with slow heavy thuds that left him breathless.

Doug was staring out the window again and missed seeing his friend's sudden pallor. "Yeah. Without the schematics for the project, the company has a real problem. I don't suppose you know where they are?"

Chase didn't answer him. He couldn't. There was pain in his head. Pain that intensified until he was sure he would explode. His hands began to throb as if in symphony with the pounding in his temples. Voices echoed in his mind. *Where are they? Tell us where they are.* Lights blinded his eyes. He shut them, but still they shimmered in front of him, relentlessly following him. He was dimly aware of someone calling his name, but the pain had increased to such a degree that he couldn't hear.

Entering the room with a tray of coffee cups in her hands, Gwenn was horrified to see Chase lying limply in his chair, his head lolling forward against his chest as if the weight were too much for his neck to support. Doug crouched in front of him, his face a study in panic, his huge hands patting futilely against Chase's pale face.

She set the tray down on the floor, oblivious to the cups that overturned and the tinkle of broken china as she rushed across the room and bent over her husband. She tilted his head back, almost afraid of what she would see. Her hand went to his throat, and she felt a surge of relief. The pulse beneath her fingers was fast but steady.

Even as the thought crossed her mind, his eyes opened and he stared up at her. "Chase? Darling, can you hear me?"

"Gwenn." Her name came out slurred with pain, and she cast a frantic glance at Doug.

"What happened to him?" Her tone was accusing.

He shrugged helplessly. "I don't know. We were talking, and all of a sudden he groaned and grabbed his head."

She barely listened. Putting her hand against her husband's forehead, she felt the dampness of sweat. "Darling, are you in pain?"

His eyes dragged open again, the pupils dilated and unfocused. But he seemed to recognize her voice. "My head. It hurts."

"Help me get him upstairs. He's got medication there, but it knocks him out. I'd like to get him into bed before I give him a pill."

Between the two of them, they got Chase up and guided his wavering footsteps across the room to the stairs, Doug supporting most of his weight. Chase was semiconscious, but the pain in his head was such that he couldn't focus his eyes or thoughts on anything for more than a few seconds. Every step sent new demons of agony to torture his pounding head.

The awkward threesome had reached the bottom of the stairs when someone knocked on the front door. Gwenn glanced over her shoulder, but there was no way she could leave Chase's side right now. She didn't have to worry about it, however. The brief knock was followed by the sound of a key in the lock, and seconds later, her brother entered the hall.

His gaze fell on the three by the stairs, his brows going up in surprise and then coming down as he strode rapidly across the wide hallway. Gwenn gratefully relinquished her place to him, knowing that his broad shoulder was more up to the task of supporting her husband than she was.

"I'll go get his medicine," she told him breathlessly. She slipped around them and hurried up the staircase. Robert didn't waste his breath on asking questions. By the time they reached the top of the stairs, both men were winded. Chase had lost some weight during his incarceration, but he was still almost a hundred and ninety pounds of near deadweight.

Gwenn had turned down the covers on his bed and had a glass of water and a pain pill waiting. She got Chase to take the tablet, coaxing him into swallowing it, knowing that he was barely conscious. She gratefully accepted Robert's help in getting her husband undressed and into bed. She was vaguely aware of Doug leaving the room but all her attention was focused on Chase's still form.

She sat on the edge of the bed, holding one of his hands and stroking her free palm gently over his forehead, feeling helpless to ease his pain while they waited for the pill to take effect. She barely glanced up when her brother touched her on the shoulder and told her that he'd wait downstairs.

Robert hesitated in the doorway, a feeling of frustration gripping him as he looked at his sister's tense figure. He wasn't accustomed to being forced to watch her suffer without being able to offer her any help. He shook his head angrily and opened the door. There wasn't anything he could do right now.

He stepped out into the hall, closing the door behind him and then stopped abruptly as Doug's bulky form straightened away from the opposite wall. The other man towered over Robert, but Robert didn't seem to notice it. His dark brows snapped together in a frown.

"Is he going to be all right?"

Robert nodded in answer to Doug's anxious question, but his frown didn't ease.

"What happened?" he snapped the question out in a voice that had been known to surprise answers out of men accustomed to sneering at authority.

Doug's eyes flashed for a moment, his resentment of the other's tone obvious. But his gaze dropped before the fierce demand in Robert's. He shrugged, running his fingers through the heavy shock of blond hair that fell onto his forehead.

"We were talking. He wanted to know about his job."

Robert's muffled curse brought his eyes back up, and his fair skin flushed a dull red when he saw the contempt there.

"You don't need to go on," Robert told him flatly. There was a moment of tense silence. "Dammit, Johnson!" The words exploded out of him, belying his claim to Chase that he never got angry. "Why the hell didn't you keep your mouth shut? You knew Chase wasn't to be upset. What were you thinking of, man?"

Doug shrugged again. "I didn't mean to say anything. It just sort of slipped out. We were talking about work, and the plans have been on my mind. They've been on everybody's mind since they vanished. You know how important they are. I just sort of asked him if he knew where they were." His eyes shifted uncomfortably about the hall, looking anywhere but at the man before him.

"What did he tell you?"

Again came a lift of those huge shoulders. "He didn't say anything. When I looked over at him, he was holding his head, and he'd gone all gray and sick looking. Hell, man, you ought to know I'd never deliberately hurt Chase. I just didn't think." This last burst out beneath the biting anger Robert's eyes lashed him with.

"You didn't think. You never think, Doug. That's the problem. You haven't thought about the consequences of your actions in the fifteen years I've known you. You didn't think when you quit school three months before you were due to graduate. You didn't think when you wrecked your car and damn near got yourself killed. You didn't think when you took off on that mind-broadening tour of Africa and forgot to tell your father that you were alive. You didn't think when you..."

"I don't care what you two are fighting about; you're going to have to do it somewhere else. I can hear you in Chase's room, and I don't want him disturbed."

Gwenn's whispered reprimand shattered the tension that shimmered almost visibly in the narrow hallway. Robert broke his words in midsentence, letting his eyes flicker over Doug one last time before he turned to his sister. "How is he?"

"He'll be just fine as soon as he gets to sleep, and you two shouting at each other isn't going to make that any easier!"

Robert drew a deep breath, swallowing his anger and allowing a calm mask to slip over his face. "Sorry, Sis. Doug and I were just leaving."

The bigger man nodded his head, eager to be gone. He whispered a good-night to Gwenn and added another apology for any trouble he had caused before practically running down the stairs.

Gwenn and Robert listened to the soft thud of the door as it closed behind him, and then Robert touched her lightly on the cheek. "How are you holding up?"

She managed a tired smile. "Today went better than I expected. We were able to talk pretty comfortably, and

Chase seemed to be relaxed." Her smile brightened slightly. "He remembered Sal. Or at least he remembered that we had a dog. That's a good sign, isn't it? It could mean his memory is coming back."

He nodded. "It could, but I wouldn't hold my breath waiting for more." He glanced at the wide watch strapped to one heavy wrist. "I've got to go. I only stopped by to see how you two were getting on. I'm due at the station in a few minutes." He put his arm around her shoulders and gave her a brief hug. "He'll be fine. Chase has always been a survivor."

Gwenn murmured an agreement and then watched him move quickly down the stairs. It wasn't until the door had shut behind him that she muttered her thought silently. Chase was a survivor. The question was, was she?

Chapter 3

It was after ten when Chase came downstairs the next morning. Gwenn had been up since before daylight. She had not slept well during the night, waking up every hour or so and leaving her own bed to go and check on Chase. She told herself over and over again that she was being foolish. Once the medication took effect, he wasn't going to be waking up before morning.

But she needed the reassurance of actually seeing him safe and sound. The month after he disappeared had made her appreciate the luxury of being able to look at him whenever she wanted. He slept soundly, not even moving beneath the gentle stroke of her hand on his forehead. In the long dark hours of the night, she sat next to his bed and whispered her love to him, telling him how much she loved him, begging him to remember his love for her.

At dawn she gave up all thought of getting any more sleep. She dressed in a pair of faded jeans and a lightweight shirt. Even at five o'clock in the morning, August in

Southern California was warm. By the time Chase came downstairs she had cleaned the big old house from top to bottom, had outlined some designs for rearranging the stock at Guinevere's Fantasy to give her more room to display the merchandise, and had managed to chew her way through the last decent fingernail she had.

She spent the entire morning feeling on edge, her ears tuned constantly for any sound that might indicate Chase was awake. It was ironic that when he did get up she happened to be outside getting the mail. Her attention was still on the mail as she entered the house, kicking the door shut behind her and giving an unconscious sigh of pleasure as the cool air-conditioned atmosphere in the house breathed over her warm skin.

"Good morning."

The greeting was quiet, nonthreatening and totally unexpected. She gasped and jerked her head up, her hands going automatically to her throat, dropping the stack of mail in the process. White envelopes rained softly onto the tile floor, accompanied by the heavier splat of magazines.

He must have just come downstairs. He stood on the bottom step looking at her, his eyebrows raised slightly in surprise, probably at the intensity of her reaction. Her eyes skimmed over him, taking in the neatly tailored perfection of his soft gray slacks and the warm rust color of the silk shirt. He looked like exactly what he was. A confident, mature executive: cool, experienced and unapproachable.

She flushed, and dropping to her knees, gathered the papers together with fingers that trembled. The tremor became more pronounced when another hand joined in picking up the more widely scattered envelopes. She finished gathering the items within reach and got to her feet, taking the remaining mail from his outstretched hand with a murmur of thanks.

"I didn't realize that wishing you good-morning was likely to cause an accident. Are you always like this in the morning?"

She managed a strained laugh as she got to her feet, the mail clutched in a death grip, her knuckles white. She could tell by the tightness in his voice that he was upset. She didn't have to think very long to come up with the reason for his anger. He obviously remembered the conversation with Doug last night that had resulted in his collapse. Now he was upset because he hadn't been told about the missing plans.

She set the envelopes down on the narrow table that stood against one wall. "I guess I just wasn't expecting you to be up yet. I'm not usually this nervous. How are you feeling?"

She turned and leaned her hips against the table, allowing her eyes to rest on his face. Her first urge was to put her arms around him and let her fingers soothe away the lines of worry that etched his features. His skin was gray; only the warm reflection from his shirt gave him any color at all. It was obvious his sleep the night before had not been a restful one. The illusion of health and power faded when she got a close look at him. He looked as if a strong breeze would knock him over.

Shrugging away her question he said, "I'm okay. I need to talk to Robert. How do I go about getting in touch with him?"

"Robert figured you'd want to see him when you got up." There was resignation in her tone. She had hoped that he could have a few days to regain his strength before being confronted with the full details of his disappearance. Obviously that was no longer a possibility. "Why don't you go pour yourself a cup of coffee, and I'll call and tell him you're waiting for him."

Chase nodded. "Thanks."

When Gwenn joined him in the kitchen a few minutes later, he was seated at the table with a mug of coffee cradled between his palms. Without speaking she got out a loaf of bread and popped a couple of slices into the toaster.

"Do you want anything with your toast?"

Chase shrugged irritably. "I didn't know I wanted the toast." Sarcasm edged the words, but it was diluted by the exhaustion that etched his face.

She set the golden-brown bread on a plate and buttered it lightly before setting it in front of him. "You have to eat something. You always run out of energy if you go without breakfast."

"Well, I'm glad one of us knows what's best for me." He had made a similar comment yesterday. Today his tone was less than amused. He pushed the plate away from him. "Whose idea was it to keep me in the dark about whatever it is that's missing from Johnson Industries?"

"The doctor said that you shouldn't be upset unnecessarily. There didn't seem to be any point in telling you about the missing papers when you wouldn't be able to do anything about them, anyway." She pushed the plate back in front of him.

He ignored it, picking up his coffee and taking a large swallow. He set the cup down, and his eyes met hers. Gwenn wanted to cry out at the raging frustration she read in those smoky green depths.

"Do you have any idea how frustrating it is to be totally at the mercy of what other people choose to tell you? I don't know whether or not anything I've been told is the truth." His mouth twisted bitterly, and his gaze shifted to stare out the window behind her shoulder. "There are times when I even wonder if I am Chase Buchanon, when I think that maybe this is all some kind of bizarre joke." His eyes snapped back to hers, their look piercing.

"I can't help but wonder what else I haven't been told. What else has been hidden from me because I'm not supposed to be upset?"

Gwenn stared at him, feeling her throat close with guilt and regret. Did her face reveal the turmoil of her emotions? Oh, God, had she been wrong to conceal the full truth from him? Was he going to hate her when he found out just how much had been left unsaid?

She jerked her eyes away from his, half relieved, half sorry for the interruption of the doorbell. "That must be Robert." She reached over to push his breakfast under his nose. "Eat your toast. I'll go let him in." She hurried out of the room before he could answer.

Twenty minutes later Chase sat next to Robert in the other man's tiny automobile. He glanced sourly across the inches that separated them. Being forced to scrunch his knees up close to his chin was not his idea of comfort. Robert's dark eyes slid over him as he started the car.

"Don't say it. You always have hated my cars. But there's no reason for me to pay for extra leg room when I don't need it," he pointed out reasonably.

Chase snorted. "*You* may not need it, but I feel like a pretzel." He closed his eyes as a fleeting image drifted through his mind. "Did you ever drive a Triumph?"

Robert glanced at him, startled. "I had a red Triumph the last year we spent at UCLA. You hated that car with a passion."

"That's because it always felt like it was designed by the Marquis de Sade. I remember wondering if I would make it out in one piece, every time I got into it."

Robert kept his voice neutral. "What else do you remember about it?"

Chase frowned for a moment and then shook his head. "It's gone. Damn! For a minute there I really remembered something, but then it all left again."

"Don't worry about it. It's a good sign. Dr. Maguire told you that you might recall things in bits and pieces. It'll all come back."

"Yeah, sure. Meanwhile, I have to just sit back and rely on what everybody tells me about myself. You knew about the papers and you didn't tell me. What else am I not being told?" he repeated his earlier question to Gwenn.

Robert turned the little car down Colorado Boulevard, blending expertly with the busy traffic as they headed into the heart of Pasadena. He chose his words with care. "Anything that you haven't been told has been out of concern for you. The doctor warned Gwenn and me both about hitting you with your entire life all at once. After all, it took you thirty-nine years to get where you are—you can't expect to relearn all those years in the space of a couple of days."

Chase's good hand clenched into a fist, and he stared out the windshield, his face a study in frustration. His head pounded as he fought to break through the thick curtain that shielded his memory. The pain intensified until, with a gasp, he was forced to abandon the struggle. His lean body relaxed back into the too small seat, and he let his eyes close.

Robert remained quiet, letting his friend fight the silent battle without interference. Chase didn't speak again until Robert pulled the car into a marked parking place in front of a low brick building. He opened his eyes as he felt the cessation of movement and turned his head wearily to look at the other man.

"I won't ask any more questions. It's too frustrating when I don't get any answers. I'm just going to have to accept that whatever I'm not told is really for my own good."

He gave a short bitter laugh as he opened the car door. "I don't really have any choice, do I?"

Robert shook his head as he watched the other man get out of the car. He hoped Gwenn knew what she was doing. Chase was not going to like it when he found out he'd been lied to, but it had to be her decision.

Chase drew in a deep breath of hot summer air and looked around the parking lot. Most of the spaces were filled, cars of all colors and makes butted up against the green strips of lawn and trees that marked the aisles. There was a sluggish stirring deep inside, and he felt his spirits rise as he and Robert walked toward the wide front doors. He knew this place.

His steps quickened, his long legs covering the distance to the doors at a pace that Robert had to strain to match. Chase thrust open the doors and stepped into the hallway, inhaling deeply. The mingled scents of waxed floors, furniture polish and air-conditioning filled his nostrils, pushing against the curtain in his mind, forcing it to open, if only just a crack.

Without hesitation, he turned left toward a bank of elevators. Robert followed him silently, entering the elevator on his heels and not saying a word as Chase pressed his finger firmly against the button that marked the top floor. When the doors slid open on an expanse of expensively carpeted hall, Chase hesitated for only a moment before moving forward. He seemed oblivious to the startled gasp of the secretary who sat in the outer office as he walked past her desk and thrust open a door.

Robert paused to murmur a low instruction to her before following Chase into the office she guarded. Chase stood next to a broad oak desk, his palms planted firmly on the sturdy surface as he leaned against it. He didn't appear to notice Robert's intrusion at first, but after a moment he looked up. The glitter in his eyes lightened them to a shimmering green.

"I remembered!" His voice rose as he repeated the phrase. "I remembered! This is my office. This desk was a present from my father. He gave it to me just before he died." His voice trailed off, and the light in his eyes began to fade. His face tightened, and the room echoed to the sound of his fist slamming against the solid oak.

"Damn! I can remember that he gave it to me, but I can't remember what he looked like! I can't even remember his name."

"David Chase Buchanon," a voice said from behind them. Your parents reversed his names when you were born to save the confusion of both of you being named David."

Chase's head jerked around at the sound of the new voice. Robert moved out of the doorway to allow the newcomer to enter the room, but Chase was only peripherally aware of his movement. His attention stayed on the man who stepped into the room.

Chase supposed that by some standards, the other man might be called old. But one had only to look in his eyes to discard the description. The eyes were a brilliant blue, clear as a morning sky in the Sierra Nevada, and piercingly alert. His height matched Chase's own, and the weight of sixty-five years of heavy responsibility did not show in the straight strength of his posture.

The stranger smiled faintly and went on without waiting for Chase to say anything. "And he looked a lot like you. His hair was darker, and he was an inch or two shorter, but the basic features were pretty much the same. Guinevere could probably dig up some old family pictures for you, if you want."

For just an instant, the heavy curtain that held back his memory stirred sluggishly. Chase felt as if it would lift far enough to tell him who this man was, but then the thick shield sank down again, leaving him with nothing but a feeling of familiarity.

"I'm sorry, sir. I'm afraid I don't remember your name, though I'm sure I know you."

The older man came forward, reached out a hand and clasped Chase's fingers with an intensity that reinforced his obvious pleasure in seeing the younger man. "I'm Charles Johnson. It's good to see you looking so well, Chase."

"Thank you," Chase murmured. "Doug mentioned you last night."

A fleeting frown creased Charles's broad forehead. "I understand my son mentioned more than just my name last night. He tells me you were very upset. In fact, I understand you were in a great deal of pain. Are you sure you're feeling up to this visit today? There's nothing that can't be discussed at a later date."

Chase shook his head. "I'd feel better if I knew exactly what was going on."

Charles hesitated, glancing at Robert, who merely shrugged, as if to say that he had no objection. With a sigh the older man turned back to Chase. "You always were too stubborn for your own good. Why don't we go to my office? We'll be more comfortable there, and I'll have some coffee sent up from the cafeteria."

A few minutes later Chase held a steaming cup of coffee in his hand and looked around the room. It was interesting to note the contrasts between the four men in the room. Doug had joined them soon after they entered his father's office, apparently alerted to Chase's arrival by some interoffice grapevine.

Charles was talking on the phone. He had taken the call reluctantly, apologizing for the delay, but Chase was just as happy to have a few minutes to consider those with him. He let his gaze dwell on each man for a moment. Robert lounged back on a comfortable leather chair in a characteristically indolent pose, his legs stretched out in front of him, the coffee cup balanced precariously against his stomach. He looked as though he might doze off at any moment, but Chase had no doubt that if required that compact muscular body would spring into action in a matter of seconds. For all his easygoing appearance, Robert Lawford was not a man to be messed with lightly.

Doug Johnson was the next to catch his attention. The big man reminded him of a caged animal. He hadn't managed to stay seated for more than a few seconds before he was on his feet and pacing over to the huge windows that filled one wall of the office. In a light suit, he looked even more enormous than he had in jeans and a T-shirt. Enormous and uncomfortable, Chase decided. It was odd, but for all his size, if Chase needed someone to back him in a fight, he would never pick Doug. There was something about the other man that made him uneasy, and no amount of reasoning with his feeling could banish it.

Charles was the last to receive his attention, and his mouth quirked in a smile as he studied the other man. He couldn't remember him, but he responded to the sight of him with an undeniable inner warmth. He had the impression that he and Charles Johnson had been very close before the kidnapping. His brows drew together in a frown, and he tapped his splinted finger against the arm of his chair. Odd that he hadn't felt the same instantaneous closeness with Gwenn. You would think his wife should inspire that feeling, if anyone did.

"I'm sorry that took so long, gentlemen."

Chase snapped out of his speculative thoughts as Charles spoke. Doug spun away from the window as if he'd been stung by a wasp and moved quickly to seat himself in a chair a little to the side of his father's desk. Only Robert didn't show a significant reaction.

Charles cleared his throat slightly. "I hadn't intended for you to be bothered with the details of your kidnapping until you had a chance to recuperate more fully. Since you have found out some of what happened, perhaps it would be best if you were given more information."

Doug shifted uncomfortably in his chair. His father's glance did not stray to him, nor did his even tone of voice alter.

"I'm grateful for everyone's concern for my health, sir. But I'm sure you can understand how I feel about being kept in the dark on something that appears to intimately concern me." Chase's mouth turned upward in a rueful smile. "It's bad enough that my own memory is hiding things from me. It only makes it worse to think that everyone else is, too."

Charles nodded. "I'd feel the same way. Well, I'll tell you what we know, which, to be honest, isn't a whole lot. On the ninth of July, you came in to work as usual. You kept all of your appointments until early afternoon. Your secretary says that you came back from lunch and appeared to be upset. You told her to cancel all your appointments and not to disturb you for anything less than all-out nuclear war. The next time she saw you was about three-thirty in the afternoon. You left your office and told her that she could go home whenever she wanted, that you wouldn't be needing her any longer."

He paused for a moment, and Chase felt the tension in the office climb. "She didn't see you again, but we know where you went from there. You went to the engineering division and took a set of top-secret documents out of a safe. You were seen leaving the building with your briefcase a few minutes later, and that was the last time anyone saw you until you stumbled onto Hollywood Boulevard last week."

He finished speaking, and there was a long silence while Chase tried to absorb the implications of what he had been told. They were unpleasant, to say the least. He had to clear his throat before he could speak evenly.

"How did I get these papers?" He kept his eyes steady on Charles, though he was vaguely aware of Doug restlessly turning his coffee cup around and around between his huge palms.

"You had the necessary clearance."

"Isn't it possible that I had a reason to want to study the documents?"

Charles shook his head slowly. "It's possible, of course, but I can't imagine what it could be. You had the clearance to look at them, but there is no reason why you would need to. Even if you did have a reason to study them, it's strictly against rules to take them out of the building, which is apparently what you did. We searched your office and every other room in the building after you disappeared. They aren't there."

Chase swallowed hard. His right hand balled into a fist until the still-healing flesh protested. "So what you're telling me is that I stole top-secret documents. That means I may have been working with the people who did this to me." He lifted his bandaged left hand.

"No!" The word burst out from Doug, and Chase let his gaze shift to him, aware of a throbbing ache settling into his stomach at the realization that he could be a thief. Doug's face was flushed, and his hands gripped the mug so tightly that Chase expected to see the heavy porcelain crack at any moment.

"No," Doug repeated in a quieter tone. "Chase would never steal from anyone, let alone the company he works for." His eyes, a paler version of his father's, darkened with the force of his emotions as he stared across the wide desk at Charles. "You can't believe that he would do that."

Charles shook his head slowly. "I don't believe it." He looked at Chase. "I want to make it clear to you that I don't have any doubts about your honesty or your loyalty to this company. After all, you own a considerable chunk of Johnson Industries. I'm sure you had a reason for taking the documents. The problem is, no matter what your reason was, the documents *are* missing. We're very concerned that they do not fall into the wrong hands."

Chase shook his head slowly. "I wish I could help you, sir. But at the moment, I can't remember anything other than a few isolated and irrelevant incidents. I can't even promise you that I didn't tell them anything. Obviously they were very anxious to know something they thought I could tell them." He lifted his bandaged hand for emphasis. "I may have told them everything I knew."

Charles shook his head. "We don't think so. This kind of information is very valuable. Whoever was trying to get it out of you is probably going to sell it to the highest bidder. The defense community is surprisingly small and, like all small communities, when someone offers something for sale, it doesn't take long for the information to spread. If they had achieved their goals with you, they would be trying to market their treasure and we would hear about it."

"Defense community?" Chase questioned. "These documents have something to do with a defense project?"

Charles nodded. "That's probably more than I should have told you, but you would have figured it out sooner or later. Johnson Industries deals almost exclusively in government defense contracts. I can't give you any more details. Personally, I trust you, with or without your memory. But I'm afraid the board of directors doesn't know you as well as I do."

Anything further he might have said was interrupted by the buzz of his intercom. He frowned and pressed the button down impatiently. "I requested that you hold my calls, Ms. Larson."

The secretary's voice was disembodied and tinny sounding. "Yes, sir. But Admiral Reynolds is on the phone, sir. He says this was a scheduled call."

The senior Johnson glanced at his desk clock impatiently. Chase was on his feet before the other man could say anything.

"Please don't even consider postponing an important call for my sake. I think you've told me everything you could, and I appreciate your honesty." He stepped up to the desk and held out his hand, returning Charles's firm clasp. "I'll be in touch with you if I remember anything helpful. I'd appreciate it if you would let me know if you get any new information."

"Of course. Don't push your mind too hard, Chase. Nothing is important enough to risk damaging your health."

Chase and Robert exited the building in total silence. Doug had left them outside his father's office, muttering that he had an appointment and brushing aside Chase's efforts to thank him for his support.

It wasn't until they were well on their way, with Chase's knees once more in danger of meeting his chin, that he realized that one of the most valuable aspects of knowing Robert Lawford was his ability to let a silence grow comfortably. He didn't fidget or make idle remarks or ask Chase how he was feeling or try to cheer him. He just accepted the other's need for quiet.

And God knows he needed some time to think. It had been bad enough to know that he didn't have a memory. He hated the helplessness of relying on others for the most basic information about himself. Now he had to consider the possibility that he had stolen classified documents and hidden them somewhere for a purpose that no one could even guess at.

The thought was not going to make it any easier to sleep at night.

Chapter 4

Gwenn experimentally poked a finger into the lump of bread dough and sighed. It looked as lifeless as she felt. She took a sip of iced tea and then jabbed at it again, but it stayed stubbornly unresponsive. Well, the yeast *had* expired six months ago. She should have just thrown it out instead of wasting her time and ingredients in the hopes that its effects might have survived long past the date on the package.

She picked up the bowl and carried it to the trash, dumping the lifeless dough in on top of the day's accumulation of junk mail. She filled the bowl with hot water, letting her attention drift out the window. The roses were heavy with flowers. Too heavy, she decided. She hadn't pruned them very thoroughly in January. In fact, she hadn't pruned them as well as she should have the year before, either. Not since Livvie had died.

Chase had suggested hiring a gardener last summer, but she had snapped that she was perfectly capable of taking care of her own gardens. Her throat ached, remembering the hurt that had momentarily flashed in his eyes before it was concealed beneath the mask that she'd helped put there.

She'd pushed him away so many times. Slapped him away any time he'd tried to reach out to her. They should have shared their grief, drawn closer, but she hadn't allowed that. And eventually Chase had stopped reaching out. It had taken his disappearance to make her realize how much she was losing.

She set the bowl in the drainer and dried her hands. Now she *had* realized how much he meant to her, and she wasn't going to lose him this time. They had a chance to rebuild something of what they'd lost and she was going to do everything she could to make sure they created something even stronger than before.

But you're building on lies, her conscience muttered.

Not lies, she argued. She hadn't really lied to Chase; she just hadn't told the full truth.

He doesn't know about Livvie and he doesn't know what your marriage was before he was kidnapped. How is he going to feel when he remembers?

"He'll understand." She hadn't realized that she was speaking out loud until she heard her words echo in the big kitchen. "This is our chance to start over, and I'm going to take it, no matter what."

She hurried out of the room, as if afraid that someone would argue with her.

Chase slipped off his suit coat as soon as he got out of Robert's Fiat. He would have taken it off before, but there was no way he could have maneuvered it off in the tight confines of the little green car. Robert backed to the end of the drive and lifted a hand in farewell. Chase returned the gesture, watching until the car was out of sight before he turned toward the house.

But he didn't walk toward it. Not right away. He stared at the front of the house, trying to call up some feeling of familiarity, but there was nothing. For all intents and purposes, the first time he had seen this building was the day before yesterday when he'd come home from the hospital. He'd been too nervous about the upcoming meeting with Gwenn to really look at it then.

Now he stood in the hot afternoon sun and studied it. It was a pretty house, he decided. There was a vaguely Spanish air about it—white stucco, with arching windows and a heavy wooden door. The red tile roof added to the image. From where he stood, he looked down the driveway that ran along the side of the house. If he tilted his head, he could see through the stucco arch that went over the drive to the four-car garage. Four cars. Two people and four cars?

Without really thinking about it, he wandered down the drive, his coat hooked on one finger and slung over his shoulder. The sun was blazing hot, and he supposed it was uncomfortable, but it felt so good just to be out in it that he didn't really mind. The memory of waking up in that basement and being so cold that he couldn't even imagine being warm again had given him a new appreciation for the hot sun.

He inhaled deeply, drawing in the heady fragrance of the roses that lined the drive. The bushes were neatly arranged in a wide bed where they'd be easily visible from the window above him. He stopped for a minute, his eyes narrowing on the window. The kitchen. That must be the kitchen window, and above that would be the windows in Gwenn's room.

He crossed the drive until he stood next to the rose bed. Lifting his hand to cup a pale yellow flower, blushed with pink, he bent to sniff the sweet fragrance, but his thoughts weren't on the flowers.

Gwenn's room.

Why didn't he share a room with his wife? The question nagged at him. It wasn't simply that they were one of those couples who had separate bedrooms. Without a memory to go on, he had to rely on instinct. And instinct told him that there were a lot of things being kept from him.

He released the flower and continued down the drive. They weren't divorced. He was sure of that. No, they weren't lying to him about being married. But his belongings had been in that room since long before the kidnapping. When he didn't think about what he was doing, he'd found himself automatically reaching for things, knowing where they were without looking.

He stopped in front of the garage door and stared at it without seeing it. So he and his wife hadn't been sharing a bedroom for quite some time. The question was: Why?

A butterfly fluttered gracefully past, breaking into his thoughts. He watched until it disappeared out of sight around one corner of the garage and then shook his head. He wasn't going to get any immediate answers. Either his memory was going to return, or he was going to have to piece things together on his own. It was a sure bet he wasn't going to get any answers out of the people around him. They were all too busy concealing things for his own good.

He tossed his suit jacket onto the grass beside the drive and, for the moment, tossed the questions with it. He opened the garage door nearest him and stepped into the dim interior. There were two cars in the garage. The one closest to him was a sleek Porsche in a silver-gray color that reminded him of Gwenn's eyes. On the other side of that was a red Aston Martin Volanté.

"The Porsche is mine, and the Aston Martin is yours."

Chase turned. Gwenn stood just inside the garage. In the dim light her hair was more brown than blond, and her eyes looked a deep, almost charcoal gray. She was wearing the same jeans she'd had on when he left, but she'd changed the soft cotton T-shirt for a bright green tank top that left her shoulders bare. Her hair was pulled up on top of her head in a pony tail, and the simple style, combined with her bare feet, made her look like a teenager.

He said as much and was rewarded by her wide smile. "Flatterer." But she was obviously pleased by the comment. She came forward until she stood beside the Porsche. "I've had Betty since right after we got married."

"Betty? For a Porsche?" He raised one brow in disbelief, and Gwenn laughed self-consciously.

"I named her for a teacher I had in grade school. She..."

But Chase wasn't really listening to her words. He was watching her face. He'd been wrong, he decided suddenly. She didn't look like a teenager. There was too much character there, too much awareness in her eyes. He let his gaze skim down the long line of her neck. He was intrigued by the shadows of her collarbone, and he had a sudden image of his tongue tracing that delicate line.

His eyes snapped back to her face, and he realized that she'd stopped speaking. He smiled at her, wondering if she could read his thoughts. Wondering if her mouth would taste as soft as it looked.

"I suspect the company would take the car away from you if they knew you'd named it something as unexotic as Betty."

Her smile widened, giving him a bewitching glimpse of a dimple high on her left cheekbone. Apparently his answer was satisfactory. Gwenn's smile slowly faded as her eyes met his. It had been so long since she'd seen that look in his eyes that for a moment she couldn't even read it.

Desire. The word tingled through her. He was looking at her with desire. The color rose in her cheeks, and her eyes dropped away from his. She felt suddenly breathless and giddy, more like a young girl than a mature married woman.

"Gwenn?" Her eyes lifted again, seeing the question in his eyes. Unconsciously she stepped forward as his hand came up. She caught his fingers before they could touch her cheek. Tears filled her eyes as she looked at the pink patches of new skin.

"Your poor hand." She kissed the palm and then cradled it against her cheek, the salt of her tears washing away the memories of pain.

The gesture was so tender, so filled with emotion that Chase couldn't move, couldn't even speak. Seeing her face resting against his palm, he felt his heart swell with emotion, with a need to protect this woman, this wife he couldn't remember.

His left hand came up to catch the back of her head and tilt her face to his. Gwenn lifted her eyelids as he bent toward her. There was so much need, so much uncertainty in his eyes that she wanted to cry out in pain.

Instead her eyes fluttered shut as his mouth touched hers, and she offered him the soft comfort of her lips. It was a gentle kiss, without demands. An exploration. For Gwenn it was like touching a memory and finding it still fresh and new. It had been so long.

For Chase it was a discovery. Her mouth was so soft and warm. He wanted to hold her forever; he wanted to sink into the clear gray of her eyes and wash away the pain and confusion. And he wanted to make love to her with a fierce desire that caught him off guard.

For an instant he wanted to take her right where they stood, pressing her back against the shiny gray Porsche and stripping her clothes off before burying himself in the heated welcome of her body. The image was so vivid, the desire so fierce that his mouth hardened demandingly for a moment, his hands tightening around her face.

It was the stab of pain in his bandaged left hand that broke the spell. With a shallow gasp Chase eased his hand away. His mouth left hers more slowly, reluctant to give up the soft territory he had just conquered.

Gwenn's lashes lifted reluctantly as Chase drew back. His eyes were filled with questions, but there was also a slumberous desire there. Desire for her, and need. He needed her. And this time she wasn't going to push him away.

He stepped back and the last of the spell drifted away. They were still standing in the garage. The sun was still blazing down outside. Nothing had changed, and yet everything was different.

"I... I guess it must be time for lunch." Gwenn glanced at her wrist and then laughed self-consciously. "I left my watch in the house."

Chase looked at the gold band on his wrist. "It's almost one." He followed her from the garage. He hadn't seen what was in the other half of the garage, but he wasn't interested in that at the moment. Right now the most important thing was to be with Gwenn, to savor those moments in the garage when he'd almost been able to believe that he really was the Chase Buchanon who was married to this woman.

Chase turned away from the window and paced restlessly across his bedroom. The thick carpet padded his footsteps, maintaining the silence in the big house. There was no traffic on the winding roads outside, nothing to break the quiet. But then, at two o'clock in the morning, anyone with any sense would be asleep.

He walked back to the window, a humorless smile on his face. Apparently, he had no sense. He'd tried to sleep, and the twisted mess of his bed was silent evidence of the failure of that attempt. He was tired, but his mind simply refused to stop churning.

Questions. God, he was so sick of questions. He wanted answers. He wanted to know who he was, what kind of a life he had led before the kidnapping. And he wanted to know what he'd done with the papers that all the evidence said he'd taken.

If Charles was right, and the information hadn't yet hit the international market, did that mean he hadn't told them what they wanted to know? He stared at the bandages on his hand as if they could answer the question for him.

His head began to throb with the intensity of his need, and he abandoned that line of thinking. But everywhere his thoughts turned, he had more questions than answers. Gwenn. Now there was one of the biggest questions.

He leaned his shoulder against the wall and stared unseeingly outside. He didn't have to close his eyes to remember the way her mouth had softened beneath his this afternoon, or to recall the tears she'd shed over his injured hand and the love he'd seen in her eyes. But if she loved him, what was wrong with their marriage? Why were they sleeping apart?

His headache intensified, and he muttered a curse, letting his thoughts go blank, asking nothing of his bruised mind. He had to take things as they came. Let his memory return when it was ready.

When the ache had subsided to a bearable throb, he opened his eyes again. Outside, everything was still. The moon shone down on the black carpet of the lawn, catching gleaming highlights here and there. He really needed to get some sleep. The doctor had given him some sleeping pills, but he didn't like the groggy feeling they left in the morning.

His eyes narrowed on one corner of the lawn. Under the heavy shadow of a huge live oak, there was a gleam that looked out of place. He stared at that point until his eyes ached, and he was just about to decide he was imagining things when a shadow detached itself from the darker gloom beneath the tree and began to creep across the lawn.

With a muffled exclamation, Chase backed away from the window. Adrenaline pumped through his veins, banishing the tiredness. They were back. It could be just an ordinary burglar, but he gave that only a moment's consideration. They didn't get what they wanted the first time, and they were coming back again. But this time he was going to be waiting.

Gwenn was deep in a dream in which Chase was holding her close and whispering how much he loved her. She snuggled closer to her pillow, a contented smile curving her mouth. "I love you. I've always loved you. We'll start over and build our marriage stronger than it ever was. I... Gwenn, wake up. Wake up."

She frowned and tried to recapture the first part of the dream. Why was Chase telling her to wake up? Didn't he know that this was a dream?

Her eyes snapped open. Chase was bent over the bed, a pair of silk pajama bottoms riding low on his hips, his chest bare. For a moment it was almost like a continuation of her dream. Now he would take her in his arms and make love to her. But, in the moonlight that poured in through the curtains, his expression was all wrong. It was hard and urgent.

"Do we have a gun?" That question shattered the last remnants of sleep. She sat up, oblivious to the thin chiffon of her nightgown.

"A gun? What do you need a gun for?"

"Someone is in the house."

She ran her fingers through the tousled length of her hair, trying to force her groggy mind to work. "There's a gun in the night table by your bed."

He turned toward the door, and she suddenly realized exactly what he'd said. Someone had broken into the house, and Chase was going to go after him. She caught him two steps from the door, her hands closing around his arm.

"Where are you going? Chase, let me call the police. Let them handle it."

He turned to look at her, his voice soothing, as if talking to a child. "Gwenn, if this man is one of the ones who kidnapped me, he might be able to tell us who's behind this whole damn mess. If we wait for the police to show up, he's going to be long gone."

"I don't care. I don't want you hurt." She pressed her forehead against the muscles in his arm, fighting back the need to cry.

His hand rested against the back of her head for a moment, offering silent comfort. "Gwenn, I want this man. They put me through hell. And I want one of them."

"But it could just be a burglar. He may not have anything to do with the men who kidnapped you."

"In that case, we don't want him stealing the silver, do we?" Though he tried to inject some lightness into his words, there was an underlying tone of deadly intent. He pulled his arm loose from her frantic hold.

"Call the police and stay in your room. I don't want to have to worry about what I see moving in the house."

He dropped a hard kiss on her trembling mouth, and then he was gone. Gwenn stared at the blank door for a moment, fighting back tears. What if he got shot? She couldn't lose him. She hurried to the phone and forced her shaking fingers to punch out the numbers that would connect her with her brother.

The two rings before he picked it up seemed like twenty. "Hello." His voice was thick with sleep.

"Robert? There's someone in the house. Chase went to get the gun."

"Stay calm, Gwenn. I'll be there in ten minutes." All traces of sleep had vanished from his voice. He was alert and efficient.

"Should I call the police?"

"I'll do it from the car. You just sit tight."

She hung up the phone and sank down onto the edge of the bed. Her knees felt as if they were made of water. Ten minutes. In ten minutes Chase could be killed or kidnapped again. She got up but then sat down again before she took a single step toward the door. She couldn't go out there, no matter how much she wanted to. Chase was right. At least this way he'd know that anything that moved had to be the enemy.

It seemed as if hours had passed while she sat on the edge of the bed and strained to hear some sound that might tell her what was going on. Maybe Chase had been wrong. Maybe there was no one in the house. There had been no gunshots. That was a good sign. With luck, whoever it was would leave without Chase seeing him. She didn't care about catching the kidnappers; all that concerned her was keeping her husband safe.

When the silence was finally broken, it was so sudden and so shocking that it took her a moment to believe she'd really heard anything. But the crack of sound was unmistakable. A gunshot. The sound was lighter somehow than what she remembered from the times she'd gone to the shooting range with Chase. It wasn't the heavy boom of his .45.

And if it wasn't his gun, then that meant someone had fired at Chase. Fired at him. But had they hit him? Was he lying somewhere bleeding? Dying?

"Chase!" His name came out on a scream, and she was suddenly struggling with the doorknob, not even remembering how she'd gotten from the bed to the door. The knob turned beneath her shaking hands, and she was in the hall. She didn't care that the pale blue of her gown made her a perfect target for anyone lurking on the stairs. She didn't care about anything except finding Chase.

She ran down the hall, the luxurious chiffon floating behind her. Tears blinded her so that she didn't even see the figure coming up the stairs two at a time. Didn't see him until he caught her in his arms, and she was slammed into a hard male chest. The scream in her throat died unvoiced as she inhaled the deep woodsy scent of his cologne.

"Chase! Oh, God, you're alive. You're alive." Her hands were shaking as she ran her palms over his naked shoulders, assuring herself that it really was him.

"Dammit, Gwenn! You could have gotten yourself killed. I told you to stay in your room."

"I thought you'd been shot. It wasn't your gun. I knew it wasn't your gun." Tears streamed down her face as she looked up at him. "I wanted to die."

Chase looked down at her, reading the anguish in her face. The adrenaline that had been pumping through him since the first moment when he'd seen the shadow on the lawn suddenly veered in another direction. He'd been shot at, could have been killed.

Gwenn had only a glimpse of the hard glitter in his eyes before his mouth came down on hers. And she responded to the demand in him without hesitation. Her hands slid up the width of his chest to lock at the back of his neck. Standing on tiptoe, she arched into his strength, offering her mouth to him.

His lips slanted over hers hungrily, his arms circling her back. She could feel the butt of his gun pressing into the small of her back, and the hard metallic presence was a potent reminder of how close she'd come to losing him. Her mouth opened to him, and his tongue slid avidly over hers, tasting her need.

"Gwenn." Her name was a groan as his free hand flattened on her back, pulling her closer, trying to absorb her into his flesh.

The sound of sirens screaming to a halt in front of the house broke them apart. They faced each other in the dim hall. Gwenn could read nothing of his expression.

"You'd better go put something on." His voice sounded shaken, but whether by the encounter with the intruder or by the explosive kiss, she couldn't begin to guess.

She backed a step away, unable to drag her eyes from him. Robert's voice booming from outside broke the last of the spell. "Chase? Gwenn? Are you all right?"

"You'd better go tell him we're alive before he wakes the whole neighborhood with that bullhorn."

With a last enigmatic look in her direction, Chase turned toward the stairs, freeing her to go to her room.

When she came downstairs a few minutes later, she was dressed in a pair of jeans and a T-shirt. She'd quickly run a brush through her hair, and a glance in the mirror had told her that she looked perfectly normal. Her color was high, but that could easily be attributed to the excitement.

Chase was talking to Robert in the hall, and the sound of their voices reached her as she came down the stairs. Lights seemed to blaze from every room in the house, and uniformed police officers combed each room.

"You should have called me first, Chase. That's my job. I don't like you taking out after this guy."

"This is my house, Robert. And it's my mind they messed with. By the time you got here, he would have been long gone."

"He's gone, anyway. A fat lot of good your heroics did. Are you all right, Sis?"

She nodded in answer to the fierce look he threw her. She came to stand next to Chase, not yet ready to lift her eyes to meet his. She wanted to put her arm through his, to assure herself that he really was there, but she didn't quite dare. They were still such a long way from having their relationship clear.

"It wasn't heroics, Lawford. I wanted to catch the guy. I wanted a chance to talk to him."

"And instead you almost got yourself killed," Robert told him acerbically. "Do you know what a scare it gave me when it came over the radio that one of your neighbors had reported a gunshot?"

"Look, it's over and done with. Maybe I shouldn't have gone after him, but it seemed the thing to do at the time. I want whoever did this to me, Lawford." There was simmering rage in the words.

Robert combed his fingers through his already mussed hair. "I know you do, Chase. I want them, too, but we don't have any reason to think that this break-in had anything to do with your kidnapping. It could have been a burglar looking for something portable to sell."

The look Chase threw him made it clear what he thought of that theory, and Robert nodded reluctantly. "Okay. I don't buy that any more than you do. It's a little too much of a coincidence. But we don't *know* any different." He turned impatiently as one of the officers approached.

"Sir, we found the bullet. It was embedded in the ceiling in the study."

"Take it in and let ballistics have a look at it. Not that they're likely to find anything helpful," he muttered as he turned back to Gwenn and Chase. "If this *was* the same people who kidnapped you, they're professional enough to get rid of the gun. Drop it in an aqueduct, throw it in the Pacific. We'll never see it." Robert tugged on his lower lip for a moment, his eyes thoughtful. "The ceiling, huh?"

"I don't think he was trying to hit me. I think he was trying to scare me off." Chase smiled grimly. "It worked. It's incredible how fast a man can duck when someone takes a shot at him. When I picked myself up off the floor, he was already halfway across the lawn, and no matter how bad I wanted him, I wasn't going to take potshots in the dark."

"How can you two stand there discussing this so calmly?" Gwenn's voice still held a shaken note of fear. They were talking about this as calmly as if it were an episode on a TV cop show. This was reality. Someone had broken into their home. Someone had taken a shot at Chase.

Both men looked at her in surprise. "How would you like us to discuss it?" Robert raised one dark brow to emphasize his point, but Gwenn wasn't interested in logic at the moment.

"I want to know what we're going to do to prevent this happening again."

"I'll put a guard on the house tonight. Tomorrow I'll see what I can do to get someone assigned to the place regularly."

"You'll see what you can do? What about catching these people? Is anyone doing anything about that? Is anybody interested in that?"

"Gwenn, stop it!" Robert closed his hands around her shoulders and administered a gentle shake. "It's over. You're upset and I don't blame you, but it's over now."

Chase watched the two of them, Robert's dark head bent over Gwenn's fair one. His good hand clenched and unclenched. He should be the one offering her comfort, and he ached to put his arms around her and hold her close.

But he didn't move. There was too much between them. His mouth twisted. Too much and too little. Not enough memories and too much tension. The kiss they had shared only minutes ago had been explosive, but it had left him with more questions than it answered.

He turned away, blocking out the quiet murmur of Robert's voice. If he could have laid his hands on tonight's intruder, maybe he would have come up with some answers instead of more questions. But he hadn't, and he was left without any more answers than he'd had before.

Chapter 5

It was a source of never ending amazement to Gwenn that the human mind could adjust to almost anything and make it seem normal. A week ago someone had broken into her home and taken a shot at her husband. At the time, she would never have believed how quickly the incident would fade when faced with the relentless tide of day-to-day living.

It was only when she'd see the bullet hole in the ceiling of the study that it all would come rushing back. Then she'd remember the sheer terror of knowing that Chase could have been shot. By the time she got home tonight, even that reminder would be gone. Chase had said he was going to repair the plaster now that the ballistics people had looked their fill.

"Gwenn, where should I put these teddies?" Her manager's voice broke into her thoughts and she shook herself out of her thoughts. Turning to look at the garments in question, she felt a rush of pride as she looked at the shop.

She'd worked hard to get Guinevere's Fantasy to this point. This year they should show a pretty respectable profit. It had taken three years to get to this point, but it had been worth every hour. The shop had been all that had saved her sanity after Livvie had died.

"Gwenn? Yoo-hoo. Are you in there?"

She blinked and focused her eyes on her manager, laughing self-consciously. "Sorry, Maggie. I didn't mean to doze off on you."

"That's okay." Maggie's gamine features widened in a smile, her green eyes alive with curiosity. "You looked like you were a million miles away."

"Not really. I was just thinking about how far we've come in the past three years." Gwenn's hand swept out to indicate the shop. "It's a far cry from the electronics store it once was."

Maggie turned to look at the long narrow room. Dark peach carpeting covered the floor in a thick layer, inviting customers to walk slowly and relax. The walls were the palest apricot, a shade that enhanced virtually every other color, while giving the shop a warm glow.

Racks of garments lined both walls, broken up by an occasional set of pale oak shelves. A small table sat against one wall with a steaming pot of fragrant coffee and a plate of cookies to offer customers an excuse to sit down and take their time with their choices.

Against the serene background tones, the merchandise was a riot of color. Everything from the palest blues and pinks to emerald green and royal purple. Silks, satins and lace spilled elegantly from every corner. Tiny French-cut panties and exquisitely flowing negligees, and every garment in between.

Maggie nodded. "It looks pretty good. The fashion shows have really helped. Business has almost doubled since you started those."

"It gives women an excuse to spend an afternoon feeling elegant and pampered." Gwenn reached out to take the hot-pink silk teddy from Maggie's hand. "This is pretty flashy. Why don't we put it somewhere where it can really be appreciated? How about next to those cream satin camisoles that came in last week? The contrast should be nice." Gwenn laughed and went back to the job she'd been doing before she let herself become distracted. As she jotted down figures in the ledger, she let her mind wander again. What was Chase doing right now? Since he'd discovered that the other half of the garage was a well-equipped wood shop, he'd spent most of his time there.

At first she'd been worried about him, but after a day or two, it became obvious that he was able to lose himself in his woodworking in a way that nothing else seemed to match. Whatever else he'd forgotten, he still handled his tools as if they were an extension of himself.

And there was an officer there to watch the house, she reminded herself. She had to remember that Chase wasn't a child. He could take care of himself. He'd lost his memory, not his mind.

"Lost again?" Maggie's question startled Gwenn, making her realize that she'd been staring off into space, her pen idle.

She smiled self-consciously and shut the ledger, dropping the pen on top of it. "Maybe I'd better help you put the new stock out. It's obvious that I'm in no condition to be doing the bookkeeping."

She stepped around the counter that held the cash register and crossed the room with Maggie. The two women worked smoothly, folding the silk garments and laying them on the shelves. Gwenn ran her fingers lightly over the edge of one shelf. Chase had built these for her before she had opened the shop. A shop-warming present, he'd called them.

"How are things with Chase?" Gwenn jerked her hand away from the shelf and threw Maggie an apologetic grin, aware that she wasn't being much help.

"Pretty good. He remembers odds and ends every once in a while. So far nothing major, but it's a good sign. Most of the bandages are gone, but it's going to be a while longer before they take the splint off his finger. He's gaining back some of the weight he lost."

"It must be tough on you. If it were me, after what you've been through, I'd just want to sit and stare at him to make sure he was really there."

"That's exactly how I do feel. I came so close to losing him that all I really want to do now is hang on as tight as I can. Robert set up a guard for Chase, so I don't really have anything to worry about. And it isn't like Chase is a helpless invalid or anything."

"How is Robert?" Maggie's tone was elaborately casual.

"He's fine. Why are you asking? I thought you were still seeing David."

Maggie shrugged. "David turned out to be a dud."

"So you're turning your sights on Robert?"

"Well, it isn't exactly that I'm turning my sights on him. In a way, they've never been off him." Her eyes slanted toward Gwenn and then away. "I've had the hots for him since the first time I met him," she confessed.

Gwenn's brows rose in surprise and she teased, "You've had an interesting way of showing it. The one time he asked you out, you turned him down, and I've lost track of the guys you've gone out with in the past three years. I'd never have guessed you were nursing a secret passion."

Maggie's flush clashed with the brilliant red of her hair, and her fingers twisted restlessly on the edge of the box they were supposed to be emptying.

"Well, you see, I really thought he was a hunk, but I knew he was the serious type."

"Robert?"

"Not serious as in *dull*," Maggie added quickly. "But serious as in settling down and marriage and all that. And I wasn't ready for that."

"And now you think you are? What brought on this realization?"

"I just suddenly realized how empty my life had been. I was so sure I didn't want to commit to any one man, so sure that I was really enjoying living the life of a single woman in the eighties, and then I woke up one morning and realized that I was going to be thirty-four on my next birthday, and there was no one to really care whether or not I got up in the morning. I want what you and Chase had... I mean, have...." She stumbled over the words, her cheeks turning scarlet beneath the scattering of freckles.

Gwen swallowed hard on the stab of pain the other woman's words brought. "It's all right," she said huskily, breaking the suddenly awkward silence. "Chase and I did have something special before...before Livvie died. We lost it, but we're going to find it again. When he disappeared, I realized just how much we'd lost, and I promised myself that, if I had the chance, I was going to do everything I could to make things right between us again."

She raised her head and smiled at Maggie, who was not only her manager but her best friend. But her relationship with Chase was not something she was ready to discuss, even with Maggie. She turned the conversation back to the original topic.

"So you think my brother is the man you want to settle down with."

"I think he might be. Do you think I'm his type?" She put on her most vampish expression.

The question was asked jokingly, but Gwenn gave it serious thought. Her eyes narrowed as she studied her friend, trying to see her as Robert might. She was only five foot one, but her small frame was curved in all the right places. Her hair was a mass of auburn curls in a shade that stopped just short of being carroty. All the ingredients of a vamp were there, except the features.

She nodded slowly. "I think you might be exactly his type."

Maggie blinked, startled at getting a serious answer to her rather facetious question. "What?"

Gwenn nodded more positively this time. "I think you might be exactly what Robert is looking for."

"Really?" The tentative hope in Maggie's voice told Gwenn just how much the answer meant to her, no matter how joking the question had been.

"Really. I think the two of you would make a terrific couple."

A discreet *ping* announced the arrival of a customer, and Gwenn left Maggie to finish folding the teddies while she got back to the business of running the shop, but the conversation lingered in her mind. Maggie's comment about wanting what she'd had with Chase had reinforced her own determination to recapture that relationship.

Chase looked up as he heard a car pull into the driveway. He didn't recognize the big gray Cadillac, but then, he didn't recognize much of anything these days. He forced back the inevitable surge of irritation that went with that thought and picked up a rag to wipe his paint-stained hands.

Propped on the workbench in front of him was a wooden goose. Painted slate blue, all it needed was the final details. He was going to paint tiny flowers over the body, giving it the appearance of an old-fashioned calico. It was a completely useless knickknack, but it had a country flavor that would go well in the kitchen.

Since his return from the hospital, this shop was the only place he felt completely at ease. He might not consciously know where things were, but his hands didn't have any trouble remembering the feel of the tools and exactly what to do with them.

Creating the wooden goose had given him a sense of control that was sorely lacking in most other aspects of his life. And it had also kept him from going crazy with nothing to do but think about the past he couldn't remember and a future he couldn't even guess at.

He dropped the rag on the bench and turned as the driver's door opened on the car. His eyes narrowed against the bright sunlight outside the garage. There was no mistaking that pale hair and those shoulders.

"Chase!" Doug shouted a greeting as he slammed the car door and walked up the drive.

Chase lifted his hand in acknowledgment, wondering what it was about Doug Johnson that made him so uneasy. He'd been friends with the man for years; they'd worked together. So why was it that the sight of him was enough to bring on the warning twinges of a headache? Even now, he could feel the tension building behind his eyes.

"Doug." The greeting was flat, and no amount of effort could put warmth in it. Doug didn't seem to notice. He stepped into the garage and looked around.

"Getting back into the woodworking, are you? It's been a while, hasn't it?"

"I don't know. Has it?" Gwenn had seemed surprised when he started spending time in the shop. But, if it had been so long, why did the tools feel so right in his hands?

Doug laughed, a high-pitched sound that didn't match the bulk of his body. "Sorry. It's hard to remember that you can't remember." He laughed again, and Chase had to restrain a wince. Doug sobered, his attractive features settling into apologetic lines.

"I'm sorry, Chase. I guess it doesn't seem very funny to you. You know how I am. I've always had a practically fatal case of foot-in-mouth disease."

"No problem. I'm not that sensitive. What can I do for you?"

Doug wandered farther into the garage, and Chase turned to watch him, trying to pin down the source of his uneasiness. Doug stopped in front of the workbench and studied the freshly painted goose.

"For Gwenn? She's going to love it. She's always loved the country look. Used to haunt the auctions looking for ratty pieces of old furniture that you could fix up for her. That oak wardrobe in her bedroom was a pile of junk when she bought it."

Chase felt the pressure behind his eyes solidify into a steady ache, and he forced himself to breathe slowly and steadily to control the pain. Maybe that was what he hated about Doug. The man knew more about his life than he did himself. And he knew more about Gwenn.

That, more than anything else, ate at Chase. How the hell did Doug know what was in Gwenn's bedroom?

Doug turned and leaned back against the sturdy bench, his blue eyes guileless. "Once you'd fixed the thing up, it looked terrific, but it still weighed a ton. I thought we were going to have to tear out a wall to get it upstairs. Robert kept trying to talk Gwenn into putting it in the living room, but she insisted that it had to go in the bedroom."

"But she cooked a huge pot of chili as a reward, and you and Robert ate enough for ten people." Chase was hardly aware that he'd spoken until Doug's eyes suddenly sharpened, and he stiffened.

"You remember?"

Chase stared without seeing him, trying to grab hold of the elusive thread of memory and pull it to unravel the curtain that shielded his past. A sharp stab of pain warned him not to push any further, and he released the wisps of awareness.

He shook his head. "I remember moving the wardrobe and then eating afterward, but it's all foggy, like an out-of-focus movie."

"Does this happen often? How much do you remember? Do you remember anything about the schematics?"

Chase felt his head begin to pound a warning, a distant echo of the pain that had caused him to collapse a week ago. He raised his brows and Doug flushed.

"I'm sorry, Chase. Dad would wring my neck if he knew I'd even mentioned the damn things to you. It's just that they're pretty important and I..." He broke off. "I'm sorry. But when you remembered something, I guess I lost my head. I hope I didn't upset you."

"No problem." Not for anything was Chase going to admit to the pounding that threatened to break his skull open. "I wish I *could* remember something useful, but so far it's just bits and pieces, nothing earth-shattering and nothing particularly useful."

"That's okay. You'll get your memory back. I didn't mean to upset you."

For all his size, at that moment Doug Johnson looked like a four-year-old begging forgiveness for some childish misdemeanor. It was almost impossible to believe that he was only two years younger than Chase.

Chase shrugged. "Don't worry about it. I know you're worried about the missing papers. Believe me, the minute I remember anything that might help to find them, I'll let your father know."

"Thanks, Chase. I appreciate..." But whatever it was that he appreciated, Chase was destined not to find out. A muffled roar announced the arrival of Robert's tiny sports car and put an end to the conversation.

It was just as well, Chase decided. Much more of Doug's undiluted company, and he had the feeling that his headache would have reached unmanagable proportions.

Robert joined them in the garage. "Hi, Chase. Doug." His greeting was even more lukewarm than Chase's had been. "I didn't expect to see you here."

The level words were a comment, not a question, but Doug shifted uneasily. "I just dropped by on my lunch break." His eyes jumped to Chase. "I'll see you around. Maybe the three of us should go out for dinner one night to Gwenn's favorite Chinese restaurant."

Chase nodded, suppressing the twinge of resentment that had struck when Doug mentioned Gwenn's favorite restaurant. It was one more example of how little he knew about his own wife.

"Sure, I'll mention it to Gwenn."

A few seconds later Robert and Chase watched the Cadillac disappear down the drive.

"How are you doing, Chase?"

"Not bad. Why don't we go into the house? Gwenn made some lemonade last night."

Robert wiped his damp forehead. "Lemonade? On a chill day like this? You're getting soft, Chase. The temperature can't be much over a hundred. What we need is some good hot coffee."

Chase grinned, feeling the throbbing in his head fade. "Maybe I'll build a fire in the fireplace, too. I'd hate to be responsible for your catching pneumonia."

He shut the garage door, and the two men crossed the lawn to the back door. As they stepped into the kitchen, the contrast in temperatures drew a sigh of pleasure from Robert. "Days like this make you wonder if California weather is all it's cracked up to be."

Chase was at the sink unwinding the paint-stained bandages on his left hand. "The lemonade is in the fridge. Why don't you pour a couple of glasses while I get rid of these?"

He rinsed his hand with warm water, trying to avoid the wrapping that held his little finger rigid. It was healing. He flexed his hand experimentally and was rewarded with only a mild twinge of pain as the movement pulled at the damaged flesh. The skin was still marked by pink patches where it was healing, but all in all, he was pleased with the progress. Maybe he could even leave the bandages off.

Chase followed Robert into the living room. The other man's eyes were closed. He looked like he was dozing, but Chase didn't doubt that he was well aware of everything that was going on around him. Robert Lawford would be perfectly comfortable if Chase didn't say a word for the next hour. Unlike Doug Johnson, who felt the need to fill every silence.

"What's with you and Doug?"

Robert opened his eyes, his stocky body tensing for a moment. "What do you mean?"

"It's pretty obvious that the two of you don't get along all that well."

The question apparently deserved some attention because Robert actually uncrossed his ankles and pulled himself higher on the sofa. Of course, it could just have been that he'd been about to slide off onto the floor. He tugged at the sleeve of his black T-shirt.

"Doug and I have never been bosom pals." He shrugged. "I guess our personalities clash."

"Was he a close friend of mine?"

Robert shrugged again. "The two of you practically grew up together." His dark eyes skimmed over Chase. "Doug is a perfect case of arrested adolescence. There's no real harm in him, I suppose, but he doesn't ever seem to grow up."

"Gwenn seems fond of him." There was an edge to the mild comment that made Robert's gaze sharpen.

"Gwenn is fond of just about everybody. Doug is like an overgrown puppy. I think he appeals to her maternal instinct."

"I suppose."

Robert didn't pursue the subject. He could have said more, could have told Chase that he had nothing to worry about. But unless he was specifically asked for advice he wasn't going to offer it. There was nothing more obnoxious than interfering in-laws.

"How's Gwenn?"

"Fine. I had to talk her into going back to her shop. She seemed to think she ought to be on hand just in case I went into convulsions or began swinging from the chandelier."

"She worries about you."

Chase shifted restlessly in his chair. "I know. I just hate feeling so damned helpless."

"When did the doctor say he'd let you start driving again?"

"Next week maybe. He wants to be sure that I'm not going to black out."

"Has Gwenn taken you to the shop yet?"

Chase shook his head, and Robert got to his feet. "I think you've got a bad case of cabin fever. Why don't you go put on something appropriate for visiting a lingerie shop, and I'll drive you down." He glanced at his watch. "The place closes in an hour or so. Gwenn can drive you home. You haven't lived until you've seen Guinevere's Fantasy."

Chase stood up more slowly, rolling the idea over in his mind. The more he thought about it, the more it appealed. Until Robert had mentioned it, he hadn't realized just how confined he was feeling. It would be nice to get out of this house for a while.

"Give me five minutes." His steps were lighter as he left the room and hurried up the stairs. He should have thought of this days ago. Robert was right; he *was* suffering from cabin fever.

Besides, maybe this time seeing something that had been familiar once would unlock the door of his memory.

Chapter 6

When the discreet chime of the doorbell announced the arrival of another customer, Gwenn didn't bother to pay attention. Maggie could take care of it. Gwenn was on her hands and knees, her head deep in the cupboard beneath the register.

It was dark in the cupboard, and her own body blocked out what little light might have come in through the open doors. But there were only a few more receipts to pick up, and it didn't seem worthwhile to try to find the flashlight, which was somewhere in the tiny storage room at the back of the shop. If she hadn't knocked over the box, she wouldn't be crawling around under here chasing little slips of paper.

At least the desk was fully enclosed. Unless someone walked around to the back, no one could see her. Of course, the long peach colored skirt covered her modestly enough though her hips undoubtedly looked six times as wide as they should. She didn't particularly want any of her customers seeing her like this.

Her fingers had just closed around the last elusive slip of paper when a quiet but definitely masculine voice spoke from somewhere in the vicinity of hips.

"Lose something?"

She jerked out of the closet, bumping the back of her head on the upper shelf as she did so. She swung her knees around and sat down on the carpet with a thump, the skirt pooling around her.

Her eyes watered from the pain of her encounter with the shelf as she looked at Chase. He sat back on his heels in front of her and, even to her blurry eyes, he looked remarkably good. The jeans were worn, and the denim molded the muscles of his thighs. A dark green polo shirt stretched across his chest, the buttons undone, giving her a tantalizing glimpse of the curling hair that dusted across his torso. Her nose twitched at the faint smell of paint and turpentine that clung to him.

"I didn't mean to startle you."

She hadn't even been aware that she was rubbing the bumped area on her head until he gently pushed her fingers out of the way and replaced them with his own.

"Are you hurt?"

"Not really." She couldn't drag her eyes away from his. The feel of his fingers in her hair brought on a tingling that had nothing to do with the mild bump on her head. She wanted to lean into his touch and have him cradle her face with his palm just like he used to do years ago, before they'd lost track of each other.

As if reading her thoughts, his hand slid down to the side of her head. The feel of his palm was wonderfully warm and familiar. She inhaled, letting her eyes drift half shut. He smelled of sunshine and cologne and...turpentine. Her nose wrinkled again in helpless response, and the budding intimacy of the moment was shattered by her sneeze.

"I'm sorry...Chase...it's the...turpentine.... It always makes me...sneeze." The words were punctuated by sneezes as Chase helped her to her feet. When he realized that *he* was the cause of her misery, he backed away, raising his hands to show that he wouldn't dream of coming near her again.

His expression was full of such comical dismay that Gwenn laughed between sneezes, leaning weakly against the counter as she tried to bring the fit under control and catch her breath.

Underneath her laughter was regret. A moment that had started out so tenderly had degenerated into a comedy routine. But the regret was only momentary. Maybe they needed to learn how to share laughter as much as tenderness. There'd been too little of both in the past two years.

By the time Robert and Maggie walked up from the front of the store to see what all the commotion was about, Gwenn had stopped sneezing. Chase stood a few feet away, his hands elaborately shoved into his back pockets.

"You two look guilty." Gwenn shook her head in answer to Robert's questioning comment.

"You know how I react to turpentine. What brings the two of you down here?"

"Robert decided I was in danger of developing terminal cabin fever, so he very obligingly crammed me into that sardine can he calls a car and took me on a quick tour of the area."

"I figured you'd be closing up shop pretty soon and Chase could go home with you."

"Oh, dear, does that mean you won't be able to take me home, Gwenn?"

"What?" Gwenn blinked at Maggie. This was the first she'd heard about taking the other woman home.

"My car's in the shop, remember?" Gwenn was about to shake her head and deny remembering anything of the sort. She knew for a fact that Maggie's Datsun was parked behind the store right next to her Porsche. But the intent look in her friend's eyes made her hesitate.

With Chase in the room, it was difficult to really think of anything else, but it wasn't hard to figure out what Maggie was aiming at. Gwenn cleared her throat.

"That's right. I had forgotten about that."

"I'm sure we could still give you a lift, Maggie," Chase said unhelpfully. "I don't think we have any appointment we have to rush off to, do we Gwenn?" For just an instant Gwenn basked in the glow of the moment. She liked the easy way the word *we* had come to his lips. It had to be a good omen.

"Oh, that's okay, Chase. The Porsche isn't really built to take three people. I can catch the bus. I think there's one that stops at the corner around six-thirty."

It was only five-thirty now, and Maggie managed to put just a hint of wistful bravery into the words. Gwenn gave her an admiring look. She couldn't have sounded more pathetic if a blizzard had been raging outside and she had been offering to walk the forty miles to town to buy food for starving children. And the look she gave Robert was just subtle enough to avoid being a hint.

The look Gwenn threw him wasn't subtle at all. Their eyes met, and the gleam in his told her that he wasn't missing any of what was going on. He let the silence drag on for another beat, and Gwenn's glare grew a little more fierce. Just when she was sure he was going to be stubborn about it, he turned to Maggie.

"I can give you a lift home, Maggie. I've got plenty of time before I have to get to work."

She didn't waste any time with false protests. "That would be wonderful, Robert." She gave him a dazzling smile before she turned to look at Gwenn. "You don't mind if I leave a few minutes early, do you?"

"Go ahead. The place is hardly a hotbed of activity at the moment."

Her smile was almost indulgent as she watched the two of them leave the store. With her usual exuberance, Maggie was talking a mile a minute, her hands gesturing widely to illustrate her story.

"Do I gather that we've just been witness to the birth of a romance?"

Gwenn turned to find Chase at her shoulder. "Maggie hopes so. I think they might make a nice couple."

Chase frowned doubtfully. "Don't you think she's a little too...excitable for Robert?"

"Maybe Robert needs someone to shake him up once in a while. I hope you don't mind waiting a little while before we leave. The shop isn't supposed to close until six and I...I..." An explosive sneeze cut off the rest of the sentence, and Chase backed away from her hastily.

"Do you have someplace I can wash up a little more thoroughly? Maybe I can get the smell off my hands."

Gwenn sneezed again, gesturing to the back of the shop. "There's a bathroom in the back."

When Chase came back out, his hands no longer smelled of turpentine. Gwenn had her back to him, sorting through a pile of brightly colored panties. The tingle at the back of her neck told her that he was in the room, but before she had a chance to turn, he had put his hand around in front of her, waving it under her nose.

She sniffed and nodded approvingly. "No turpentine. But I don't think lavender is your scent."

"Well, at least you're not sneezing." He dropped his hand and she expected him to move away. Instead he let his fingers drift into the pile of bright silk on the desk. The contrast of his hand among the delicate garments was evocative. It reminded Gwenn of all the differences between a man and a woman.

She wondered if he could hear the ragged catch in her breathing. She could feel the length of his hard body just inches away from her back. If she turned, would she see desire in his eyes? A hunger to match hers? Was he unaware of the effect of his nearness?

"I think this would be a wonderful color for you," he said huskily, his breath stirring her hair.

She had to blink before she could focus her eyes on the scrap of silk he held up. Bright scarlet, the panties were of the sheerest of laces, a delicate web of threads meant to tantalize and beckon. Gwenn followed the movement of his hand as he brought the tiny garment up to her face as if to compare the color to the flush in her cheek.

Her eyes fluttered shut as the silk touched her skin. He cupped her cheek in his palm and Gwenn turned to face him, obedient to the gentle pressure of his hand. The only contact between them was his hand on her face. She tilted her head as his fingers slid the delicate garment down along her throat, tracing the contours of her collarbone. The flame-colored lace seemed to leave a trail of fire wherever it touched.

"Definitely your color." The words were a murmur against her lips, the merest breath of sound. He let his hand drop as his mouth met hers. Now the only contact between them was his lips tasting the warm response of hers.

The muted chime of the doorbell drew them apart, but they didn't hurry. Gwenn's eyes felt weighted as they opened to meet the slumberous green of her husband's. For once, she didn't see any shadows there. She saw nothing but her own reflection and the desire he made no effort to conceal.

"You have a customer."

She nodded, but she didn't turn her head to see who'd come into the shop. If Chase hadn't stepped away, she would have stayed frozen just where she was. But he moved back, freeing her to attend to the woman who stood on the other side of the shop, ruffling her way through a rack of nightgowns.

Chase stayed out of the way while Gwenn helped her customer select a garment. He wandered idly around the shop, and Gwenn found herself watching him, giving the customer only half her attention.

What did he think of Guinevere's Fantasy? He'd helped to create the place, building shelves, encouraging her when it began to seem like the dream would never become a reality. The night after the shop's grand opening, he'd taken her out to dinner and toasted the newest entrepreneur in the family.

Did those hidden memories give him a warm impression about the shop, or were his feelings influenced by the past few years, when work had become her way of running away from him?

After the customer left, Gwenn shut and locked the door, turning over the sign to indicate that they were closed. It was still a few minutes before six, but for once she was going to quit early. She hurried through the routine of locking up and turning on the alarm system. She was acutely aware of Chase every second.

Her last stop was at the desk, where she ignored the duties of counting out the receipts. She'd do it in the morning. Right now she wanted to be with her husband. She took her purse out from beneath the counter and was about to turn away and announce that she was ready to go when a scrap of scarlet lace caught her eye.

Feeling like a sneak thief in her own shop, she snatched the scandalous pair of panties off the counter and stuffed it into her purse. It wasn't time yet, but one of these days she'd wear these for Chase and let him judge for himself whether or not they were "her color."

"I hope you're not under the mistaken idea that you're being subtle about Maggie."

Gwenn glanced up from the shrimp she was peeling and met her brother's eyes. He was seated on the counter across the kitchen sink from her, a habit their mother had tried in vain to break him of.

"What do you mean? What about Maggie?" She didn't have any real hope of convincing him that she was innocent of any scheming, but the question might stall him long enough for her to decide exactly how much to tell him.

Robert leaned over and grabbed a sliced carrot from the plate beside her. "It's a good thing you didn't want to become an actress. You'd have starved to death." He crunched the carrot. "The two of you were about as subtle as a kamikaze pilot last week. If Maggie wanted me to offer her a lift home, why didn't she just come out and ask?"

"Maybe she felt shy about imposing on you. With her car in the shop..."

His snort made her break off in midsentence. "Her car was parked right next to yours, Gwenn. Chase and I had already been around the back looking for a parking place."

He had her neatly caught, but Gwenn wasn't going to go down without a fight. "How do you know it was hers?"

"A dark blue Datsun, nasty dent in the left front fender, license number JHA 455. That's her car."

Gwenn dropped the shrimp she'd just picked up and turned to look at him. "How come you know so much about Maggie's car? You even know her license plate number."

He snatched another carrot off the plate. "I have my sources," he said mysteriously.

"So if you knew she didn't need a ride, why did you offer one? You knew she wasn't going to be stranded waiting for a bus." She slapped at his marauding fingers when he reached for a water chestnut. "Get out of the vegetables, or I won't have enough for the stir-fry. And answer my question."

He shrugged. "I've had my eye on Maggie ever since you hired her. I asked her out once or twice, and she turned me down, so I figured I'd just bide my time for a while. I knew she'd get tired of playing the field sooner or later, and that's when I'd pounce." He demonstrated his pounce by snatching a carrot out from under his sister's nose.

Gwenn was too stunned by the accuracy of his words to even notice the petty theft. It was like hearing Maggie's words all over again. "Modest, aren't you?" she finally managed.

"Just truthful. I mean to have Maggie. She knows it and I know it. It's just a matter of coming to an agreement as to where and when."

"It would serve you right if she told you to go jump in a lake. You're too sure of yourself, Robert Lawford. Would you get out of the vegetables!" She smacked his hand when he would have snitched yet another carrot, and Robert drew back, giving her a hurt look.

"How could you strike your own flesh and blood? The brother who raised you from childhood? I was just trying to stave off hunger with a meager carrot stick."

Gwenn ignored his heart-wrenching speech and moved the plate out of his reach. "If you reach for that plate again, you're going to pull back minus a few fingers," she threatened. She continued with her task of peeling the shrimp. "The way you eat, I could spend the rest of the night cutting up food and never get dinner on the table. And now that Chase's appetite is back to normal, I don't want to skimp on dinner. So stave off starvation with a glass of water."

He recognized when he was beat and shrugged philosophically. "I suppose I can survive until dinner. How is Chase, by the way? He seems to be looking better every time I see him."

Gwenn's mouth widened in a smile, and her eyes took on a happy sparkle. "He's getting better even faster than the doctor expected. He got permission to drive again, so he's been taking the Aston Martin out in the afternoon and just driving around looking at things." Some of the pleasure faded from her expression. "I think he keeps hoping that he's going to see something that will unlock his memory."

"No luck?"

"Not so far. The doctor said it may come back in bits and pieces. But I know Chase is getting frustrated. The few things he does remember are mostly just little details. Not all that important by themselves."

She forced her hands to move again, stripping the last shrimp out of its shell. "I hope he remembers soon."

"Do you?"

The question was so quiet that it took a moment for her to realize what he'd said. She'd reached for the faucet and was about to turn on the cold water so that she could rinse the cleaned shrimp, but she froze, the movement uncompleted. She turned to look at Robert, her eyes wide with shock.

"What do you mean? Of course I want him to remember. Why wouldn't I want that?"

"Because of just what he's going to remember. I'm glad things are going well for the two of you right now, but when he regains his memory, he's going to know that things weren't going at all well between you before the kidnapping."

"Well, he'll understand why I didn't tell him about that. He knows the doctor said he shouldn't be upset. Besides, it wouldn't have served any purpose to tell him about it. I haven't exactly lied to him. I never told him everything was perfect."

"What about Livvie?" he asked quietly. "You can't say you haven't lied about that. How's he going to feel when he finds out about Livvie?"

Gwenn's eyes dropped to the sink, and she reached down to push idly at a discarded shrimp shell. "Chase will understand. I did it for his own good."

"Did you? Are you sure that was the only reason, Gwennie?" The childhood nickname brought tears to her eyes. She shook her head, unable to answer his question around the lump in her throat, and Robert went on. "I know things were pretty bad between the two of you before the kidnapping. You wouldn't be human if some part of you didn't look on this as a chance to make things go back to the way they were when you were first married."

His voice was gentle, but his words were blunt. "I don't think there's anything wrong with that dream, as long as you remember to keep it separate from reality. No matter what happens between the two of you now, when Chase gets his memory back, he's going to be upset and hurt and angry.

There's nothing you can do about that, but just be sure you don't keep anything from him that you don't have to."

The silence in the kitchen stretched for several seconds while Gwenn weighed his words, searching her heart.

"I really do want him to get his memory back, Robert. I know I haven't always been there for him in the past," she admitted with difficulty. "But I want to be there for him this time. And, if he hates me when he remembers everything, I'll just have to face that when the time comes."

"I think Chase loves you too much to ever hate you. I just don't want you to lose track of the real situation."

The back door swung open, breaking the strained silence. Gwenn turned away, blinking rapidly to get rid of the tears in her eyes. Robert shifted his position on the counter to look at Chase, raising his brows when he saw what the other man was carrying.

Chase stopped inside the door, his eyes skimming back and forth between Robert and Gwenn. "Something wrong?"

Gwenn shook her head without turning. She was apparently engrossed in some task at the counter. Robert shrugged. "Nothing's wrong except that your wife is a hard, cruel woman. Here I am, on the verge of starvation, and she's refused me even a morsel of food. She even threatened to do me bodily harm."

Since he looked the very picture of well-fed indolence, Chase took his complaints with a grain of salt. "I suspect if Gwenn threatened you, it was only to keep you from eating us out of house and home."

Gwenn laughed, still without turning, and Chase wondered if it was only his imagination that heard an unsteady note in that laughter. Certainly, more had been going on that a squabble over Robert snitching too many bites of food. They were concealing something from him.

The familiar anger was muted. If they were lying, it was because they thought it was best. Nothing he could say would convince them otherwise. Until he regained his memory, he couldn't begin to guess at what caused all the undercurrents that flowed around him. His anger was directed more at this own stubborn inability to remember than at those who thought they were doing the right thing. Now was not the time to fight with either of them.

He cleared his throat. "I noticed there was an empty spot on the wall over there, and I thought this might fill it in." He was amazed to discover how nervous he was as Gwenn turned to look at him. Without saying anything else, he handed her the whimsical wooden goose.

She gasped, and he saw that her hand was shaking slightly as she reached to take it from him. His hand was shaking a bit, too. Would she like it? Wife or not, he knew so little about her taste—another thing his memory had robbed him of. She stared at the simple carving for a moment without speaking and then pulled it close against her chest, as if cradling something precious.

"Oh, Chase. It's wonderful. Thank you so much." She stepped closer, her face tilted to his, and it seemed the most natural thing in the world to drop a kiss on her soft mouth.

There was no doubt that she liked the plaque. So why was he sure that the tears in her eyes had their source in whatever she and Robert had been discussing and not just in her pleasure over his gift?

He was still asking the question at one o'clock in the morning. He stared at the dark ceiling over his bed, wondering if he was becoming paranoid, looking for hidden meanings that didn't exist. Maybe Gwenn's tears had been caused by nothing more than pleasure, maybe she hadn't been oddly subdued for the remainder of the evening.

And maybe he hadn't really lost his memory.

He sat up and swung his feet out of bed. The night air was warm on his bare chest, and he ran his hand exploringly over the muscles there. Physically, he was improving by leaps and bounds. Flexing his fingers now brought no more than a distant twinge of discomfort. If it weren't for the splint that still covered his little finger, it would be easy to forget that he wasn't back to normal.

Restlessly he stood up and crossed to the bathroom. He flipped the light switch and then narrowed his eyes against the sudden brilliance. Leaning on the counter, he stared at the face in the mirror, comparing it to the face he'd first seen at the hospital.

He'd adjusted to the fact that this was his face. He didn't remember it before that awakening in the hospital, but he'd grown accustomed to seeing it when he looked in the mirror. He'd gained weight since he'd come home, and it showed. His cheeks were less hollow, his mouth less pinched. His eyes had lost some of the vacant look. There were memories behind those eyes, but only the memories he'd created since the cellar.

Staring into the mirror, he sought answers to questions he was half afraid to ask. Who was Chase Buchanon? A warning throb began to pulse in his temples, and with a muffled curse he spun away from his reflection, snapping the light off as he left the bathroom.

Maybe a glass of milk would help him get back to sleep. He opened his bedroom door quietly and stepped out into the hall, but he didn't head for the stairs. Instead he stopped and stared at the door across the hall from his.

Was Gwenn asleep, or was she lying awake thinking about all the things she hadn't told him? And just what were those things?

Something had been seriously wrong with their marriage, and it had driven them to separate beds. How much time had passed since he'd made love to his wife? The ache that answered that question said that it had been a long time.

He crossed the hall to lay his palm flat against the closed door. What would she do if he were to open that door? Would she welcome him, or would she turn him away?

He stood there for a moment longer, aching to feel her warmth against him, and then he turned away. The milk was forgotten as he stepped back into his own room. He wanted her, and he wanted answers but, for the moment, he'd leave things as they were. He wasn't quite ready to rock the boat.

Gwenn turned the pieces of sizzling bacon and then picked up an egg. Behind her Chase was setting the table. The quiet domesticity of the moment soothed her tense nerves in a way nothing else could have. This was the way it should be. The way it *would* be, she promised herself fiercely.

Out of the corner of her eye, she could see the wooden goose Chase had given her. She smiled. Whenever she began to have doubts about their future, she had only to remember that simple gift, and her optimism was renewed.

Chase dropped a piece of silverware, and it clanged to the floor. His muffled curse echoed it and Gwenn's smile faded. As the days went by he was getting more and more frustrated, and he still couldn't remember his past. The doctor could only repeat that amnesia was a poorly understood phenomenon, and the best he could offer was that Chase's memory would return whenever he could deal with it.

It was poor consolation to Chase. Gwenn knew he felt able to deal with it now. He wanted to get on with his life, look to the future. But how could he look to the future when he didn't have a past?

And then the past rushed in on her with a speed that took her breath away.

"Did I ever make an oak cradle?"

"What?" Was that her voice? It sounded so normal.

Behind her she could hear Chase stir restlessly and then the thud as he set down a plate. "I was looking through some plans that I found in the shop yesterday. One set was for a cradle. There were notations on it, like it was something I'd made."

He stopped speaking, but Gwenn couldn't have said anything if her life depended on it. After a moment Chase spoke again, and she could hear the frustration in his voice.

"I thought I could remember it, too. It was oak, and I put some carving in the base and headboard." He hated having to ask her something that he should have known. She could hear that in his tone.

Don't lie to him if you don't have to. Robert's warning came back to her, but she didn't have any choice. How could she tell him that the cradle he remembered was in the attic?

"You did make a cradle, and I think it *was* oak. It was for some friends of ours."

"Friends? Do they still have it? Could I see it? I have this feeling that it was important. If I could see it, I might remember something more."

She felt as if she were bleeding to death. How could she lie to him, and yet how could she tell him the truth?

There was a shallow crunching sound, and suddenly her hand was filled with a cold, sticky substance. She looked down, wondering if she'd see her own blood pouring out. But it was only an egg, the shell crushed by the pressure of her fingers.

"John and Amanda moved to New York a couple of years ago," she lied calmly.

She could feel Chase's disappointment even before she heard it in his voice.

"So much for that idea. It probably wouldn't have worked, anyway." He sounded so discouraged that Gwenn wanted to cry. Instead she threw the mess in her hand into the sink and rinsed the egg from her fingers.

When she turned to look at him, her smile was only a little strained. "I just had a great idea. Why don't I call Maggie and tell her to manage without me for today? After breakfast I'll pack a picnic lunch, and we'll drive to Descanso Gardens and spend the rest of the day there."

Chase had to force himself to return her smile. He'd been so sure that the cradle held some clue to his past. It was getting harder and harder to hang on to his patience.

"Sure. Why not? Maybe I've been spending too many hours in the shop."

Chapter 7

"You used to love this place. We came here a lot before we were married."

"What happened after we were married?"

"We still came here a lot," Gwenn answered promptly, throwing him a smile.

Despite his disappointment over yet another dead end, Chase could not help but be cheered by her mood. If there was a slightly feverish air to her happiness, he was sure it was just his imagination. He steered the Aston Martin around a sharp corner and forced himself to relax.

The weather was exquisite, he was regaining his health and he had a beautiful woman beside him who just happened to be his wife. Just because he didn't have a memory, the papers he was suspected of stealing still hadn't turned up, and there were, quite possibly, men who wanted to kidnap him again, that didn't mean that he shouldn't count his blessings.

The absurdity of his thoughts drew a genuine laugh from him. He turned his head to meet Gwenn's questioning eyes and shook his head, still chuckling.

"I couldn't possibly explain."

Gwenn didn't really care why he was laughing. All that mattered was that he seemed happy. The cradle was forgotten, at least for the moment. Her smile widened into a grin, and she threw her arms out to embrace the wind that rushed over the convertible.

Today she wasn't going to worry about the past, the future or anything but making sure that Chase stayed as happy as he seemed to be at this moment. They were going to steal this one day out of time.

On an early weekday afternoon, the picnic area was almost empty, and they had their choice of tables. They chose one that fell under the shade of a huge live oak, and Gwenn unpacked their lunch. Chase had complained loudly about the weight of the basket when he'd loaded it into the car but, once the food was spread in front of him, he didn't seem to think she'd brought too much.

Neither of them had been much in the mood for breakfast, so they fell on the fried chicken and potato salad as though they were famished. They squabbled amiably over the last drumstick and were almost too full to eat any of the brownies.

Gwenn put the remains of their meal back into the basket, but neither of them was in any hurry to leave. Their laziness was rewarded when a shy quail tiptoed out from beneath the shelter of some bushes and pecked at the ground. They stayed perfectly still, hardly daring to breathe, but something must have startled it. It disappeared so quickly it was easy to believe it'd never been there at all.

"Come on, lazy. Let's go see the gardens."

Chase mumbled a protest as he got to his feet and lifted the basket, much reduced in weight. "I thought *this* was the gardens."

"This is just the picnic area. We haven't even entered the gardens proper."

After Chase had put the basket back in the car, they paid the small entrance fee and walked along the cement walkway that led into the garden.

"What do we see first, the rose garden, or shall we strike right out into the wilderness?"

"The wilderness? You didn't tell me to bring my hiking boots. After all that food, I think we should start out slow and easy. Let's try the rose garden."

It seemed the most natural thing in the world for Chase to take her hand, and Gwenn found herself keeping close to him, leaning her head on his shoulder when they stopped to admire a particularly beautiful rose.

The afternoon drifted by without worries or cares. It was as if, when they'd walked through the gate, they'd left the real world on the other side. They wandered through the gardens, with Gwenn pointing out the varieties that matched the ones she had planted at home. Several times she stopped to dig a pencil and a wrinkled scrap of paper out of her jeans pocket, so that she could write down the name of a variety to add to her collection.

Chase had no way of knowing that this was the first time in more than two years that she'd considered adding new roses to the garden. For the first three years of their marriage, it had been a tradition that the two of them would sit down and decide what new colors and types they should add.

Chase didn't know the significance of their discussions, but Gwenn did. If she tried, she could almost imagine that the past two years had never happened. Except that nothing could ever bring Livvie back. But she wasn't going to think about that today.

After they'd thoroughly explored the rose garden, they wandered over a bridge that crossed a narrow stream. Once past the stream, they might have been seeing the land, as it had been a hundred years ago. Live oaks covered the acres and acres of hillside. And the quiet was so intense that it was hard to believe they were surrounded by city in all directions.

"I wonder if this is how the first explorers saw this area." Chase kept his voice low, as if he was reluctant to break the silence.

"I don't know. If it is, it's no wonder that they decided to stay. Oh, look! There's a squirrel."

Her hand tightened on his arm, drawing him to a halt. Chase watched the squirrel bustle about, pausing now and again as it found something on the ground that looked edible. But he found his gaze being drawn to the woman beside him.

In worn jeans and equally well-used T-shirt, with her hair drawn back in a simple braid, she looked about sixteen. Her skin was creamy smooth, and it was only when she smiled that the tiny creases beside her eyes gave away her age. But she looked even more beautiful to him then.

"Isn't he pretty?" The squirrel's antics drew a soft laugh from her.

"Beautiful."

Something in his tone told her that he wasn't talking about the squirrel, and she turned to look at him. Her breath caught in her throat at the expression in his eyes. There was desire there, but there was also love.

"Do you think they have a rule about kissing in front of the animals?"

"I don't know." Her voice was soft and breathless as he turned her to face him. She rested her hands on the yellow T-shirt he wore. Beneath the thin fabric she could feel the crisp texture of his chest hair, and beneath that she could feel the steady beat of his heart.

It felt so good just to be close to him, to be able to touch him and feel the solid thump of his heart. It had been so long, and she'd come so close to losing him forever.

He slid his hand up her back, tracing the ridge of her spine until his palm rested on the nape of her neck. He tugged gently, urging her closer, and Gwenn eased her hands upward until her arms circled his neck. She met his mouth halfway.

The kiss was warm and undemanding, but there was a passion underlying it that told her there was no lack of desire. They drew apart, and Gwenn slowly lifted her eyes to look into the green of his.

"I think I'm falling in love with you." He hadn't planned to say the words, but once they were out, he wasn't sorry. Gwenn's eyes widened in shock, and Chase laughed self-consciously.

"Maybe that sounds foolish. We're married. I *should* be in love with you." Still Gwenn said nothing. His hand moved restlessly against her back.

"Gwenn, I know that there was something wrong with our marriage, even before the kidnapping. No." His fingers covered her mouth, and the scrape of the splint against her cheek reminded her of the need to let him discover the past on his own. But she had to bite her tongue to hold back the urge to tell him everything.

"Don't say anything. I'm not asking what it was. Right now, I'm not even sure I *want* to know what it was. Let's just take today and not think about the future or worry about the past. Let's have today for us."

"Oh, Chase." She blinked against the tears that filled her eyes. It couldn't have been easy for him to lay his feelings out in the open. She wanted to be able to tell him that he was wrong—that there'd never been a problem in their marriage.

The kiss they then shared was full of promise, and neither of them noticed when the squirrel crept a little closer and then sat upright to stare at the two humans who'd invaded his domain.

They lingered at Descanso until the hot summer sun had slipped low in the western sky. There were other people at the garden, but as far as Gwenn and Chase were concerned, they might as well have been alone. They held hands like young lovers, stopping to share a quiet kiss now and then, talking a little. The past was taboo, and the future was uncertain, so they spoke mostly of impersonal things that were made personal by the intimacy of the moment.

As Chase guided the Aston Martin between the high gates that led out of the parking lot, Gwenn had the melancholy feeling that something beautiful was coming to an end. When they returned to the house, they'd be going back to the real world. If only they could pretend for a little while longer.

"Let's go out for dinner." Chase's words so closely echoed her own thoughts that for an instant, Gwenn wondered if she'd spoken them herself. Her delighted smile told him how much she liked the suggestion.

An hour later Gwenn was struggling with the zipper at the back of her dress when Chase knocked on her door. She hesitated a moment, staring at her reflection in the mirror. The zipper was definitely stuck. If she didn't have help, she could get neither in nor out of the teal silk dress she'd chosen.

She drew a deep breath. This was ridiculous. Chase was her husband; he'd helped her zip a dress before. But that had been a long time ago. Until the kidnapping they'd been two strangers who happened to share the same last name.

"Come in."

Chase stepped into the room with curiosity. It was the first time since his return from the hospital that he'd been in here long enough to really get a good look. The night of the break-in hardly counted. Then the room had been dark, and he'd had other things on his mind. The room suited Gwenn, he decided instantly. Soft feminine blues contrasted with the antique oak furniture. The wardrobe Doug had mentioned stood in one corner. A wide bed with oak foot- and headboards dominated the room.

But all that he noticed with his peripheral vision. From the moment he stepped through the door, he couldn't take his eyes off Gwenn. Gone was the casual, girlish look of jeans and T-shirt. This wasn't even the polished image she presented when she was dressed to go to her shop.

Tonight she was completely feminine. From the narrow straps that crossed her shoulders to the soft swirl of a skirt that stopped at midcalf, everything about her was soft and inviting.

"I'm...ah...having trouble with my zipper. Do you think you could help?"

Only then did he notice that she had one hand behind her back, apparently holding her dress together.

"Sure. I think I can work a zipper." She turned her back to him as he approached, revealing the stubborn tab caught in the delicate silk halfway up its track. Gwenn released her tight grip, and Chase bent his head over the task. The clumsiness he felt had nothing to do with the splint on his finger.

She'd swept her hair up in a soft Gibson girl style, leaving several tendrils free to curl enticingly. Her nape was only inches from his mouth, and he was aware of the delicate scent of her perfume. Even when zipped, the dress only came midway up her back, and the length of her spine enticed him. He wanted to forget about the zipper and ease his hands beneath the thin silk, sliding them around to cup her breasts. He wanted to find the pins that held her hair in place and pull them out one by one until the silken strands cascaded over his hands.

The pool of light cast by one table lamp near the dresser was bright enough to allow him to see what he was doing but left the rest of the room invitingly dim. He was vividly aware of the bed only a few feet away.

Gwenn wondered if he could feel the faint tremor that shook her when his fingers touched her back. She stared at the pale wood of the dresser, almost afraid to look in the mirror, to see them together. Her eyes lifted slowly.

Chase's head was bent down, his eyes on the recalcitrant zipper. The lamplight picked out the reddish highlights in his hair. The green silk shirt he wore was one she'd bought him when they were first married, and she knew the way his eyes were heightened by its color. He'd regained most of the weight he'd lost, and the gray slacks molded his hips, emphasizing the flatness of his stomach.

She didn't have to close her eyes to picture the mat of red-brown hair that covered his chest, arrowing down across his stomach. She could feel the quickened beat of her pulse. He tilted his head to get a better angle on the stubborn zipper, and she felt his breath against the back of her neck, raising goose bumps of awareness.

"I think I've got it." Was his voice huskier than usual, or was it her imagination?

His hands remained on her back as his eyes lifted to meet hers in the mirror. His eyes were brighter now and smoldering with a beckoning promise. There was a question in their depths. She was incapable of answering it verbally, but she didn't need to say anything. He read the response in the smoky gray of her eyes, in the flush that mantled her cheeks, in the disturbed rhythm of her breathing.

The zipper moved beneath his fingers, sliding smoothly downward until it stopped at the base of her spine. The narrow straps held the bodice up as Chase's palms flattened against her back before sliding around her rib cage and coming to a rest just below her breasts. He hesitated, giving her a chance to change her mind.

Her eyes locked on his, Gwenn let her back arch, wordlessly urging him to end the torture. Chase exhaled, and excitement flared in his eyes as his hands slid upward, cupping her breasts. Gwenn's breath left her on a shuddering sigh, and her head fell back onto the ready support of his shoulder.

His thumbs rubbed across her nipples, tightening the flesh into almost painful sensitivity. With her eyes closed to savor the intense pleasure, Gwenn shook the straps loose from her shoulders, letting the bodice fall to her waist.

She felt more than heard Chase's sharp intake of breath, and she opened her eyes to see the two of them reflected in the mirror. The sight of his hands against the milky flesh of her breasts was incredibly erotic. He caught her nipples between the thumb and forefinger of each hand, rubbing delicately until he drew a muffled whimper of pleasure from her.

There was a gleam of satisfaction in his eyes as he continued to toy with her breasts with one hand while the other slid down her stomach. Watching his broad hand press against her flesh, Gwenn had a fleeting moment of gratitude for all the hours she'd spent doing exercises she hated.

His fingers traced the waistband of her panty hose, sliding just inside the nylon, teasing gently before he let his hand slide beneath it. His hand paused as it reached the top of her satin panties, and Gwenn held her breath. And then his fingers slid over the fabric, cupping her through its gossamer thinness.

She tried to turn—to go into his arms—but he held her still. "Watch." The word was whispered against her ear an instant before his teeth tugged at the lobe, his tongue circling the diamond stud there.

"Chase." His name was an aching plea, but he refused to let her move.

"Watch." And Gwenn was helpless to do anything else. Her fingers clenched and unclenched. Deprived of anything to hold on to, she could only watch her reflection in the mirror.

"Your breasts feel so soft and silky." His tongue feathered along the sensitive skin beneath her ear, his breath stirring the tendrils of her hair. "I'd like to taste them, to feel them harden under my tongue just like they are now."

Gwenn moaned, arching her back into the warm pressure of his hand. His fingers continued to brush gently back and forth across the thin fabric of her panties, teasing, tantalizing, hinting at pleasures to come.

There was nothing in the world but the two of them in this dim room, and the things he was doing to her, saying to her. It had been so long. She hadn't realized how much she missed his touch until he'd been taken from her, and the weeks since his return had added fuel to the fire that she'd thought burned out long ago.

"I can feel you quivering, Gwenn. For me?" His finger found the center of her need and rubbed it tantalizingly, still with the frustrating layer of cloth between them.

"Chase, please." She could hardly hear her own voice for the pulse that pounded in her ears. But she had no trouble hearing every word he said, feeling every touch. The pressure that was building inside was a hot wave of passion. Years of denial and of need built behind it, pushing the wave ever higher.

The furred length of his arm was like a steel band across her stomach, and her hand found the hard muscles there, her nails digging in to anchor herself as he pushed aside her underwear and his fingers at last touched the moist welcome of her.

Gwenn stiffened for a moment at the almost painful intimacy of his touch, and then she melted against him. Chase stroked the delicate folds, drawing her closer and closer to the peak she sensed rushing toward her. She twisted in his arms, seeking relief for the hot tightness that gripped her body. And he gave it to her, his thumb brushing gently across the heat of her need and then returning with a more demanding caress.

"Chase!" His name quivered in the air as she stiffened in near agony, her neck arching back as the pleasure took her. His fingers continued to rest against her, sensing that she needed that contact; that to withdraw too soon would leave her bereft.

If it hadn't been for the support of Chase's arms about her, Gwenn would have sunk to the floor. Her quivering knees could never have supported her. She shivered as his hands slowly left her, coming to rest on her waist, turning her into his arms.

She lifted her eyes to his face, half afraid of what she might see there. Would he be disgusted by the wanton response he'd drawn from her so easily? But his eyes were warm and slumberous, still holding a promise. Against her stomach she could feel the pressure of his desire and, though she wouldn't have believed it possible so soon, the feel of him brought a renewed tingle of anticipation.

Her fingers drifted slowly down his shirt, sliding buttons through buttonholes as she went. The buckle on his belt eased apart beneath her touch. His hands caressed her hips, and her dress gave up its last tentative hold and dropped to the floor.

Words didn't seem necessary. Outside, the warm summer night was still, but no more so than the room inside. The silk shirt left his shoulders and joined her dress in tangled abandon.

She murmured a protest when he bent to lift her into his arms. "You shouldn't. You might hurt yourself."

He shook his head. "The only hurt I'm worried about is the one I want to ease in you."

He carried her the few feet to the bed and set her down on the thick carpet. He slid his hands inside her panty hose and pushed them down over her hips, going to his knees as he eased them down her legs. Gwenn braced her hands against his shoulders as she stepped out of her hose.

He caught the fragile lace that formed the top of her panties between his teeth and tugged gently. With his hands assisting, the narrow garment slid down her legs, leaving her naked.

"Chase, let me. Don't...ah." The cry was torn from her as his tongue gently tasted her still-quivering flesh. His hands cupped her buttocks, pulling her forward to meet the delicate torture of his mouth.

Gwenn's hands left his shoulder to tangle in the russet brown of his hair but whether to pull him closer or push him away, she couldn't have said.

Chase's own desire was too demanding for him to drag out the moment the way he would have liked to.

His hands were shaking with need as he eased Gwenn back onto the bed and quickly rid himself of the rest of his clothes. When she finally felt the hard length of his body touching hers, the sensation was so exquisite it was almost unbearable.

Her fingers dug into his hips, drawing him still closer, urging him forward. The aroused need sought the heated warmth of her. Their eyes met, and he rested against her, teasing them both with the realization of how close they were to completion.

She wet her lips with the tip of her tongue, and with a low groan, Chase bent to taste that moisture. His tongue eased into her mouth at the same instant that his body sheathed itself in hers.

Gwenn hadn't realized how empty she'd been until this instant when that emptiness was filled. She'd been only half alive without Chase, her emotions dulled, her body unawakened. It had been so long since she felt complete. So long.

Chase fought for control in the swirling pleasure that threatened to engulf him. She held him so snugly, as if she were made for him alone. He lifted and thrust, feeling her hips arch to receive him, to deepen the contact. Her soft whimpers drove him closer to the edge and, paradoxically, held him back. He wanted to prolong her pleasure, wanted to feel her exploding around him.

But he was only a man, and when he felt the delicate contractions of her body tighten on his, he could prolong the moment no longer. He buried his face in the thick fall of her hair, only aware of her arms around him, in the entire world, only aware of her.

His hard body shuddered over her, and Gwenn tightened her arms, letting the pleasure sweep her away.

The slide back to earth was slow. It was several minutes before Chase gathered the energy to lift his weight from

Gwenn's limp body and shift to the side. Even then, he pulled her against his side, needing to feel her close. Gwenn snuggled her cheek into his chest, savoring the scent of his damp skin.

"We didn't make it out to dinner." His voice was a rumble beneath her ear.

"Didn't we? Funny, I feel remarkably full."

His arm tightened for an instant, squeezing her against his side. "I can't say I feel much like going out now, either."

Gwenn stifled a yawn. The physical and emotional release of weeks—or was it years?—of tension had left her drowsy and relaxed. Chase rubbed his cheek against the top of her head, and a contented smile touched her lips, but she didn't bother to open her eyes. There were so many things to discuss, but she was so sleepy. They could talk in the morning.

Chase listened to the even pattern of her breathing, and he also smiled. She was snuggled against him like a kitten seeking warmth. His hand stroked absently at her back as he stifled a yawn of his own. It was too early to be going to sleep, but he couldn't imagine doing anything else.

In the morning they would talk. He'd make her see how silly it was to continue keeping his own past from him. Whatever it was, they could talk about it. Maybe talking about it would help him regain his memory.

The light was still on, and the curtains were still open, but he couldn't gather the energy to get up. The long walk through the gardens, the tension of the past weeks and the explosive lovemaking had left him tired and contented. Tonight he'd sleep with his arms around his wife, and tomorrow they'd talk.

Now, more than ever, he wanted to get his life back together, to straighten out the past and look toward the future. And right at this moment he could really believe in the future. A future that held Gwenn.

Chapter 8

It was early when Chase awoke the next morning, but the sun was already pouring in through the open curtains. For the first time since waking in the hospital, he didn't have a nagging feeling of not belonging in the body he wore. This morning he felt contented with his world. He didn't have to look far for the source of that contentment.

He raised himself up on one elbow, careful not to disturb the bed's other occupant. During the night Gwenn had rolled onto her back and was sprawled comfortably over a good portion of the bed. It was easy to see that she was used to sleeping alone. He wondered how long had it been since they'd shared a bed.

Reaching out to brush a lock of hair back from her face, he studied her features as if they could give him the answers to all his questions. Quite a while, he decided. It had been months since they'd shared a bed, maybe even years. Her response had been everything he could have dreamed of, but her body had possessed the feel of a woman who'd been without a lover for a long time. It had been almost like making love to a virgin, and he had needed all his willpower to love her gently.

He let his fingers touch the delicate contours of her collarbone, exploring the vulnerable hollows there, testing the steady beat of her pulse. The night had been hot enough to make covers unnecessary. Hot enough in more ways than one, he thought with a half smile. Her body lay open to him, vulnerable in the bright sunlight. She might not like being quite so exposed if she were awake, but he couldn't resist the urge to explore her with his eyes.

Her breasts were flattened by her position, but he could easily remember the weight of them in his palm, the taste of them on his tongue. She'd told him that she burned easily and never exposed herself to the sun, so her skin was a milky white, delicate, feminine.

His finger trailed down the valley between her breasts and came to a halt in her belly button. He knew she hated to exercise but considered it a necessary evil, so the skin on her stomach was smooth and firm, soft and silky with narrow white lines across the delicate skin.

He drew his hand away slowly, feeling his head begin to pound. He couldn't drag his eyes away from those damning marks. Stretch marks. The kind of stretch marks a woman gets from carrying a child.

The pounding grew steadily worse.

He sat on the bed next to Gwenn, gently rubbing lotion onto the swollen mound of her belly.

"I look like a beached whale." Her voice was mournful, with a hint of tears that told him how badly she needed reassurance.

"You look beautiful." And it wasn't a lie. She was beautiful, rounded stomach and all. "Come on, in a few weeks

you'll be holding a little baby in your arms. Eustace if it's a boy or Xenia if it's a girl."

As he'd intended, she laughed, even if there was a slightly watery sound to it. "It's a good thing we agreed that I get to name the baby. Your taste is dreadful. If it's a boy, we're going to name him David Chase after your father, and if it's a girl, we'll name her Olivia after my mother. We can call her Livvie."

Livvie.

The pain intensified until he thought his head would explode. He rolled away from Gwenn and sat up on the edge of the bed, cradling his head in his hands. Confused images spun through his mind: a tall dark-haired man who he knew was his father; a younger Robert Lawford; Gwenn in an ivory lace gown, her eyes wide with nervous tension as she walked toward him down a church aisle.

And a laughing little girl with strawberry blond hair who ran toward him with unsteady steps and held up her hands to be lifted into his arms. Who called him Daddy.

A muffled groan of pain tore from his throat, and he got to his feet, staggering out of the room. Behind him lay his clothes and Gwenn's, tangled together in suggestive intimacy. Gwenn stirred once as he opened the door, and her brows came together in a frown as if something had intruded into her sleep. Then she turned her face into the pillow and relaxed again.

Gwenn awoke suddenly, her heart pounding as if she'd been running. She sat up in bed, her eyes wildly searching the room, and then collapsed back against the pillows with a sigh. A bad dream. That's all it had been. Then she noticed Chase wasn't beside her. She sighed again, this time a happy sigh. The fear from the dream was already fading.

It would have been nice to have him beside her when she woke, but that was a small cloud on the golden glow of her happiness. Her hand drifted dreamily over his pillow. Just to know he'd been there was enough to make her feel as if all was right with her world.

She sat up and swung her feet off the bed, giggling as she caught sight of the abandoned scattering of their clothes. She could pick things up later. Right now she wanted to see Chase. She wanted to feel his arms around her again and his mouth on hers.

Her steps were light as she hurried over to the wardrobe and found a soft cotton robe. The fabric was light, but it wasn't quite transparent. It hinted at far more than it revealed, and the robe gave her a feeling of femininity that few garments could match.

She ran a few strokes of the brush through her hair, smiling at her own image in the mirror before she crossed the hall to Chase's room. It wasn't going to be his room much longer, she promised herself. After last night, there wouldn't be any reason for separate bedrooms.

She tapped lightly on the door and then pushed it open. The room was empty. She cocked her head, listening for the sound of the shower. There was no sound from the bathroom. He must be downstairs. Maybe he was fixing her breakfast in bed. When they were first married, he'd sometimes surprised her with a tray for breakfast. And, more often than not, the food had grown cold while they made love.

She smiled at the memories and left the room, turning down the hall to the stairs. But before she could take a step, her senses told her that there was something out of place. She turned slowly to face the end of the hall opposite the stairs. There wasn't much to see: the door to what had once been a nursery but had been converted to a storage room two years ago; a framed print that Chase had bought for her on their first anniversary.

And the door to the attic. A door that hadn't been opened since Chase returned home. A door she'd deliberately kept locked. When Chase had asked her about it, she'd dismissed it, saying that the attic stairs weren't safe, and they hadn't gotten around to repairing them.

The door was now wide open, gaping onto the steep flight of stairs in a way that was anything but inviting.

She didn't have to wonder anymore where Chase was.

Full attics in Southern California were a rarity. It was one of the things she'd loved about the house, one of the reasons she hadn't minded the time and trouble involved in modernizing the old home. An attic was in keeping with antiques and rose gardens. After Livvie had been born, they'd talked about finishing the attic and widening the stairs, making it into a living space.

Now, Gwenn thought as she forced her feet to climb the steps, she wished the attic didn't even exist. But it was a futile wish. It was there, and if it hadn't been, the memories it held would simply have been stored somewhere else. Chase would still have found them.

He'd turned on the lights, and the bare bulbs illuminated the unfinished space with harsh clarity. Sunlight poured in through the small panes of glass that marked either end of the attic. Dust motes danced in the brilliant streams of light. It was hot with the accumulated heat of summer.

Chase sat on the edge of an ancient stuffed chair, one of Gwenn's purchases that she'd never gotten around to refinishing. He was wearing a pair of faded jeans, but he hadn't bothered with a shirt. His elbows rested on his knees, and his head was bent, his eyes on something he held between his hands.

Gwenn didn't have to move closer. She already knew he held a silver-framed photo of a smiling toddler, her green eyes alight with mischief. Until three days before Chase had returned from the hospital, that photo had sat on Chase's dresser, and a duplicate had sat on hers. In the past two years, it had been one of the few things they'd shared.

He must have heard her approach, but he didn't lift his eyes from the portrait until she stood right in front of him. Even then, he didn't acknowledge her presence until she spoke his name.

"Chase?" Her voice was hesitant, uncertain. Frightened.

His shoulders twitched as if that one word was a stinging lash across them. For a moment Gwenn thought he was going to ignore her, refuse to admit she was there, but then his head lifted slowly until he looked up at her.

She had been prepared to see anger, pain, confusion. But the raw agony in his face struck deep into her soul. His eyes were red rimmed but dry, like a man's who'd spent days under a burning desert sun. Deep lines cut into the skin around his mouth, and his lips were flattened out in pain.

"Chase." She dropped to her knees and reached out instinctively, needing to offer him comfort. His withdrawal was immediate. Nothing so melodramatic as pulling physically out of reach. It was a mental and emotional retreat that was unmistakable. Gwenn let her hands drop before she touched his.

"Chase, I—"

"Damn you." The words were uttered in a flat, empty voice.

She winced, her eyes dropping to the photo he held. "I'm sorry you found out like this. I—"

"How could you shut me away from my own child?"

"The doctor said you—"

"It has nothing to do with what the doctor said. You've been trying to shut me away from Livvie ever since she died."

"That's not true." Gwenn blinked back tears, trying to marshal her thoughts. "I was grieving, Chase. I hurt."

"Do you think I didn't grieve? Do you think I didn't hurt? She was my daughter, too. I loved her just as much as you did."

"I know. I didn't mean..." Her voice trailed off as she realized what he was saying. "Chase, you remember Livvie! Your memory. Do...can you...?"

"I remember almost everything." But there was no interest in his voice, no relief.

Gwenn reached out to touch the back of his hand, her fingers trembling. "Darling, that's wonderful. When did this happen? How do you feel?"

Chase let his eyes drift over her face. Excitement shone in her gray eyes, and a tentative smile was on her lips. His gaze shifted to her hand. He said nothing for a long moment, and then he quite deliberately moved his hand away from hers. Gwenn's soft gasp echoed in the quiet space.

"When I woke up this morning, I just wanted to lie in bed and look at my beautiful wife." His voice was level, but bitterness threaded through the quiet tones. "I was thinking how well everything was going to work out. Whatever had been wrong with our marriage, I was sure it wouldn't be anything we couldn't overcome. And then I saw the stretch marks on your stomach. They're very faint. I might not have noticed them if the sun hadn't been shining so brightly."

Gwenn unconsciously tightened the belt of her robe, as if trying to conceal the damning marks. "I...I wanted to tell you, Chase."

His eyes flickered to her face. "No, you didn't." The flat denial took her breath away for a moment. "You didn't want to tell me because you didn't want to share Livvie with me."

"That's not true! Chase, the doctor said you weren't supposed to be upset. How could I tell you about Livvie?"

"You've been trying to deny that I had anything to do with Livvie ever since the accident. I think you resented the fact that you had to give me credit for sharing in her conception."

"No! That's not true."

"When I lost my memory, you didn't have to worry about sharing Livvie anymore. I didn't even remember her."

"No!" Gwenn struggled to find the words to tell him how wrong he was. "It wasn't like that at all."

He set the photo down and reached out with one hand to gently push the cradle that stood nearby. An oak cradle with delicate carving on the head and foot, love in every line.

"Why didn't you tell me about this when I asked about it yesterday morning? I told you that I had a feeling it might be important."

"I was afraid it might upset you. How was I supposed to explain what it was doing up here?"

"You could have told me that we were storing it for friends. That way I would have had a chance to see if it unlocked my memory."

"I didn't think of that."

"You thought up that story about John and Amanda moving to New York pretty promptly."

"That was because they did move."

"They moved to Santa Monica, Gwenn. That's not exactly New York."

"All right!" She took a deep breath and tried to think calmly and clearly. "I didn't like lying to you, and I probably should have figured out a way to tell you the cradle was up here without telling you about Livvie. But I didn't think of it in time."

"Of course you didn't. Because you didn't want me to get my memory back."

"That's not true! I *did* want you to get your memory back."

She might as well not have bothered to speak. Chase wasn't listening. "You know, what I don't understand is why we've been playing this whole game of happy families. What did you think was going to happen when I regained my memory? Did you think things were just going to go on from here as if the past two years hadn't happened?"

"Of course not." But her voice lacked strength because there was a part of her that *had* wanted exactly that to happen. "Chase, when you were kidnapped, it made me realize how much I still cared for you."

"Really?" He pulled his hand away from the cradle, setting it in motion. The sound of the rockers rubbing against the wooden floor was a quiet counterpoint to the emotions that shimmered in the air.

"Yes, really!" Gwenn snapped her reply and then swallowed hard, trying to force down her own anger. He was putting her on the defensive, and they weren't going to get anywhere if all they did was snap at each other. She forced herself to go on more calmly.

"I wanted a chance to put things right between us."

"How could you put things right when I couldn't even remember what had been wrong?" He got to his feet and moved away from her, but the sloping ceiling forced him to turn back after only a few steps.

Gwenn stood up slowly, her fingers twisting nervously in the belt of her robe. "Maybe it doesn't make a lot of sense right now, but it did at the time."

"Have you forgotten the state our marriage was in before the kidnapping?"

"No." For the life of her, she couldn't have added anything to that one syllable.

"Then how could you have thought that things could be put right just by pretending that nothing was wrong?"

"Maybe it was a stupid idea, but I'd come so close to losing you." He ignored the plea in her voice, or maybe he didn't even hear it.

"Losing me? You've been pushing me away ever since Livvie died. First, you couldn't stand to sleep with me, then you could hardly stand to talk to me. It got to the point where I felt like the sight of me was enough to make you sick."

"All right, all right! I admit I was wrong!" Her voice echoed in the attic, and she took a deep breath before forcing her tone to something under a shout. "I did push you away, and I'm sorry for it. But that was two years ago, Chase. I can't change what happened then. I just wanted to try and fix it now."

"You can't fix something with lies. And you can't fix it by pretending it was never broken. You suggested a divorce, Gwenn. Did you think that was something else I was going to conveniently forget?" He ran his fingers through his hair, and if Gwenn had been able to see through the tears in her eyes, she might have noticed that his hand was shaking.

But all she heard was the cold anger in his voice. "I didn't really mean that, Chase."

"You sure as hell sounded like you did."

"I didn't know what else to do. We hadn't been able to talk to each other in so long."

"And you thought a divorce would make it easier to talk?"

"No!" She'd long since lost the battle with tears, and they trickled down her cheeks in silvery streams. She sniffed and searched futilely through her pockets for a tissue. When she didn't find one, she wiped her nose on the back of her hand, sniffing like a hurt child.

Chase watched her without saying a word. The sunlight caught on the muscles of his shoulders and chest, giving him the gleaming look of a statue. And as far as Gwenn could tell, he was about as responsive as one.

"Maybe I thought that suggesting a divorce might force us to talk to each other."

"Why not just say that you wanted to talk, if that was what you really wanted?"

She sniffed again and lifted her shoulders in a defeated shrug. "I guess I thought it was too late for that."

The simple words summed up so much. Too much pain, too many unspoken hurts, too much silence. It was so quiet in the dusty attic that the silence almost had sound. They stood only a few feet apart, but they looked at each other across a gulf of heartache that seemed uncrossable.

Too late. The saddest words in the language.

It was Chase who finally broke the silence, his voice rough with pain. "Maybe it is too late. For all of it."

"No! Chase, please!"

Her fingers shook as she reached out to him, but he didn't seem to see her. Through a wall of tears she saw him shake his head, and then he turned and walked away, picking his way across the cluttered floor without hesitation.

"Chase!" But she might as well have been talking to one of the dust motes that floated on a sunbeam. She heard the stairs creak beneath his feet, and then there was only silence.

Her hand came up to try and still the quivering of her lips. She seemed to stand there for a very long time, eyes wide open and focused on nothing at all. After a while she heard the muffled roar of the Aston Martin's engine, and then even that was gone, taking Chase with it.

Slowly, as if she were a very old woman, she lowered herself into the chair Chase had been using. At her feet Livvie's picture smiled up at her, and she stared at it for a moment before it disappeared behind a flood of tears. She wrapped her arms around her waist and rocked slowly back and forth, letting the scalding tears trickle down her face.

She was so alone.

Chapter 9

Chase had come too close to losing his life to risk it foolishly, no matter how angry he was. But it took all his self-control to resist the urge to slam his foot on the gas pedal and see if speed would help to ease the burning ache in his gut. The winding roads that led down out of the Flintridge hills were enough to discourage that idea all by themselves.

He drove aimlessly, his mind still trying to sort out all the confusing images that kept pouring in. It was like watching a choppy film biography of the life of Chase Buchanon. Sometimes the memories trickled in one by one, and then a sudden flood of images would spill into his consciousness.

He was blind to the streets and houses passing outside the car. He didn't even notice the breeze that spilled over the windshield and tousled his already rumpled hair. It wasn't until he found himself parking along a curb that he realized he'd had an unconscious goal all along.

Robert. Anger flickered to life inside him. Robert had lied to him, too. And with a hell of lot less excuse. He swung out of the car and slammed the door shut. Instinct made him pocket the keys, but he didn't bother with putting the top up or locking the doors.

It was only when he noticed an elderly lady eyeing him cautiously from the sidewalk that he realized the picture he must make. He'd thrown on a shirt, but he hadn't bothered to button it, and it hung open over his jeans. He'd put on tennis shoes but no socks, and with his uncombed hair and the anger that undoubtedly hardened his features, he looked something less than a respectable citizen.

He gave a mental shrug and didn't blame the woman when she hurried out of his way as he came around the hood of the car. If he looked as bad as he felt, he'd have gotten out of the way, too.

He took the stairs to Robert's apartment two at a time. He didn't have a watch, but he knew it had to be fairly early in the morning. It hadn't been too long after dawn when he'd woken, and though it seemed like centuries ago, he knew that not more than hour or so had passed.

Robert never got up before noon if he had a choice, and Chase took great satisfaction in pounding his fist on the apartment door, knowing that he was probably dragging the other man out of bed. He had to knock twice before the door opened and Robert stared out at him groggily.

"Chase. What the hell?" He pushed open the screen door with one hand and smothered a yawn with the other. He'd thrown a robe on, and he tightened the belt as he shut the door behind Chase. He ran a hand through his hair, shaking his head as if trying to shake himself awake.

"I'll put some coffee on," he muttered, stumbling toward the kitchen. "I know you don't remember this, but I'm not a morning person so don't expect me to be coherent before I've had some coffee."

Before he made it to the kitchen, there was another knock on the door. He stopped and turned, his brows coming together as he started toward the door.

"It's like Grand Central in here this morning," he muttered. "Maybe I need a butler."

From where Chase stood, the open door blocked his view of the new visitor but he didn't have to wonder about her identity for long. Robert barely had the door open a crack when Gwenn's voice came tumbling into the room.

"Have you seen Chase?"

Robert blinked. It didn't take a genius to figure out that something was wrong here. Silently, he opened the door wider and Gwenn stepped into the apartment, coming to an abrupt halt when she saw Chase.

Chase said absolutely nothing. She'd followed him here, let her speak first. At the moment, he had nothing to say to her.

"Chase, I was so worried."

He raised one eyebrow. "I've been driving a car by myself for a long time."

Robert cleared his throat ostentatiously. "I think I'll go take a long shower to wake up." His eyes flickered worriedly over the pair but whatever was wrong was strictly between them and the last thing he wanted was to get involved in a fight.

Gwenn gave him a strained smile, thanking him without words for giving them some privacy. She watched him walk into his bedroom, close the door and, a moment later, heard the fainter click of the bathroom door. She turned back to her husband, her smile fading.

"Are you all right?"

"I'm fine. I've been driving a car for a long time, Gwenn. You didn't need to follow me as if I'd just gotten my license."

"I didn't follow you. I just got worried and I thought you might come here."

"You'll have to excuse me, but I don't see the distinction between that and following me. I'm not a child, Gwenn. I don't need someone checking up on every move I make."

Gwenn swallowed hard, trying to force down her own anger. It wasn't going to do anybody any good if she also got angry. They needed to be able to talk rationally and calmly.

"I wasn't checking up on you. You left before we'd had a chance to really talk and I knew you were upset."

Chase clenched his hands into fists, stunned by his base urge to destroy something. There was so much anger combined with pain bubbling up inside that he couldn't even separate the two emotions into some coherent form.

"I thought we'd said everything there was to say," he got out tightly.

"Chase, you have to listen to me."

"No!" The word exploded into the room, cutting Gwenn's voice off. She took an involuntary step back, her eyes wide.

Chase struggled for control, running his fingers through his hair and breathing deeply. "No," he repeated more quietly. "I don't have to listen to you. I've listened to you ever since I came home from the hospital. You've lied, or colored the truth, or whatever polite euphemism you want to use and I don't want to hear it anymore."

"Chase, you're not being fair! The doctor said you weren't to be upset if it could be avoided. I didn't tell you any unnecessary lies."

"Unnecessary lies? That's an interesting concept. I wasn't told anything about my life. Did you think I was too stupid to figure out that something was wrong with our marriage? I lost my memory, Gwenn, not my mind."

"The doctor wanted you to have a chance to heal, physically and mentally. I was just trying to give you a chance to do that."

"You lied to me about my own child, Gwenn. Did the doctor tell you to lie about Livvie?"

For a moment, Gwenn wanted to say that the doctor *had* said to keep the truth about Livvie from him. But it would be a falsehood and the last thing they needed right now was another lie.

"He left that up to me."

"And you thought it might be a nice idea to not tell me about her. There's something very sick about your whole attitude, Gwenn. As if, if you pretend I had nothing to do with Livvie, she's not really dead."

The movement was so quick that neither of them had a chance to expect it. Her palm connected with his cheek, the sharp sound of the slap echoing in the small room. They froze for a moment, Gwenn's hand dropping back down to her side, her fingers clenching over her tingling palm. Chase made no move to touch the darkening welt where her hand had connected. It seemed as if neither of them dared to even breathe.

Gwenn broke the silence, drawing a deep breath, her words spilling out rapidly. "I'm tired of you acting as if I didn't tell you about Livvie because I had some nefarious plot in mind. Maybe it was a mistake but I did it because it seemed the best thing to do at the time."

She blinked rapidly, trying to clear her eyes of the tears that insisted on gathering. "I know how much you hurt when Livvie died. I shut you out then. I admit that. In some ways, it was much easier for me because I was able to get it out in the open and cry on Robert's shoulder. You held it all in and, by the time I realized what was happening, it was too late. I'm sorry for what happened then but I'm not going to apologize for not telling you about Livvie when you got home from the hospital. And I'm not going to apologize for worrying about you."

The tears spilled over and she turned toward the door, fumbling in her pocket for her car keys. "Tell Robert goodbye for me." The polite words came out on a muffled sob and Chase took a step forward, half lifting his hand toward her before letting it fall. Gwenn saw none of this. She was already on her way out the door.

Chase stood motionless in frustration as the door closed behind her. There was so much anger and confusion raging inside him that he didn't know what to say or do. All he knew was that he couldn't offer Gwenn the comfort she needed. Not right now.

He turned impatiently as the bedroom door opened and Robert stepped into the living room. His brother-in-law's eyes narrowed slightly when he saw that Gwenn was gone.

"All through talking?"

"Gwenn said to tell you goodbye."

"You want to tell me what's going on?"

Chase shrugged. "I got most of my memory back this morning." It was ironic. If someone had asked him to guess what his reaction would be to regaining his past, he wouldn't have answered regret. But there was a part of him that regretted being jerked out of the fantasy world that he and Gwenn had been creating.

"You don't sound real happy about that."

The anger that had driven Chase here was not quite gone but the confrontation with Gwenn had left it muted, without urgency. He followed Robert into the kitchen and leaned in the doorway, watching his friend start the morning coffee ritual.

"It hasn't been quite the bowl of cherries I had hoped."

Robert's sharp glance told him that his comment had been recognized for the understatement it was but he didn't probe further. Whatever was going on between Gwenn and Chase, they were going to have to work it out between them. The last thing he wanted was to get involved in his sister's marital problems.

"What do you remember about the kidnapping?"

"Nothing."

Robert turned, for once startled into a quick movement. "Nothing?"

Chase shook his head. "Absolutely nothing." He dragged the words out for emphasis.

"Well, hell." The laconic comment surprised a short, humorless laugh out of Chase.

"That's one way to put it. On the way over here, I tried to piece together the last things I remember and I think my memory goes up to a day or so before the kidnapping but after that, it's a complete blank."

"So you have no idea where the schematics are or why you took them?"

"None at all. The last thing I remember clearly is a... conversation with Gwenn." Not even to his best friend could he bring himself to admit that she'd suggested a divorce. Even now, the memory was enough to make him feel as if he were suffocating.

"No clue at all about the papers?"

Chase frowned. The throbbing in his splinted finger set up an annoying counterpoint to the painful throb at his temples.

"I... knew there was a problem. There was something at the company that was bothering me." He pushed harder at the fog surrounding the memory and then gave up with a gasp. He lifted his hand to his forehead, pressing against the pain there and he was hardly surprised when his fingers came away damp with sweat. "That's all there is. I come up against a blank wall when I try to push further."

Robert handed him a cup of coffee. "Don't worry about it. It'll come back sooner or later. Drink this while I finish dressing. We should probably go down to Johnson Industries and let Johnson know what's going on."

He disappeared into the bedroom and Chase folded himself onto the sofa, letting his head fall back, trying to blank out all the confusing thoughts that fought for precedence. So much had happened in such a short time. He'd gone from waking up on top of the world to falling into hell in a matter of minutes.

Once the curtain was ripped open, memories had poured through at a frightening rate. He'd stumbled from Gwenn's room only to collapse on his own bed, his pulse pounding like a drumbeat inside his skull. It was only when the flood of memories slowed that he really grasped all the things he remembered.

He was still trying to come to terms with the fact that the things he remembered were his life. It was like having a stranger inside him. There was the man who'd awakened in the basement, who had no memories prior to that. And then there was the man who'd lived in this body for the last thirty-eight years.

Regaining his memory was not quite the simple process he'd assumed it would be. In some ways he was even more confused now than he had been before. He had just as many questions and so few answers. And so many of the questions revolved around his wife.

Gwenn. Last night he'd been so sure he was in love with her. Their lovemaking had been so perfect. An explosion that had been as much mental as physical. No wonder, he thought cynically. It had been two years since he'd touched her, two years since they'd shared a bed. That was a lot of abstinence to make up for.

He opened his eyes as Robert came back into the room. Swallowing the last of his coffee, he got to his feet. He couldn't find the answers to his marriage right away but maybe he could find some of them to his professional situation. After all, the curtain had opened this far; maybe his old office would open it the rest of the way.

Gwenn set down the phone and wrapped her arms around her waist in a vain attempt to get warm. But the chill she was feeling had nothing to do with the temperature, which was already soaring into the eighties outside. This was an inner chill. So deep and abiding, it made her wonder if she would ever be warm again.

Maggie had said that there was no problem with her managing the shop today so at least that responsibility was taken care of. After the painful confrontation with Chase at Robert's apartment, there was no possible way that she could have gone in to the shop and looked bright eyed and eager to help her customers.

She sniffed, rubbing the back of her hand across her nose and then sniffed again before firming her mouth and getting to her feet. Crying wasn't going to change anything and she'd already shed enough tears this morning to flood the entire Los Angeles Basin.

But her determination was badly shaken when she stepped into her bedroom and was confronted with the tumbled sheets, the imprint of two heads on the pillow. Even more painful was the sight of their clothes lying across the floor in tangled intimacy.

Stunned by the hurtful reminders, Gwenn leaned against the doorway, momentarily unable to take another step. She'd been so happy last night. For the first time since Livvie's death, she'd really believed in the future. A future that held Chase and perhaps, eventually, another child.

Last night had been as close to paradise as she'd ever come and it had all been torn away from her before she had more than a glimpse of what it could be.

She forced herself upright, tamping down the pain to a managable level. She wasn't going to give up. She was going to fight to keep her marriage together, to regain the love they'd once had.

A few tears escaped as she picked up their scattered clothing and folded Chase's things. She hesitated for a moment before carrying them back to his room. Last night she'd been sure that they'd be sharing a room again. But everything had changed since last night. With a sigh, she left his clothes stacked on his bed and pulled the door shut behind her. They'd lived apart for two years, they'd survive a little longer.

"But I don't understand. How can you have regained all of your memory except the part about the kidnapping? That doesn't make any sense."

"Doug, I think that's enough." Charles Johnson didn't raise his voice, but his quiet words were enough to cause his son to break off in midsentence. Doug threw his father a sullen glance and sank back into his chair without another word.

"Are you sure it was wise to come here, Chase? Perhaps you should have gone to see your doctor first."

Chase took a reviving swallow of steaming coffee and then shook his head. "To tell the truth, Charles, I don't know what I should have done first. Physically, I'm tired, but then, it's been a rather eventful day, so that's hardly surprising. I don't really think Dr. Maguire is going to be able to tell me much about how most of my memory returned but why I'm still missing part of it. A rather vital part," he added ruefully.

"It seemed important to let you know what was happening. I know how essential those missing papers are to the company. I did have a rather forlorn hope that being in the building might trigger the last of my memory."

"Don't push yourself too hard. We've got engineers working to replace those schematics. The government isn't happy about the delay but, up to this point, our record has been unblemished, and they're giving us a little room to work."

Chase set his coffee cup down and shook his head. "I have to tell you, Charles, that I'm anxious to get the plans back but I'm even more anxious to know who kidnapped me." His eyes were distant, and he unconsciously rubbed his splinted finger. "Whoever did this stole my identity, and that's not something I'm likely to forget real soon."

"I understand that. I'd feel much the same myself. Whoever did this should be caught and punished. We need the schematics, but you need your peace of mind just as much." His heavy brows came together in a scowl that made it easy to see how he'd successfully controlled a growing company.

"I've never been able to understand how a human being can sink to preying on other humans. It must take a particular kind of mind to be able to do something like this."

"Unfortunately there are a lot of people who have that kind of mind." Robert shrugged without shifting from his usual slouched position. "In my job, you see a lot of it."

"If you don't like it, maybe you should find another line of work." Doug's comment brought the eyes of the other three men to him, and he shifted uncomfortably.

"Somebody has to take care of controlling the criminal element," Robert said mildly.

"And you're doing a wonderful job, too. Look what happened to Chase."

"Doug, that's hardly fair," Charles said.

Robert waved a hand, dismissing Charles's attempt to defend him. "Unfortunately the police haven't won the battle yet. The old saying that 'crime doesn't pay' isn't quite true. If you get away with it, it can pay very nicely.

"Whoever kidnapped Chase could have sold those papers for a healthy sum on the international market. One consolation in this mess is that *we* may not know where the papers are, but neither does the enemy. Hopefully we'll find them before they do."

Robert's tone was even, without any hint of resentment over what had amounted to a personal attack, but Doug squirmed uneasily in his chair. For all his size and years, he reminded Chase of a small boy being judged by his elders. But the thought was more tolerant than it would have been before he'd regained his memory.

He and Doug Johnson had practically grown up together, but their relationship had never been like the easy friendship Chase shared with Robert. When they had been young, the two year discrepancy in their ages had set them apart. Chase was always the elder, the stronger, the leader.

But it hadn't been just the age difference that caused difficulties. Charles Johnson was an honest businessman and a good friend, but he was a stern father. To counteract that, Doug's mother had been indulgent to a fault. When she had died, Doug had been left to his father's fair but unbending care, but the damage had already been done.

As Robert had said, Doug had simply refused to grow up. He rarely considered the outcome of his actions. He was fun loving and entertaining, but it wasn't wise to depend on him for anything further.

For years Chase's relationship with Doug had been that of an older brother. There were times when he wanted to throttle the other man, but balancing that desire was his understanding of what had molded him.

The look Charles threw his son made clear his dislike of Doug's attitude, though he didn't say anything out loud. Instead he turned to Chase.

"If you feel like coming back to work, your position is still there. We've had people filling in for you, but I don't mind telling you that we haven't found anyone with your flair for marketing. We'd love to have you back."

"That's very flattering, but does the rest of the company share your enthusiasm?"

Charles waved one hand dismissingly. "There was some doubt at first; I won't deny that. But as time goes on, it becomes more and more obvious that you were very much the victim in this whole mess; sympathy has swung firmly to your side. You're not going to run into any hostility. If you feel up to it, the job is still yours."

Chase considered for a moment, On the one hand, he wasn't sure he was ready to jump right back into his old life. But he couldn't put it off forever. Besides, this would enable him to put some distance between himself and Gwenn. He couldn't think clearly in a house that was permeated with her presence.

He nodded slowly. "I'd like that. I think it would do me a lot of good to get back into the swing of things. Besides, I took those papers from here, maybe something in the building will trigger the missing pieces of my memory."

"Good. Good." Charles stood up and reached across the desk to shake Chase's hand, his expression making it clear that he approved of this decision. "It'll be good to have you around."

A few minutes later Chase, Robert and Doug stood in the hall outside Doug's office.

"It really will be great to have you back, Chase. I'm one of the people who's been filling in for you, and I'm afraid Dad hasn't been too pleased with the job I've been doing." He shrugged his wide shoulders and grinned. "I just don't have your way with the buyers."

"Maybe after so long away from it, I don't have a way with the buyers, either."

Robert leaned his shoulder against one wall and looked as though he might doze off at any moment. Doug shifted from one foot to the other, nervous tension radiating from his big body.

"Do you really think that working here might trigger your memory?"

Chase shrugged. "I don't know. It's worth a try. Something's got to work sooner or later."

"I bet Gwenn was thrilled about your memory coming back."

Chase thought of the image he had of Gwenn when she'd stood in the dusty attic, tears streaking her face, one hand held out to him as if in supplication.

"Yeah." He didn't even care if the flat answer was revealing. Doug didn't seem to notice that Chase wasn't interested in pursuing the topic.

"She was really worried about you."

"Yeah." What was it that made him want to thump Doug on the top of the head every time the other man mentioned Gwenn? With his memory restored, he no longer wondered about Gwenn's feelings for Doug. Robert had been right when he'd said that Doug was like a lost puppy and Gwenn had a soft spot for strays.

He moved his shoulders in an irritated gesture, trying to ease the tension that seemed to have settled at the back of his neck. Too much had happened in the past few weeks. He was on edge. Robert seemed to sense his irritation.

"We should probably run you by the doctor's and let him take a look at you."

"I suppose so. See you around, Doug."

"Sure. We still haven't managed that Chinese dinner. We'll have to do that soon."

"Sure. Give me a call."

He was on edge. That was all. There was a drumming inside his head, and he was feeling irritable. He'd already had a full day, and he still had to go home and deal with Gwenn. He still wasn't at all sure what to say to her. His irritation really had nothing to do with Doug.

It was all Gwenn. Just as everything in his life seemed to come back to her, sooner or later.

It was always Gwenn.

Chapter 10

Gwenn spent the time after Maggie left wandering from room to room, trying to find something to occupy her hands and distract her thought. But nothing could hold her attention long. When Chase came home, they'd be able to talk more calmly. Neither of them had been prepared for the events of the morning. After some time apart, maybe they'd both be a little more rational.

But, despite her best efforts to think optimistically, the house felt achingly empty. It was so quiet and still, as if it had never held any life. And that wasn't true.

Even before Livvie was born, this house had been a home. The birth of their child had only rounded out the family Gwenn and Chase had already become. She'd been twenty-two when Robert introduced her to Chase and, from then on, there hadn't been another man in the world for her. They'd been friends before they'd become lovers and their marriage had been the inevitable extension of their love.

She wandered into the living room and sat on the sofa. She picked up her needlepoint and worked a few stitches but her mind wasn't on the colorful array of wool and she put it down after only a few moments.

"I'm not going to lose him. Not after all we've been through." The words echoed in the quiet room, forcefully. "We're going to get through this together. I'm not giving up now."

But she knew how empty that vow would be if Chase didn't share her determination. Did he want to save their marriage? Or did he feel there was too much between them to ever bridge the yawning gap that separated them? Did he remember the good times or only the bad?

She sniffed, but then became determined not to cry again. When Chase came home, she was going to be calm, controlled and ready for a rational discussion. Against her will she sniffed again. She'd cried enough today. Chase wasn't going to find her in tears when he got home.

If he came home.

The lonely thought pierced all her determination. He might not come home at all. And then it wouldn't matter how much she wanted to save their marriage; she couldn't do it without him.

The tears spilling onto her cheeks were slow and painful, full of despair. With a sob she drew her feet up under her and curled into a corner of the sofa, burying her face in her hands and giving in to the pain.

The lamp cast a soft pool of light over her, accenting the gold in her hair and catching on the brilliant skeins of wool that lay on the end table. Gwenn sobbed until she no longer had the energy to draw a steady breath, until her throat was raw and aching.

She was so tired. Tired of the tension and uncertainty. Tired of constantly wondering about her own motives and worrying about Chase. At the moment she felt as if she was tired of living.

Chase opened the back door quietly. It was only nine o'clock, but there was a chance that Gwenn had already gone to bed. He hoped she was asleep, and he suppressed the niggling little voice that said it was unlikely she'd just calmly retire after the events of the day.

The kitchen was empty. One light over the sink provided dim illumination for the big room. He set his car keys down on the table and looked at the cabinets, remembering Gwenn's excitement when they had been installed. He'd spent months on those cabinets, finally finishing them only a week before Livvie was born.

Everything he saw brought back a new flood of memories. Things that had belonged to his grandparents, things he and Gwenn had bought together. All the places they'd kissed and made love. His eyes darkened, and his mouth softened in a smile as he remembered the night he'd made love to Gwenn on the kitchen table, ignoring her giggling protests that it was a thoroughly decadent thing to do. Those protests had turned to moans of pleasure.

He shook his head, ruefully aware of the inevitable physical response to the memory. That recalled a more recent event, Gwenn melting against him the night before. He recalled the feel of her heated skin, the taste of her on his tongue, the moist welcome of her body.

A twinge of pain made him realize that he was clenching his fists. He had to make a conscious effort to relax them, slowly uncurling each finger until his palms lay flat on the tabletop.

They'd always been good in bed, and, until Livvie's death, he'd have sworn they had everything. But losing their child had ripped them apart, shown the fatal flaw in the fabric of their marriage. They hadn't been able to handle the bad times.

He shook his head and picked up the car keys. It had been a long day, and he was too tired to try to deal with anything more tonight. The session with Dr. Maguire had been long and gruelling, and left him feeling as if his skull had been turned inside out.

His footsteps were slow as he flipped out the kitchen light and went into the hall. He was halfway to the stairs when he realized there was a light on in the living room. He stopped and hesitated. He didn't want to talk to Gwenn tonight. He wasn't sure he even wanted to see her. The hurt was still too new and tender. But it would be childish to pretend she didn't exist. Besides, if she was waiting for him, common courtesy demanded that he let her know he was home safe and sound, if a little worse for the wear.

He stopped in the doorway, his face softening as he took in the scene before him. Gwenn was curled up in one corner of the sofa, her hair spilling around her face. Chase crossed the room quietly, feeling his heart twist at the tear stains that marred her smooth cheeks.

She looked so forlorn and so lovable. And he did love her. That was what made it so hard to forget what had gone before. He was afraid of being hurt again. Would she turn away the next time they faced a crisis?

He shook his head. There was no immediate answer for his question. Maybe there never would be. In the meantime, she obviously couldn't be left to sleep where she was.

He bent to lift her into his arms, trying not to notice the gentle scent of her perfume as he cradled her against his chest. He glanced at the lamp and decided it could stay on for tonight. Gwenn stirred as he carried her into the hallway and started up the stairs.

"Chase?" His name was a sleepy mumble, and her arms lifted automatically to encircle his neck.

"Go back to sleep. I'm just putting you to bed."

She snuggled her face into the opening of his shirt, her breath tickling the dark mat of hair.

"I was worried about you."

"I'm sorry. I should have called." In the darkness he felt safe letting his arms tighten around her.

"We need to talk." She hadn't opened her eyes, and he knew that she was only half awake.

"Not tonight." He pushed open her bedroom door with his foot and carried her to the bed. For just an instant his mouth brushed her forehead and then he set her down. He eased her slippers off and unsnapped her jeans before pulling up the sheet.

"We need to talk, Chase." She mumbled the words around a yawn, and he almost smiled. She was hardly in any condition to have a serious talk.

"Not tonight," he repeated. "Go back to sleep." Before he could even admit to the urge to crawl into bed beside her, he turned and left the room, pulling the door quietly shut behind him.

Gwenn woke slowly the next morning, coming up from the depths of a wonderful dream in which Chase was laughing with her and saying how much he loved her. Even when asleep, she somehow knew that reality wasn't going to be nearly as nice, so she resisted the bright sunshine that called for her to wake.

It was a losing battle, and with a groan she opened her eyes and rolled over to look at the clock. Nine-thirty. And the shop opened at ten. Maggie could open without her, but it wasn't fair to expect the other woman to handle everything alone. After all, Gwenn was the owner.

She threw the sheet off, sat up and then stopped, puzzled. Why was she still wearing her clothes? Chase. He'd carried her up to bed. She remembered snuggling against him and feeling the warm strength of his arms around her. Had she just imagined his mouth touching her forehead?

Gwenn scrambled out of bed, Maggie could hold down the fort for a little while longer. Right now Chase was the number one priority. They needed to talk.

After a quick shower Gwenn pinned her hair up in its customary chignon before applying light touches of make-up. She wanted to look her best for the talk with Chase, and knowing that she looked good would give her some added armor.

She smoothed her fingers over the pale gray skirt and warm pink silk shirt. The combination was flattering and elegant, exactly the right clothing to wear to Guinevere's Fantasy. But was it the right thing to wear for her talk with her husband? She fretted over her reflection, trying to decide if the combination made her seem too distant.

She picked up a bottle of perfume and sprayed a touch of it at her wrists and throat. Chase had once said he liked that particular scent. Her fingers were shaking as she set the bottle down and she cursed mentally.

She was getting too worked up over this. She and Chase were adults. They were going to be able to sit down and have a rational discussion. She wasn't expecting to work out all their problems at once, but they had to start somewhere. Squaring her shoulders, Gwenn took a deep breath and then broke into a reluctant smile. She looked like a soldier facing court martial.

As it turned out, she needn't have worried about how she looked. It didn't take long to see that Chase wasn't in the house. His room was empty, the bed so neatly made that she wondered if he'd even slept in it. There was a coffee cup on the counter but no sign that he'd fixed himself anything to eat.

She peered out the window over the sink, leaning forward until she could see the garage, but the shop door was closed. With the temperature already creeping toward eighty, he wouldn't be working in there without some air. As she turned away from the window, she saw the note.

It was stuck to the refrigerator with a magnet, and her breath caught at the memory. When they were first married, Chase would leave her a note on the fridge anytime he left before she awoke. Sometimes it was one or two lines from a favorite poem, or a promise to take her to dinner, or an invitation to a weekend getaway for two. And sometimes it was just a note to tell her he loved her.

Despite herself, her hand was trembling as she slid the folded piece of paper out from under the magnet and opened it.

Gwenn

I'll be spending the day at work. I think it's best if I jump right back into the thick of things. Don't worry if I'm home late.

Chase

Well, at least he wasn't asking for a divorce or telling her that he was moving out. She blinked back tears. It was a perfectly polite, perfectly impersonal message.

"What did you expect, dummy? Did you think he was going to tell you he loved you?" Her whisper echoed in the empty kitchen. At least he'd bothered to let her know where he was. He cared enough to avoid worrying her, and he did refer to this as home.

"You're grasping at straws and you know it." But the brisk comment didn't stop her from drawing what hope she could from that little piece of paper.

With a sigh she tossed the note in the trash. She didn't want to add that to her precious collection of love notes. Whatever happened, she wasn't likely to look back on this as a wonderful moment in her marriage. Chase would have left much the same message to a housekeeper.

She hurried upstairs to get her purse. She would go to the shop. She didn't want to spend another minute in this empty house so she'd head over to the shop. The emptiness in the house reminded her too strongly of what her life would be like without Chase.

Not that the shop didn't hold memories, too. Everywhere she looked, she could see something Chase had built or helped her choose. But he'd never spent much time there after it opened, so she wasn't reminded of him in his absence.

In addition, Maggie's company helped. Throughout a day that seemed endless, her best friend's presence kept Gwenn from going crazy. Maggie dealt with the customers, freeing Gwenn to do paperwork and handle the stock. Unfortunately, the only paperwork that got done was in the form of meaningless doodles that she didn't even notice she'd drawn.

Gwenn's thoughts went round and round in circles to match the motions of her pen. Had she made the right choices, and had she made them for the right reasons? She hadn't told Chase about Livvie. Surely that had been the best thing to do. There'd been no reason to upset him with that knowledge. He was already struggling with the fact that he had a wife he couldn't remember. How much harder would it have made it if he'd known that they'd had a child? No, that had been the right choice, and she'd make it again, even knowing the consequences.

But maybe her reason for making that decision hadn't been as altruistic as she'd like to believe. Chase had seen it as another way for her to shut him out, to deny his involvement with Livvie. Had that been in the back of her mind?

She'd loved Livvie, and after the accident there had been times when she'd resented Chase's grief. And she'd felt as if he couldn't possibly understand her feelings. He'd only been Livvie's father. What could he know of the pain of carrying a child for nine months, nursing, loving her and then seeing all the promise cut short?

In her more rational moments, she'd realized that Chase's pain was just as acute as her own, but by then the barriers had been already drawn, and she hadn't been able to reach through to share their grief. Instead she'd pushed him away even more, unable to bear his sorrow in addition to hers.

Even before he'd been kidnapped, she'd begun to realize how much they were losing. But she hadn't admitted even to herself that what she wanted more than anything else in the world was to save their marriage. The week before Chase had disappeared, she'd suggested a divorce.

She closed her eyes, remembering. The idea of dissolving their marriage wasn't something she actively thought about. She hadn't actively planned on blurting out the suggestion. But Chase had been sitting across the table from her, absentmindedly eating cold cereal and reading the paper. That was the way they had always spent the few meals they shared—in silence, with no communication, their glances rarely crossing.

Suddenly she'd remembered the way they used to spend their time together. Not always talking but always aware of each other. And she'd seen the future stretching out in front of them. Never talking, rarely looking at each other.

She'd opened her mouth to ask if he'd pass the sugar and found herself suggesting a divorce. Chase had frozen, his eyes slowly lifting from the paper to meet hers. Looking back, she could see the stunned pain in his eyes, but at the time, all she'd realized was that he didn't say much. He'd folded the paper and stood up, picking up his half-full bowl and carrying it to the sink. He'd rinsed the bowl and set it on the counter before turning to look at her again.

"You do whatever you think best."

And that was all he'd said before he picked up his briefcase and jacket and strode out the back door. She'd sat there without moving and listened to the sound of the Aston Martin's engine as he'd backed down the drive and onto the street.

She shivered now, remembering how lost she'd felt. Suggesting divorce had been a desperate attempt to shock them out of their silence. But she'd been so afraid to admit to her feelings that she hadn't even understood her own motives.

Understanding her reasons now didn't make it any easier to explain them to Chase. And she still hadn't answered her own question. Had she kept knowledge of Livvie from him because she wanted to protect him or because she was still trying to deny his right to grieve?

"Well, there's nothing like seeing someone hard at work."

Gwenn jumped, startled out of her preoccupation. Robert leaned against the front of the counter, his mouth smiling but his eyes watchful and concerned.

"How long have you been there?" Gwenn shuffled together her papers as if she'd written something important and not a bunch of squiggles that would probably drive a psychiatrist insane if he should attempt to analyze them.

"In the shop—about five minutes. Standing in front of you—just a few seconds."

"Did you stop by to see Maggie?"

"We have a lunch date but I also wanted to see how you were doing."

"Not too bad." She gave him a pale smile. "I've done better. Have you seen Chase?"

"As a matter of fact, my car is in the shop so Chase brought me down here."

Gwenn stiffened, coming to her feet as if she'd suddenly discovered she was sitting on a tack. "Chase is here?"

"In the flesh."

She smoothed her hands over her hair nervously as she came around the counter. Robert's casual, "You look fine," did nothing to soothe her panicked thoughts.

There wasn't enough time. She didn't know what to say to him. But she didn't have any real choice in the matter. Chase and Maggie stood next to the front door, Chase's suited figure seeming to dwarf Maggie's petite frame. Chase looked up as Robert and Gwenn approached and Gwenn felt her heart start to thump heavily as their eyes met for just an instant.

It seemed like only seconds later that Maggie and Robert were walking out the door. For once, her brother ignored the pleading looks she threw him. Chase was her problem and Robert wasn't going to stick his nose in and he wasn't going to run interference for her, either.

The silence in the shop seemed to echo after the door closed behind them. Nervously, Gwenn turned the shop sign to closed. Whatever was going to be said, she didn't want to be interrupted by someone looking for a girdle guaranteed to take eighteen inches off her waistline.

"How are you?" Her eyes flickered up to his and then away.

"Not too bad. How are you?"

"Just fine." She began to fidget with the basket of sugar packets that sat on the little tea table.

"We need to talk."

Her fingers tightened around the basket and she couldn't bring herself to look at him. What if he was going to suggest a divorce? "I know. But I don't think either one of us is ready to make any major decisions right now."

If he heard the trembling note of fear in her voice and guessed its origin, Gwenn couldn't tell. "I agree. But we can't go on living in the same house if it's going to be a war zone."

"Agreed." She stole a look up at his face, seeing the lines of exhaustion that bracketed his mouth. "I don't want that any more than you do."

"Maybe we could just set everything aside for a while. Until I regain the rest of my memory, perhaps."

Her head jerked up. "The rest of your memory? I didn't know you didn't have it all."

He shrugged as if to dismiss the problem but she could see the tightness in his face. "I've got everything back up until the kidnapping. But the kidnapping itself and the month I was missing are gone."

Gwenn stared at him, forgetting for the moment the tensions that lay between the two of them. She knew how much he'd been counting on regaining his memory to clear his name and to be able to put faces to his kidnappers.

"Oh, Chase, how awful for you." She reached out to touch his arm and the muscles knotted beneath her fingertips. Her hand dropped away immediately and she shoved it into the pocket of her skirt. She thought she read a momentary regret in his eyes in the instant before she looked away but that could have been just wishful thinking. "It must be very frustrating." Her voice had flattened out.

Chase's hand clenched into a fist as he resisted the urge to reach out to her in apology. But he couldn't do that. Too much had been said. Too much was left to say. Emotionally, they were both battered and bruised.

"I'll cope," he said flatly. "I just wanted to suggest that we try, for a little while at least, to just kind of leave the past in the past. We're going to be living together and I don't think either one of us wants it to be like an armed camp."

"Sounds fine to me." The thought of living in the same house with Chase and pretending that they were strangers sounded very close to Gwenn's idea of hell but it was better than not living with him at all.

Chase shifted uncertainly. "Well, I guess I'd better get going."

Gwenn nodded, struggling against the urge to cry. Crying wasn't going to change anything now. He hesitated for a moment as if wanting to say something more and then muttered a soft curse under his breath before spinning and walking out of the shop. The door rattled shut behind him and Gwenn thought it was one of the most final sounds she'd ever heard.

But it wasn't final, she reminded herself. He was asking for some time. Time they could both use. She poured herself a cup of coffee and set it down on the little table. She automatically turned the sign back to open. She didn't feel like dealing with customers but it was very bad business to be closed when you should be open.

When the bell rang a few minutes later, she looked up, pinning a friendly smile on her face and hoping it was someone with a wrong address. The smile relaxed into surprise as Doug Johnson's bulky figure stepped into the shop.

"Doug. What a surprise." She held out her hand and he took it, squeezing it for a moment before smiling down at her.

"I haven't seen you in a while."

"Well, I guess we've both been pretty busy." Looking at him, she was sure that he hadn't come in for idle chitchat. "What can I do for you?"

Doug shifted uneasily, as if uncomfortable with her bluntness. "Well, it's about Chase, really. He was back at work today."

"He wanted to get right back into things. I guess he felt he'd taken enough time out of his life."

Not that Chase had discussed it with her or would listen to her opinion but there was no need for Doug to know that.

"I suppose I understand how he feels. It must be pretty tough to lose your memory."

A masterpiece of understatement if she'd ever heard one, Gwenn thought but she didn't say it out loud. "It's been hard on Chase."

She began to refold a stack of silk panties on a nearby shelf, her hands moving automatically as she neatened the bright fabrics. Doug shifted uncomfortably from one foot to another, sticking his hands in his pockets and then pulling them out again, as if not quite sure what to do with them.

Gwenn stifled her impatience. She'd known Doug almost as long as she'd known Chase and she'd learned that he took his own time when he had something to say. Whatever he wanted to discuss with her, she couldn't rush him into it.

"Would you like a cup of coffee?" The offer was made as much for her own sake as his. He obviously had something to say and he might as well be comfortable until he was ready to say it. And she didn't really want to be alone with her thoughts right now, anyway.

She poured him a cup of coffee and waved her hand at one of the chairs that sat next to the table. "Have a seat."

Doug looked at the delicate chair and shook his head. "I don't think so. It looks as if it might collapse if I tried to sit on it. You've really made this into a going concern, haven't you?"

"We should see a pretty fair profit this year." There was quiet pride in her voice.

"You've worked hard, though."

"Yes." Her eyes narrowed, thinking of all the hours she'd put in here. "Sometimes I wonder if it's really been worth it." She murmured the comment more to herself than Doug, wondering if things might have been different in her marriage if she hadn't used the shop as an escape.

She took a sip of coffee. "You said you wanted to talk to me about Chase."

"I guess I've been beating around the bush, haven't I?"

"A bit." Sometimes, she understood Robert's impatience with Doug. "Is there something wrong?"

"No. At least, not yet." He set the cup down and shoved his hands in the pockets of his suit pants, destroying their expensively tailored line. "Do you think that going back to work might really trigger the rest of Chase's memory?"

"I don't really know. It seems as likely a theory as any. Why?"

"What was it that triggered it the first time?"

Gwenn had to make a conscious effort to keep her hand from going to her stomach. There was nothing she could do about the flush that warmed her cheeks. It was a perfectly natural question.

"He saw something familiar that just seemed to break it loose."

Doug didn't seem to notice how stilted her answer was. He ran his fingers through his hair, disarranging it into charmingly boyish waves.

"Then the same thing could happen again, couldn't it? He could see something at work that would trigger the rest of his memory and then he'd remember who kidnapped him."

"I suppose it could happen that way." She tilted her head to one side, studying his face. "That would be a good thing, wouldn't it? If Chase gets his memory back, we'll be able to pick up the men who kidnapped him and he'll remember where those papers are. Why do you look so worried?"

"It's nothing, really. Just a thought I had."

"What thought?" Gwenn was losing patience with this whole conversation. If he had something to say, why didn't he just say it?

"Nothing, really. I don't want to worry you with it."

"Doug, if you don't tell me what you're talking about, I'm going to see just how tight that necktie will get."

Startled, Doug grinned at her. "Do you think you could reach it?"

"I'll get a stepladder. Tell me what's bothering you."

"I really shouldn't have said anything at all to you." Seeing her impatience about to explode, he shrugged apologetically. "It just occurred to me that, if the guys who kidnapped Chase find out that he might regain his memory, it could put him in danger again."

This was his big revelation? Of course it would put Chase in danger. When had he been out of danger?

"I suppose that's true but I think Robert has probably planned for that."

Doug's face tightened subtly. "Sure. I guess I didn't think of that. Your brother's working pretty closely with the government on this one, isn't he?"

"Well, Chase is his best friend. Even if it wasn't part of his job, he'd be pretty concerned."

"Yeah." He took one hand out of his pocket and looked at the gold watch that circled his wrist. "I guess I'd better get back to the office. And I suppose you have better things to do than sit here talking to me."

Gwenn stood up and followed him to the door. "It's nice to know that you're concerned about Chase."

"Sure. No big deal. Chase has always been like a brother to me. In fact, sometimes, I think my father thinks Chase is his favorite son." His laughter held a bitter note.

"I think Charles knows exactly who his son is," Gwenn said gently.

"To his everlasting regret, I'm sure." Before she could think of anything to say to that, he pulled open the shop door. Traffic noise intruded on the quiet atmosphere of the shop and end-of-August heat battled with the air-conditioning.

Doug turned in the door and looked down at her, his expression uncharacteristically solemn. "Take care of yourself, Gwenn."

"Sure. You too." He bent and dropped a kiss on her forehead and then he was striding away.

Shaking her head, she shut the door, closing out the heat and noise. She had the distinct feeling that there was more to Doug's visit than she knew, as if he hadn't said everything he could have.

The news that Chase might be in danger was hardly a revelation. He'd been in danger all along. Still, she'd mention the conversation to Robert when he brought Maggie back and she'd mention it to Chase tonight.

Assuming Chase came home tonight. And, assuming that, if he did come home, he would be willing to talk to her at all.

There was so much they needed to talk about. Maybe Doug's visit would provide her with an opportunity to at least break the ice.

She shivered as she walked past one of the air-conditioning vents and cold air wafted over her. She just hoped that the ice wasn't so thick that it refused to crack.

Chapter 11

Chase shut the door of the Aston Martin before leaning in the open top to pick up his suit jacket and briefcase. He glanced at the silver Porsche on his way out of the garage. So Gwenn was home. He wasn't sure whether he was glad or sorry.

He shut the garage door and crossed to the back entrance, stepping into the warmth of the kitchen. It was almost eight o'clock, but the room was filled with appetizing aromas. He inhaled, sorting out the smells of tomato sauce and garlic.

Gwenn was standing at the counter with her back to him as she cut slices from a loaf of crusty bread. She was wearing a pair of yellow slacks and a bright blue sleeveless shirt. He'd been with her when she bought that outfit. Chase found it was still a new experience to be able to remember things at will. He often found himself calling up details of the most casual incidents, as if to prove to himself that he could.

He remembered that they'd been in a little boutique in Pasadena, and Livvie had been with them. Gwenn had bought the slacks because they were a color that would go with everything, and the fit was perfect. But she'd bought the blouse because Livvie had thought it was a pretty color, and she'd also managed to get her sticky little fingers on it before either of them could stop her.

His face softened at the memory. Once Gwenn got the fingerprints off the blouse, it had turned out to be one of her favorite garments. She'd once worn it a lot, but he hadn't seen her wear it since Livvie died. He'd assumed that she'd thrown it out.

Hearing the door slam, Gwenn turned away from the counter. She'd left her hair down, and she pushed it nervously back from her face as their eyes met briefly. Chase turned away, setting his briefcase and jacket on a nearby chair and reaching up to loosen his tie.

Between them lay years of silence and the pain of those few minutes in the attic. He ran his fingers through his hair, delaying the moment when he'd have to look at her again.

"I thought you might work late, so I planned on a late supper. I . . . I hope you're hungry."

Chase hadn't eaten anything but the cup of coffee and doughnut his secretary had brought him at his desk almost twelve hours ago, but the thought of food was less than appealing. What he really wanted was a hot shower, a bed, and at least ten hours of sleep.

He started to shake his head and then caught the hopeful look in her eyes. He discovered that no matter what lay between them he couldn't bring himself to disappoint her.

"It smells good."

"Maggie's mother gave her a whole bunch of homegrown tomatoes, and she passed some of them on to me so I thought I might as well use them. It's just a tomato-garlic sauce on spaghetti. Nothing fancy or heavy or anything." Her voice trailed away, and she gestured lamely with the serrated knife she held. "I guess I'm babbling."

Chase shrugged. "It doesn't matter."

"It's just that..."

"Just leave it, Gwenn." His voice was gentle but implacable. If she'd planned on having a major discussion about their marriage, he wanted to make it clear that this wasn't the time for it.

Gwenn hesitated, absently testing the point of the knife with her finger. She'd braced herself to talk to Chase tonight. They were going to get everything out in the open. She'd worn clothes that reminded her of happier times, and she'd hoped they might do the same for him. She'd planned a light supper that they would share, perhaps talk a little about unimportant things and lead the way into the main point of the evening.

But now, looking at him, she could see that it wasn't going to work out that way. His skin was gray under the light tan he'd acquired over the past few weeks. If he wasn't actually asleep on his feet, she had a feeling it was sheer willpower that prevented it. She swallowed her disappointment and smiled nervously.

"There's some iced tea in the fridge. Dinner will be in about fifteen minutes, so you've got time to relax a bit."

"I think I'll skip the tea for now and just go change. Thanks."

Gwenn managed another smile, a little more relaxed this time. She'd waited a long time to pull her marriage back together, and a little while longer wouldn't matter that much. It didn't make any sense to try to have that all-important talk when Chase was obviously too tired to think straight.

She watched him leave and then turned back to her dinner preparations with a sigh. Part of her was relieved to be able to put the whole thing off. That was the way they'd been living for so long that it had begun to seem normal. Never talking out problems. Barely even talking to each other.

But that wasn't the way it was going to work anymore. Too much time had been lost already, and she wasn't going to live the rest of her life in a half marriage. She sawed vigorously at the loaf of bread. The old saying about half a loaf being better than none no longer applied. If she couldn't have a real marriage with Chase, she'd rather have nothing. It hurt too much to go on the way they were.

Twenty minutes later she stirred a wooden spoon through the scarlet sauce simmering on the stove and glanced at the clock again. She'd told Chase to come in fifteen minutes. She set the spoon down and went to the sink to poke at the rapidly cooling colander of pasta. If he didn't hurry, the meal was going to be ruined.

Five minutes later she dumped the lump of spaghetti in the trash and turned the burner off under the pot of tomato sauce. Her temper was simmering as violently as the bubbling liquid. If he didn't want to eat with her, he could have just said so. In a fit of temper, she tossed the tray of garlic toast into the trash along with the spaghetti.

She was just about to toss the well-seasoned sauce in with the rest of the meal when common sense got through the hurt anger. She set the pot back on the stove. The whole thing didn't make sense. This wasn't like Chase. He had a temper to match the red that highlighted his hair. It was well controlled and he rarely lost it, but when Chase got angry, he did or said something to let you know about it. He wasn't the type to go in for petty game playing.

If he wasn't doing this deliberately, what was going on? Her feet were already carrying her out of the kitchen as numerous possibilities crowded into her mind. He'd fallen, hit his head and was unconscious. The kidnappers had come back, knocking out the guard in front and silently entering the house. He'd fallen asleep in the shower and drowned. The amnesia had returned, and he didn't remember that she was cooking dinner.

This last thought was so crazy that she stopped on the landing to get control of herself. If Chase had knocked himself out, she would have heard the thud when he hit the floor. She took a deep breath and moved cautiously to a window, opening the curtains a crack and peering out into the drive. There was the guard, sitting in his car. She could see the glow of his cigarette as he lifted it to his mouth. That ruined the theory of kidnappers.

She let the curtain fall and walked down the hall to Chase's room. It was something simple. Perhaps his watch had stopped, and he didn't realize what time it was. She knocked quietly, but there was no sound, so she pushed the door open and stepped inside.

It didn't take her long to find the reason for Chase's absence. The answer was so obvious that she put her hand over her mouth to hold back the half-hysterical giggle that threatened to escape. Chase lay sprawled across the bed. His eyes were closed, his mouth was slightly open, and he was fast asleep. No fall, no kidnappers. He'd simply fallen asleep.

She tiptoed across the room, but there was really no need for quiet. From the way he was sleeping, she didn't think anything short of a bomb dropping was going to wake him. He'd managed to take off his shirt and shoes, but he was still wearing his pants. She unbuckled the belt and loosened the waist before lifting his legs into a more comfortable position.

She stood up and looked down at him, feeling her heart ache with love. There were so many good things to remember in their marriage. It was hard to understand how they'd gotten so far off the track. She brushed a lock of hair back from his forehead. He looked so vulnerable. It was hard to imagine that this was the same man who'd been so furious when he'd found out her deception.

She shut off the light and left the room, pulling the door quietly shut behind her. She was suddenly aware of how tired she was. The emotional roller coaster of the past few days had left her drained. Maybe Chase had the right idea. She stifled a yawn as she walked down the stairs. After she put away the uneaten spaghetti sauce, she'd take a warm bath and go to bed.

Maybe it would be best to have a little more time to heal before they tried to work out their problems. Maybe they were both too emotionally battered right now.

Over the next few days Chase and Gwenn achieved a fragile balance in their relationship. The morning after the uneaten meal, Chase apologized profusely for missing dinner, and Gwenn assured him that she understood.

The conversation was calm, even cordial, but the words could have been exchanged by two complete strangers. There was nothing to suggest that they had made passionate love only two nights before, nothing to suggest the emotional upheaval that had caught both of them. They acted like nothing more than casual acquaintances.

That was exactly how their relationship stayed. Poised on a knife edge between the past and the future. Each of them wanted to avoid previous mistakes, but neither of them was sure that they had a future. They were emotionally worn thin and avoided anything that might shake their carefully established balance.

They spoke little, and when they did, it was on impersonal, unthreatening subjects. After a few days Gwenn began to feel like Alice through the looking glass. She was an outsider looking in and was observing the odd living arrangements of someone who happened to look like her.

The balance had to be broken. They had to talk, but what would happen then? Was she going to lose what little she had? If she couldn't have all of Chase, was she willing to settle for the occasional glimpse of him? And, what was he thinking and feeling? What went on behind those enigmatic eyes?

Gwenn might have been comforted to know that in many ways Chase's thoughts ran parallel to hers. He was aware of the delicate balance they'd set up and how easily it could be upset. Any way they moved, it could plunge into turmoil. Things couldn't stay the way they were, but he couldn't bring himself to push for a change.

If he'd thought that returning to his job was going to solve any problems, he was disappointed. It helped him to avoid Gwenn and gave him time to lick a few emotional wounds, but it created problems all its own.

Regaining his memory didn't make him the same Chase Buchanon he'd been before the kidnapping. In fact, he was finding that in many ways his memories almost seemed to be those of another man's. The doctor assured him that this was to be expected. After all, he *was* a different man than what he'd been before the kidnapping. He'd been changed by his experiences, those during his captivity that he still couldn't remember and those since his awakening.

Intellectually he accepted this. But it was mentally exhausting to feel as if he were two separate people. And he didn't escape it on the job. The old Chase knew the ins and outs of his work, the tasks to be performed, the people to be contacted, what to say and what to do. The new Chase not only didn't know the job, but also found he didn't really *want* to know it.

He tried to tell himself that it was just the bizarre situation. He was still finding his feet. As soon as he felt at home in his mind, he'd feel at home in his job. But, searching his memory, he realized that the boredom and dissatisfaction had been there long before the kidnapping. He hadn't been ready to acknowledge it then. His marriage was an empty shell; how could he admit that his job was rapidly becoming the same?

Chase shook his head and laid down the stack of information he was supposedly studying. The mild throbbing at his temples had become a constant companion, so familiar that he hardly noticed it on a conscious level. He took off his reading glasses and set them on the desk, pinching the bridge of his nose with thumb and forefinger for a moment in an attempt to alleviate the pressure behind his eyes.

Leaning back in the heavy leather chair, he let his eyes wander around the office. It was the epitome of subdued luxury: wood paneling, thick carpet, leather-and-wood furniture. Everything spoke of money and power. His income matched the office, and though he'd inherited enough money to make working a matter of personal choice, he'd always enjoyed the satisfaction that came from doing his job well.

But he'd changed. All the things he'd set out to achieve in college had been attained. He'd proved that he could handle a demanding job. With the investments he'd made over the years, he was modestly wealthy in his own right, so he didn't need the family wealth.

He was rich, relatively young, and he held a powerful position in a successful company.

He was also bored out of his mind.

No. It was nothing as definite as boredom. It was a niggling dissatisfaction, a feeling that he'd locked himself onto a narrow pathway and there was a lot of life passing him by.

He shook his head and picked up his reading glasses. The last thing he needed right now was to let himself get caught up in a midlife crisis. He had to get his personal life in order, and needed to decide where his marriage was going.

As always, thoughts of Gwenn brought a confusing rush of emotions: tenderness and anger; desire and hurt; need and uncertainty; love and hate. There were no neat and easy answers.

Also, no matter how he felt about the job, until the missing schematics were found, he owed Johnson Industries everything he could give them. He probed cautiously at his memory, always hoping that this time the dark curtains would part and he'd be able to grasp at those last missing pieces. But his memory remained stubbornly inaccessible, and he gave up the effort with a frustrated breath.

Where were those damn papers? Why had he taken them and what had he done with them? Who'd wanted them badly enough to torture him for information? And were they still after the papers?

The answer to the last question was provided in an unexpected and unwelcome manner. In the short week and a half since he'd returned to work, Chase had picked up his old habit of going to work early and leaving late. In the months after Livvie's death, it had been a way to avoid the big house that seemed to echo with lost laughter.

So, it was after dark when he turned the Aston Martin into the driveway. The dark sedan that belonged to the officer who'd been assigned to follow him made the same turn and parked to one side of the driveway. Chase grimaced as he pushed the button to open the garage door. He hated being followed around, no matter how unobtrusive his tail tried to be.

He pulled into the garage next to Gwenn's Porsche. Swinging his long legs out of the car, he stood up, stretching his back before turning to lift his briefcase off the passenger seat. He shut the garage door and turned toward the house and then stopped. Too many lights were on inside.

A frisson of uneasiness ran up his spine, and his pace quickened. Why on earth would Gwenn have turned on so many lights? She couldn't possibly be in six rooms at once. He pulled open the back door, stepped into the kitchen and then came to a dead halt, feeling his heart lodge in his throat.

The room looked as if a tornado had struck it. Cupboard doors hung open, and pots and pans littered the floor. The canisters had been tipped over, their contents mixed and strewn across the counters. Everywhere he looked there was evidence of destruction.

Gwenn.

His heart began to pound in a heavy, choking rhythm. What if she'd been at home when this had happened? What if the people who'd done this were still here? He silently set his briefcase down and crossed to the nearest counter. His fingers closed over the hilt of a butcher knife, the knuckles whitening with the force of his grip.

He slipped his feet free of his shoes and crossed the kitchen silently, stopping to listen before stepping out into the hall. His stockinged feet made no sound as he climbed the stairs, keeping away from the center of the staircase where a creaking floorboard might give him away.

He stopped at the top of the stairs and looked down the hall. Light spilled out of both his bedroom and Gwenn's, but there was still no sound but the too-rapid pounding of his own heartbeat. His fingers tightened purposefully on the hilt of the butcher knife. He started down the hallway.

Gwenn.

That was the only thing he could think of. Where was she? Was she hurt? He stopped, his back to the wall next to her bedroom door. Not a sound came from inside, but he was sure someone was there. His nostrils flared as if to pick up some scent that would tell him what lay on the other side of the wall.

He eased around the edge of the doorway, half afraid of what he might find. The room was in shambles. Clothing spilled from open drawers, creating gay trails of color across the thick carpeting. Closet doors hung wide open, revealing dresses torn from the hangers and tossed carelessly onto the floor.

All of this Chase noticed with his peripheral vision. The only thing he really saw in those first seconds was a still figure seated on the torn disarray of the bed. The room was empty except for the two of them.

"Gwenn?" He set the knife down on a delicately made table, the contents of which lay on the floor, apparently cleared by the expedient method of an arm swept across the top.

She didn't move, and it took him but an instant to reach her side. Only when he dropped to his knees next to her did she seem to become aware of his presence. She lifted her head slowly, and Chase felt a burning mixture of rage and pain when he saw the dazed look in her gray eyes.

"Are you all right?" The urgency in his tone seemed to get through to her, and she nodded slowly. "You're not hurt at all?" He ran his hands over her shoulders, searching for some sign of injury. He only remembered to breathe again when he failed to find any damage.

"I wasn't here. I came home to find the place like this."

"Thank God!" He stood up, lifting her to her feet with him. He was unaware of the bruising force of his grip on her arms, unaware of the emotions revealed in his face and voice. All that mattered was that she was safe and sound. He pulled her against him, his arms tightening convulsively about her.

"I thought something had happened to you. That was all I could think of. Thank God you're all right."

Gwenn lifted her head, her eyes searching his face. Had he been worried about her only because he still felt tied to her by the bonds of the past five years, or was it because he still loved her?

She couldn't clearly read the emotions in his eyes. There was a mixture of worry and concern there. But was love there, too? Before she had a chance to decide the answer to that, the shrill wail of sirens shattered the air.

Chase seemed to become aware of his grip on her and pulled away his hands as he took a step back. Gwenn had to stifle the urge to reach out and hold him to her, but this wasn't the time to demonstrate their confused feelings.

"I guess that must be the police. I called them when I saw what had happened."

Chase nodded, glancing around the trashed room. "I doubt if they're going to find anything in this mess, but they should know what's going on.

"What were you doing up here? You should have left the minute you realized someone had broken in. They could have still been here." There was an edge to his voice.

Gwenn shrugged, knowing he was right. She was saved answering him as the sirens moaned to silence in front of the house. Seconds later Robert's voice echoed up the stairs.

"Chase? Gwenn? Where the hell are you?" The three of them met at the top of the stairs, and Robert put his arms around his sister, giving her a quick hug before releasing her.

His eyes skimmed over her, checking for injury before moving over Chase in the same assessing way.

"Are you two all right?"

Chase nodded. "Neither one of us was here."

"Neither one of you should be here now. I don't suppose you've thought to check to see if anybody is still around."

Chase answered for both of them. "There's no one on the first two floors. I don't know about the attic. I was just about to get Gwenn out when you arrived. With all the noise you made, I don't think you're going to be able to sneak up on anybody, if they're still here."

"When a call comes in that a house has been broken into, our first priority is to protect the residents of the house; our second is to catch the criminals. I'd rather scare a burglar off than catch him right after he's panicked and shot the homeowner. Get outside and let my men go through the place."

Gwenn followed him downstairs, acutely aware of Chase's large presence right behind her. The three of them stood on the lawn while several police officers went through the house from top to bottom. Gwenn tried to control the shivers that ran through her frame.

In the first few minutes after she'd seen the disaster that had been made of her home, she hadn't been able to really grasp what had happened. Now, standing outside and watching yet more strangers go through her house, reaction was beginning to set in.

Robert reached for the zipper of his light windbreaker, but Chase was there ahead of him. Gwenn gave him a strained smile as the warmth of his suit jacket settled around her shoulders. It wasn't the air that was cold. The autumn night was balmy and warm. The chill she felt came from inside.

"Why don't you tell me what happened?"

She shrugged in answer to her brother's question. "I can't tell you anything that you can't see. I got home about twenty minutes ago. When I walked into the kitchen..." She broke off, remembering the destruction in what had always been her favorite room.

Chase's hand came to rest on her shoulder, giving her silent support. Gwenn leaned into that support, not caring about his reason for offering it. She needed it too much at the moment to question its source.

She took a deep breath and went on, her words hurried, as if she had to get them out quickly or not at all. "I couldn't believe what I was seeing at first, but then I called the police, and that's really about all there is to it."

"Didn't the officer you talked to tell you to leave the house?" Robert's irritation was easy to read in his voice.

"I don't know. To tell the truth, I don't think I really listened to anything she said. I was so upset." She shrugged apologetically.

He looked as if he wanted to say something more, and then he shook his head slightly. "What's done is done." He turned as a man came up to him, and Chase nodded as he recognized the officer who'd been assigned to follow him the last few days. "Did you see anything, McCready?"

McCready shook his head. "Not a thing, Lieutenant. I followed Mr. Buchanon home from work and parked as usual. It wasn't until the squad cars started arriving that I realized something was wrong. The house looked quiet."

Robert gave Chase a disgusted look. "I suppose you didn't think to let the man assigned to protect you know that there was something wrong."

Chase shrugged without apology. He hadn't thought of anything but making sure that Gwenn was all right. Robert shook his head and turned back to the officer.

"Don't worry about it. Whoever searched the house was gone long before you arrived. Why don't you go help search the grounds?"

The officer turned and left, and his place was promptly taken by another man who'd come from inside the house. "We've searched thoroughly, Lieutenant, and there's no sign of any intruders."

"What about any evidence to point to who did this?"

"I don't think there's any of that, either. The best chance for fingerprints is in the kitchen. There's a lot of surfaces there that could be dusted."

Robert ran his fingers through his hair, his dark brows hooking together in a scowl. "Block that area off." He glanced at Chase and Gwenn. "I'll have the fingerprint team come in tomorrow morning and dust. I don't think twelve hours is going to make much difference."

He turned to his sister and brother-in-law. "We can go back in, now. Just stay out of the kitchen."

Gwenn stopped on the threshold of the living room, her eyes skimming over the drawers that had been torn out of the mahogany secretary, the figurines broken on the hearth. She blinked back tears, resisting the urge to turn and bury her face in Chase's shirt and cry her eyes out. His fingers tightened on her shoulder, as if sensing how she felt.

"Definitely someone who knew what they were doing." Robert's eyes skimmed over the damage professionally.

"They were after those damn papers." Chase's words were more a statement than a question, but Robert nodded in answer.

"I'd say so. But I think they were also delivering a warning."

Gwenn jerked her eyes away from the mess of a room and stared at her brother. "Warning?"

Robert ignored the frown Chase directed at him over Gwenn's head. "I think they're letting you know that they still want the papers. My guess is that they know you've regained part of your memory. That's making them very nervous."

"Then they could be planning on kidnapping Chase again?" Gwenn's voice shook slightly as she asked the question.

Chase's frown deepened into a scowl, but Robert pretended not to notice. "Maybe." He waited a second to let that thought sink in before he continued. "I think both of you should go somewhere safe for a while."

Chase's hand left Gwenn's shoulder, and he turned away, avoiding her eyes. "I'm not letting anybody push me out of my home."

"It would only be for a little while, Chase. Just until Robert catches these people."

Robert's mouth quirked slightly in acknowledgment of her faith in him, but Chase was already shaking his head.

"No. I'm not going to run away. I'm not the criminal here. Besides, if I go into hiding, there's nothing to draw them out. How are you planning on catching them without something to bait a trap with?"

"What makes you think I'm planning on setting a trap?"

"Because I know you. You're not going to sit around waiting for them to make the first move."

"You're right," Robert acknowledged grudgingly.

"Then you need me here, and you and I both know it. I'm the best bait you have." His eyes met Robert's with cool determination.

Gwenn's quiet voice broke into the silent struggle. "Chase, maybe Robert is right. Maybe you should just lay low somewhere for a while. Let him find something else to use as his trap."

Her eyes were wide gray pools of concern, and Chase wanted to be able to take her in his arms and hold her close and tell her that everything was going to be all right. But he couldn't. There was still too much left to be resolved between them. And he couldn't promise her that everything was going to be all right because he didn't know that it was.

"Gwenn, other than the papers, *I'm* what these bastards want. In fact, even if they had the papers, they'd probably still want me because, when I regain the rest of my memory, I can identify them. We can't just sit around waiting for them to grow old and die. I don't want to live in hiding, and I don't want to walk around knowing that I'm a target."

Gwenn heard the truth in what he was saying, but she didn't want to acknowledge it, didn't want to admit that this was the best thing to do. She turned to her brother with a silent plea in her eyes. She wanted him to tell her that they didn't have to do it this way.

Robert met her eyes, and his mouth set in a straight line before he slowly shook his head. "Chase is right. I can't ask him to be a target, but he is the best bait we can offer."

Gwenn lifted her fingers to her mouth to stifle the sob that wanted to escape. Her eyes closed for a moment while she dealt with the realities of the situation, and then she straightened her shoulders and took a deep breath.

"If both of you think this is the best way, I can't argue with it, but I don't have to like it."

"It shouldn't take long. They must be getting anxious, from the looks of this place." Chase glanced around the room to emphasize his point. "By the time you get back, I'll have the house cleaned up and you..."

"Get back? Get back from where?" Gwenn broke in without apology.

Chase turned his eyes back to her. There was a stubborn look on her face that made him tense warily. "Gwenn, there's no reason why you should stay here. I thought you could go visit your aunt up in Seattle. You haven't been to see her in a long time. In a few days or weeks, this will all be settled and . . ."

"No."

Chase looked at Robert who hurried to fill the sudden pause left by her flat negative. "Chase is right, Gwenn. There's nothing to be gained by you staying here. In fact, you might even be in the way."

"No." Her eyes flickered from one man to the other, and she tightened her hold on Chase's jacket, drawing it closer around her as if to gain strength from it. "I'm not going."

"I appreciate the offer, Gwenn, but I really don't need someone to hold my hand."

"I'm not going off to stay with Aunt Alice, like a good little girl. If you're staying, I'm staying." She turned to face her husband straight on, knowing that Robert would go along if Chase accepted her decision. "We've had problems but we're still married, Chase, and I'm not going somewhere safe while you stay here playing cops and robbers. If you're staying, I'm staying."

Chase looked at Robert, but this time Robert just lifted his shoulders in a shrug, telling him wordlessly that he was on his own. Chase looked at Gwenn, reading the stubborn determination in her usually soft gray eyes.

"I don't want you here."

The flat rejection hung in the air between them. From the corner of his eye he saw Robert tense, but his attention was concentrated on his wife. He had to convince her to leave. Gwenn winced, and for a moment her lower lip trembled, but then her delicate jaw hardened, and her mouth firmed.

"Tough. I'm staying. You can just pretend I'm not here."

Despite his exasperation, Chase couldn't help but admire her determination. He'd lost the argument. He admitted that, and now he had to back down gracefully. But Gwenn made that unnecessary. With a dignity that was at odds with her mussed hair and the man's jacket still shrouding her shoulders, she turned and left the room without another word.

Chase thrust his fingers through his hair and then looked at Robert. "She can be the most pigheaded woman."

"Don't look at me. I'm a model of reason."

"She gets it all from you. When your parents died and left her with you, they couldn't have known that you were going to raise her to be stubborn, unreasonable..."

"And I suppose you're a model of reason?" Robert arched one brow in question, and Chase broke off in mid-tirade.

"You don't agree with her staying here, do you?"

"No. I'd rather she went to stay with Aunt Alice, but you can't tell me that you'd have reacted any differently if the situation had been reversed. Would you go off somewhere safe if *she* was in danger?"

"Of course not! But that's different."

"Careful. Your sexist tendencies are showing."

Chase's hair was ruffled into a wild tangle by his fingers as he glared at his best friend. "Is there something wrong with wanting her to be safe?"

"Nothing at all. But you can't say that she's unreasonable when she's doing exactly what you would do in her position."

"Don't hit me with logic," Chase complained irritably.

"I'll try to avoid it in the future. Look, I've got to go file a report on this. I'm going to leave some men here tonight. That won't look overly suspicious, considering what's happened tonight. We'll get together tomorrow and work out the details of how we're going to play this game."

"Fine. Just make sure that Gwenn is protected."

"She's my sister, remember? I'll take care of her."

Chase didn't move as Robert clapped him on the shoulder and then went out into the hall. He was still standing in the middle of the torn-apart living room when Robert called a quick good-night and the front door shut behind him and his men.

The big house was suddenly quiet again. Gwenn was upstairs somewhere. His shoulders knotted at the thought of her putting herself in danger because of him. She might be Robert's sister, but she was his wife, and he'd make sure she stayed safe. He couldn't depend on anyone else for that.

Now he had to go find her and try and explain that he hadn't meant to hurt her. He shook his head. Sometimes it seemed like they'd never done anything but hurt each other.

Chapter 12

Chase locked up the house, though he felt that it was rather like shutting the barn door after the horse was already gone. There was a squad car parked out front, and he knew that Robert had stationed a couple of men in the back.

As he climbed the stairs, he was aware of the lateness of the hour and his own weariness. He almost welcomed the chance to be bait in a trap. He wanted this part of his life settled and didn't want to wonder anymore about who had kidnapped him and if they were still after him.

He reached the top of the stairs and stopped, his head cocked to one side. There was a sound that he couldn't identify immediately. The sound was coming from Gwenn's room. With that realization came recognition.

She was crying.

He stopped, leaning one fist against the wall outside her door as he listened to the quiet sobs. Should he go in? Or should he leave her to her sorrow? Wasn't that what had gotten them in trouble in the first place? Too many months of lonely sorrow, too little sharing. Were they going to start the same old patterns again?

The first that Gwenn knew of his presence was when his fingers rested tentatively on her shoulder. Her breath caught as she tried to swallow a sob. She looked up at him, her eyes the soft gray of a cloudy morning. Chase sank onto the bed beside her and put his arm around her shoulders. The gesture was hesitant, as if he expected her to reject his comfort, but she leaned into him like a tired child.

"I feel so violated." The words were choppy, separated by half sobs as she struggled to get her breath.

"I know."

"They had their hands on my clothes."

"We'll get you a whole new wardrobe."

She laughed raggedly. "I don't think that's going to help. I just hate the thought of strangers being in my bedroom, touching my things. Look, I found this on the floor."

Chase looked at the garment she held, and his memory presented him with the last time she'd worn it. He reached with his free hand to catch the bit of lace between thumb and forefinger.

"Do you remember it?" Gwenn's voice was husky with tears. "I wore this on our wedding night."

"I remember. You went into the bathroom to change, and when you came out, the light was behind you. You looked like an angel dressed in pale satin."

"I was so nervous, but then you held out your hand, and you looked at me as if I was the most beautiful thing you'd ever seen."

"You were. I was afraid to touch you for fear you'd turn out to be a dream."

"A slightly pregnant dream."

"You were the only one who thought you looked pregnant. And it wouldn't have mattered if you'd been about to deliver triplets. You were still the most beautiful thing I'd ever seen. Do you remember the last time you wore this nightgown?"

"On our third anniversary. I wore it every year on our anniversary."

"And every year you were more beautiful."

"I haven't had it out in years. Not since..."

"Not since Livvie died."

"I guess a lot of things changed then."

He slid his arm away from her shoulder, and Gwenn almost cried out at the pain of that small loss. Though he didn't move away physically, she had the sense of him retreating mentally.

"You stopped talking." His words were quiet, but she thought she read pain in the simple statement.

"It hurt too much to talk."

"Did it hurt any less to keep silent?"

"In the long run, no. But at the time it seemed less painful."

"I loved her, too."

"I know. I knew it then, but I felt...I don't know. I guess I felt guilty. I was afraid you'd blame me."

"Blame you? For what? You weren't driving the car when it was hit."

Gwenn twisted her fingers in the pale peach satin on her lap. She'd never tried to explain her feelings, and it was hard to find the words she wanted. She'd held the thoughts in for so long.

"If I hadn't been so set on starting Guinevere's Fantasy, I would have been home with Livvie. She wouldn't have been with a baby-sitter, and she wouldn't have been in the car at all."

Chase got up, thrusting his fingers roughly through his hair as he paced away from her. She watched him uncertainly. Logically, she knew she wasn't to blame for Livvie's death, but she'd carried the emotional guilt for so long that she almost expected him to turn and blast her for what she'd done.

"Gwenn, I encouraged you to start up the shop. It was something you wanted, and I wanted you to have it. You didn't abandon Livvie. Cindy was a wonderful sitter, and Livvie was very happy spending time with her. If we're going to start handing out blame, then I deserve a share of it, too, because I was supposed to pick Livvie up that day. I called Cindy and asked her if she could take Livvie home because I was running late."

"You can't blame yourself for that." She jumped to his defense without hesitation. "Cindy often drove her home, and nothing had ever happened before. The accident was one of those things that couldn't have been predicted or prevented."

"Exactly. So you can't blame yourself for what happened." He caught her neatly in her own logic. "Did you think that I blamed you?" The question was voiced with difficulty, and Gwenn's answer came the same way.

"I don't know. I guess I never reasoned it out. But at the hospital you seemed to draw away. You didn't want me to touch you or hold you."

He thought back to those terrible hours when they'd waited for some news, torn between hope and despair while a tiny life struggled within a badly broken body. A struggle that was gradually lost.

"I didn't mean to push you away. It's . . . not easy, sometimes, for a man to deal with his emotions. I was hurting so much and I was so scared. I think I was afraid that if I let you close to me, I'd break down and howl like a baby."

"I wouldn't have cared. We could have cried together."

His mouth twisted. "I felt as if I had to be strong. I couldn't let go, because I had to stay strong for you. I guess that instead I made you feel like I wasn't there for you, at all."

"When the doctor told us that...that she was...gone, you put your arms around me, but you were so rigid. I could feel such anger in you. I thought you hated me."

"No. Never." He crossed to her in two quick strides and knelt down in front of her. He reached out as if to take her hands and then stopped, letting his hands fall to his sides. "I *was* angry. But I wasn't angry at you. I wasn't angry *at* anybody. I was angry over what had happened. I was angry because it helped me deal with the grief. It had nothing to do with you."

"Why didn't you tell me that?"

"Why didn't you tell me what you were feeling?" he countered.

"I thought you had drawn away. I thought you didn't want to know."

"And I thought *you* didn't want to know how I felt."

"Oh, God. What a waste." She felt wearied by the futility of what they'd gone through. "If only we'd talked."

"I tried to reach you. Remember? About a month after the funeral. We'd just gone to bed, and I put my arms around you, and you pushed me away and told me you thought it would be best if one of us moved into the spare bedroom for a while."

"And you went. If you cared, why did you go?"

"What was I supposed to do? You were looking at me like I was about to rape you, for God's sake. Of course I left."

"I thought you were just feeling obligated."

"Obligated to make love to you?" His brows shot up. "Gwenn, when did I ever make you feel like making love with you was a duty?"

"Never. But everything had changed."

"I still loved you. That hadn't changed."

"But I didn't *know* that. By then, I was beginning to think maybe you'd never loved me."

"Why would I have married you?"

"Because I was pregnant."

"Gwenn, that doesn't make any sense. I asked you to marry me before you found out you were pregnant. The only change it made was that we pushed the wedding up a bit."

"I thought maybe it was just because Robert was your best friend, and you felt guilty about sleeping with me."

"That had nothing to do with it. I won't deny that your brother wasn't any too happy when he found out we were sleeping together, and he did threaten to tear my head off if I hurt you, but the only guilt I felt about sleeping with you was because you were so young. I felt like I should have been noble and given you a chance to fall in love with someone closer to your age.

"I didn't marry you because of your brother or because you were pregnant. I married you because I loved you so much that I couldn't imagine living without you."

"Oh." Gwenn couldn't get more than that one syllable past the lump in her throat.

Chase stood up and paced restlessly across the room. "Why didn't you tell me about Livvie when I got back from the hospital?"

"The doctor had said that you shouldn't be upset, that we should let your memory come back on its own as much as possible. I honestly thought it would be better for you that way."

He stood next to her vanity and absently set several bottles upright. "Are you sure that's the only reason?"

She didn't answer immediately, feeling that it was important that she answer him as honestly as possible. "I guess there was a part of me that wanted to pretend that nothing had gone wrong with our marriage. Every time I thought of Livvie, it brought so much pain that maybe I wanted to pretend even she'd never happened. But once I *couldn't* mention her to you, I found myself wanting to remember all the good times, all the wonderful things about having her. I'd tried so hard to forget for the past two years, and then suddenly the opportunity was there to kind of go back in time."

She lowered her eyes and smoothed the satin gown against her knee. Chase said nothing. He waited for her to find the words she wanted.

"When you disappeared, I thought I'd lost you forever. And that made me realize just how much we'd lost already. When you were found, I felt as if I'd been given a reprieve, as if this was a sign that it wasn't too late. And I suppose I did look on it as a chance to start over again."

"To pretend," Chase said. She glanced up, and met his gaze and nodded slowly.

"To pretend. But I didn't do it to hurt you, and I didn't think in terms of shutting you away from Livvie. Maybe I didn't think very clearly at all. I was just glad to have you back."

"And what about the divorce you asked me for? Did you forget about that, too?"

"I didn't want a divorce, Chase. I just wanted us to talk to each other. We'd been living like strangers for so long."

"Well, asking for divorce is a hell of a way to go about patching up a marriage."

"If it wasn't what you wanted, why did you just tell me to do whatever I wanted? Why didn't you argue with me?"

"I didn't have time to think about arguing. One minute I was eating a slice of toast, and the next I'm being asked for a divorce."

"But what about later? What about after you'd thought about it? You hardly said a word to me after that."

"Gwenn, I was hurting. And I was angry. It seemed to me that you were willing to throw away five years of marriage over the breakfast table, but then I had to face the fact that, for the past two years, there hadn't been much to throw away. There was...something going on at work that had me worried." He rubbed at his temple, trying to soothe the annoying throb of pain that came whenever he tried to think of the days before the kidnapping. He shook his head abruptly.

"I don't know. There was a part of me that just wanted to walk away from it all. There was a part of me that saw divorce as... not entirely a bad thing."

Gwenn lifted the satin gown and buried her face in it. She didn't want him to see the way pain stabbed through her at his words. For a moment she faced the possibility that he might not feel their marriage was worth saving. Maybe the past had taken too much out of them, and there were too many flaws in the fabric of their life together.

She had to force her voice past the burning pain in her chest. "And now?"

"Now?"

"What about our marriage now? How do you see it?"

She couldn't raise her eyes to his face, couldn't bear to see the regret that might spell the end of hope. She could only smooth her trembling fingers over and over on the gentle satin of her gown.

"I don't know," he said flatly.

She nodded, blinking back the surge of tears that stung her eyes. "Where do we go from here?"

"At the moment, I think we should both go to bed. It's been a hell of a night. In the future...I honestly don't know, Gwenn. I wish I did. Five years of marriage isn't something you throw away easily, but we didn't make it through the bad times very well. What's going to happen next time?"

There was no answer to that question, and Gwenn didn't try to give him one. She wanted to tell him that it would be all right, that they'd learned their lesson and, if there was a next time, they'd pull together—not apart. But she couldn't promise him that any more than he could promise her.

"We can't work anything out tonight." The weariness in his voice made Gwenn realize how tired she was. "Tomorrow we can get started cleaning up the mess our visitors left."

"Chase!" The urgent tone caught his attention as he moved toward the door. He stopped and turned toward her. Gwenn's fingers twisted frantically in the gown she'd just spent so much time smoothing. "Don't go." The words were barely above a whisper, but he had no trouble hearing them. She could see the impact of them in his eyes.

"Gwenn, I don't think..."

"I don't want to be alone tonight." Her eyes were wide and pleading. "It's a big bed. Couldn't you stay here?"

He hesitated a moment longer, but there was so much vulnerability, so much need in her eyes, and he realized that he didn't want to be alone, either. He smiled crookedly and slid his palm over the switch by the door, leaving the room illuminated only by the small bedside lamp.

Gwenn stood up, setting aside the nightgown. It took her only a few moments to strip off her skirt and blouse. She didn't feel self-conscious undressing in front of him. Tonight they'd laid bare their souls.

As she stepped out of her slip, Chase's hand appeared in front of her, holding out his shirt. She was frozen for a moment, and then she reached out take the gray silk garment. Her eyes traveled up the length of his arm to his face, seeing memories in his eyes.

"You used to like to sleep in my shirts." His hand dropped away, and she had the feeling that he was suddenly uncertain about the wisdom of evoking such memories.

"It always made me feel so close to you," she whispered. "So loved." He turned away without answering, but Gwenn knew that he was remembering the good times, more than the bad.

A few minutes later, she snapped off the lamp, letting darkness close out the disaster of the room. They'd made the bed with fresh sheets. Gwenn couldn't bear to sleep on the sheets the vandals had touched. They smelled fresh and clean but all that mattered was the warm musky scent of Chase next to her.

With the silk of his shirt against her skin and his strong presence in her bed, for just a little while, she could believe that everything was going to be all right. And, when Chase hesitantly slipped his arm under her shoulder and pulled her close, she couldn't doubt that he needed her at that moment just as much as she needed him.

Her cheek fit his shoulder as if meant to be there and her arm slid across the flat planes of his stomach as she cuddled into his warmth. The evening had been emotionally exhausting but they'd brought so much out in the open. Surely they'd be able to work everything out.

Chase lay beside her, vividly aware of her feminine form cuddled so close to his side. His palm flattened against her back, pulling her against him and his free hand stroked slowly up and down her side. It was a movement meant to soothe, to offer comfort.

Gwenn held her breath as his fingers brushed against the side of her breast. They'd delved into so many memories tonight. This was one more. Lying in bed together, Chase's hands on her body. The memories it conjured up were evocative and she found herself shifting restlessly, a shimmering warmth building in the pit of her stomach.

Only half aware of her movement, she turned slightly so that when his hand swept up her side, his palm cupped her breast. His fingers froze and neither of them dared to breathe. The room was dark, absolutely still. She couldn't see his expression but she could feel the tension in those long fingers. He hesitated and she thought he might draw away, might reject her half-voiced offer.

And then her breath escaped in a sob when his fingers tightened, his thumb brushing over the silk of his shirt, finding the rise of her nipple and teasing it to full arousal. Her hand slid up his chest, exploring the furred surface, tracing the lines of his ribs and then finding the slight bump of his masculine nipple and pinching gently. Her reward was the sudden tension in his body.

He shifted, pushing her onto her back. She could dimly make out his shoulders as he leaned over her.

"Gwenn, are you sure?" The question was almost rhetorical since he was already slipping buttons free of buttonholes, spreading the shirt open to bare her to him.

"I'm sure. I need you, Chase. I need you."

Despite the desire that burned ever higher in both of them, their lovemaking was slow, almost languid. The emotional turmoil of the evening had left them needing a peaceful union. A slow build to explosion.

There was a tenderness in the way his hands slid over her body. It was almost as if they were trying to recapture the warm security they'd once had. Chase's tongue curled around a swollen nipple, his hands sliding down her body to the golden triangle of curls that concealed and yet tantalized.

Gwenn arched as she felt his fingers against her. Her hands slid down the curve of his spine, exploring the muscular length of his thighs before sliding around his body to cup the heavy weight of him in her palms.

"Gwenn." Her name was groaned out against her breast and suddenly, they no longer felt as if they had all the time in the world.

Her legs parted for him. Her hands closed over him, leading him to the very portal of her need. He stopped, his body heavy along hers, his head coming back as if to judge her expression, even in the darkness. Her eyes searched the shadowy planes of his face, seeing the faint reflection of his eyes an instant before his head blocked out all the light and his mouth closed over hers.

His body claimed her at the same moment that his tongue laid claim to her mouth. She whimpered deep in her throat, arching upward in eager acceptance of this dual invasion. The taste, the smell of him, each little movement brought the past rushing back on her. When they'd made love before, she'd been always conscious of the fact that he didn't remember her. But now, there were no secrets between them.

Her legs wound around his hips, urging him still deeper. The heavy weight of his chest crushed her breasts, abrading already aroused nipples. The tension was building inside her, tighter and tighter, drawing her deeper into the web he was spinning. Her head twisted against the pillows as the tension spiraled to an almost unbearable level.

When it snapped, she gasped, going rigid beneath him, barely aware of his thick groan as his body arched over her. The pleasure was so intense, so powerful that she couldn't breathe for a long, painful moment. He collapsed onto her, forcing the air from her lungs, drawing a muffled whimper of completion from her lips.

"Gwenn. Gwenn." Her name was a murmur against her shoulder.

Her hands stroked slowly up and down his damp back, drawing him closer. She didn't ever want to lose this closeness. She wanted to be able to hold it forever. But she knew there was still too much between them, too many things left unsettled. Tonight had been an interlude but it would be foolish to build too much on it. Foolish to hope for too much.

Chase looked up from his desk as the door to his office opened. Doug stuck his head around the edge of the door and Chase tried to smooth his frown into a smile.

"Are you busy?"

"I can spare a few minutes." He shuffled the papers he'd been examining into a neat stack, slid his reading glasses off and laid them on top of the papers. "What can I do for you?"

"Actually, I just came to see if there was anything I could do for you."

Chase raised his brows in silent question.

"I heard about what happened to your house last night."

"News travels fast."

"This is a small company."

"With a jungle drum, from the sounds of it." Chase's eyes never left the other man as he sat down across the desk. Doug always looked uncomfortable and out of place in a suit. His tie was never quite straight, and the jacket concealed the bulging muscles of his arms and chest, making him look bulky rather than muscled.

Those wide shoulders lifted in an apologetic shrug. "Well, you have provided some pretty interesting gossip lately. It isn't every day that one of our executives is kidnapped and then returns without his memory."

"I suppose it does provide a lot of grist for the gossip mill."

"Sure. And then when your house is ransacked, that just adds to the legend."

"Legend?" Chase raised one brow. "I hardly think of myself as the stuff of legend."

"Well, Johnson Industries has always been a rather quiet little company. You've kind of shaken the place up a bit." He smiled, and Chase found himself noticing the perfection of his teeth and wondering if he'd had them capped. He didn't remember them being quite so dazzling when they were in college.

Doug paused, waiting for Chase to say something. When the other man was silent, he shifted in the chair, as if trying to find enough space for his body.

"Anyway, I heard about what happened to your house, but I didn't hear any real details."

Chase shrugged. "There's not much to tell. Gwenn got home about twenty minutes before I did and found the place in a shambles. There doesn't seem to be any evidence to tell us who it was or what they were after. Robert's got a fingerprint team in there this morning, but he doesn't expect to find anything."

"That's too bad. Any major damage?"

"Doesn't seem to be. More of a mess than anything else."

Doug's eyes widened. "I just realized that if I hadn't asked you to help me with the Gunderson project last night, you might have surprised the guys who did it."

"I'd thought of that but I'll forgive you." Chase's mouth twisted ruefully.

"Forgive me? You should be thanking me. You didn't come out too well last time you tangled with these guys."

"What makes you think it was the same people who kidnapped me?"

"Wasn't it?"

"I have no idea."

The silence stretched awkwardly, and Chase began to wonder if Doug had something more to say. Doug finally spoke again.

"Well, whoever it was, I guess they left the place in a mess. Do you need any help with the cleanup?"

"I don't think so. I'm going to go home in a few minutes. I had a meeting this morning that I couldn't really put off, or I wouldn't even have come in."

"If you've got work to do, I could go stay with Gwenn this afternoon. You know me. I never have much to do. Dad only keeps me on the payroll because it would look embarrassing to have his only son apply for welfare. I could keep her company until you got home."

Chase stared at the other man silently for a moment, trying to decide why it was that he wanted to lunge across the desk and hit him every time he mentioned Gwenn. It must be that he was just overtired. With Gwenn in his arms, he'd found it impossible to sleep, finally dozing off around dawn and waking up two hours later.

There was a sharp snap and he looked down, mildly surprised to find that he'd broken the earpiece off the reading glasses. Doug's eyes followed his, widening slightly as he saw the damage. Chase dropped the broken pieces and forced his hand to lie still on the desktop.

"Thanks, Doug. But I'm about ready to go home. Maggie got her little sister to take care of the shop, so she's with Gwenn this morning."

"Are you sure you don't need any help? I'm a whizz with a broom." In the past Chase would have told Doug to come on over, knowing that the other man had few friends and he was probably looking for some company. But somehow things had changed.

He shook his head. "Thanks, but I don't think we're going to need any help."

"Oh." Doug seemed to sag slightly in his chair. Chase watched him, resisting the urge to drum his fingers on the leather blotter. He glanced at his desk clock. Another sixty seconds, and he was going to go home and leave Doug sitting there. Why didn't he take the hint and go away?

"What do you think they were looking for?"

Chases's green eyes met the pale blue of Doug's. "What makes you think they were looking for anything?" he asked coolly.

"Well, it seems pretty obvious, doesn't it? I mean, they didn't take anything, so they had to be looking for something."

"Who told you they didn't take anything?"

Doug's eyes widened and then shifted away. He shrugged. "I guess I just assumed they didn't because no one mentioned theft."

"Ah, yes. The jungle drums." Chase let the silence stretch, trying to explore the source of his unease. "Well, as best as we could tell, nothing was taken. And actually, they didn't destroy much, either. A few broken ornaments, but not wholesale destruction."

"Wonder what they were after." Chase said nothing, and Doug waited a moment before lowering his voice confidentially. "Do you think they were after the papers?"

"Could be."

"I guess they didn't find them."

"I don't really know. I don't remember where they are." He couldn't explain why he didn't tell Doug that his gut feeling was that the papers were still wherever he'd hidden them.

"Sure. Dumb question. You'd think I was the one with amnesia."

Chase smiled, but he couldn't put any real warmth into the conventional gesture. He glanced at the clock again and stood up. "I really have to get home. I didn't like leaving Gwenn, even with Maggie to keep her company."

Doug got to his feet. "Sure. I don't blame you." He reached out with his blunt fingers to toy with a letter opener that lay on the desk. "You know, I've always really envied what you and Gwenn have. I just can't seem to come up with anything that lasts. Maybe it's because after they made Gwenn, they broke the mold."

"Could be." Chase made a conscious effort to relax his white-knuckled grip on the folder he'd picked up. Doug had never made any secret of his admiration for Gwenn. Why was it so annoying all of a sudden? He shook his head, trying to clear the ache from his temples. Maybe it was just because his own relationship with Gwenn was so unsettled right now.

He grabbed his suit jacket from the back of the chair and shrugged into it, anxious to get out of his office. The big room seemed to have shrunk all of a sudden, and he felt claustrophobic.

Doug followed him out into the hallway, shoving his hands into the pockets of his pants. "I guess I'll see you around, Chase."

"I'll be back to work in a couple of days." Chase punched the button for the elevator and tried to decide why it was that he wished it was Doug's nose he was punching.

He stepped into the elevator with a feeling of relief, lifting a hand in farewell. As the doors closed, shutting off his view of Doug's rather doleful expression, he dismissed the man from his thoughts. He had more important things to think about than why he found himself so short-tempered with Doug.

Last night's talk with Gwenn had left him with a lot to think about. He'd left before she was awake this morning, grateful that he didn't have to face her until he had a chance to cope with all the conflicting emotions running around in his head.

Now he was on his way home. He'd be seeing her in a matter of minutes, and he was no closer to knowing what to say to her than he had been earlier today.

His mouth twisted in a rueful smile as he stepped out of the elevator. Being totally confused was beginning to seem almost normal.

Chapter 13

An unacknowledged wound cannot heal. Hidden away from the fresh air, it will gradually fester and poison its host. But, once brought out into the open, the very act of admitting the wound exists has a cleansing affect, allowing the healing process to begin.

Talking about past hurts did not wipe the slate clean for Gwenn or for Chase but it allowed the wounds to start healing. There was still tension between them but now it was caused more by uncertainty than anger. Neither of them knew where their relationship was headed.

As long as Chase's full memory remained elusive, the past was still too much with them to allow them to predict where the future would take them. They walked carefully, trying not to disturb the tenuous balance they'd achieved.

The tensions were different than those they'd dealt with over the last two years. For one thing, this time, they both admitted that the tension existed—there was no pretending that everything was just fine.

And there was a new sexual tension between them. Making love had made them sharply aware of each other. That awareness had been smothered by anger and hurt for a while but once the anger began to fade, the awareness slipped in almost unnoticed. Though they never mentioned the second time they made love, it was there between them, adding to the already existing tension.

Chase found himself watching Gwenn. When she sorted through skeins of wool for her needlepoint, he would remember the feel of those fingers on his skin. If she licked her lips after eating a juicy orange, his mouth would tingle as if tasting the tart juices on her tongue.

In the past two years of their marriage, he'd hardly touched his wife: a kiss on the forehead at Christmas, a helping hand under her elbow when they went to the theater. On some deeply buried level, he'd been aware that there were a lot of sexual needs going unfulfilled. But at first he'd been dealing with his own grief, and his needs had been for human contact far more than sex.

He'd dealt with his grief by burying himself in his work. Perhaps if he'd forced Gwenn to talk about what they were both feeling at the time... But there was no sense in wondering what might have happened if they'd handled things differently. They could only go forward from this point in time.

And right now he wanted Gwenn with an intensity that made him wake in the middle of the night, shaking with need. No matter how many times he told himself that there were things that had to be settled in their relationship before they made love again, his body hadn't quite gotten the message. It didn't care about anything but slaking a long-denied thirst in the soft welcome of Gwenn's body.

But that had to wait. Now was not the time for letting physical ties affect their relationship. So they hovered in a never-never land between intimacy and distance—sharing some confidences, keeping some secrets. Sometimes they acted like total strangers, and at other times they talked with an intimacy that's only possible between two people who know each other very well.

"How are things going at work?"

At Gwenn's question, Chase glanced up from his meal, meeting her eyes for a moment before looking away. They'd come a long way in the week since their home had been torn apart, but they both retained a tendency to avoid eye contact.

"Not bad."

Gwenn watched him take a bite of salad and restrained an urge to sigh. There was so much distance between them. She picked through her own salad, stabbing a sliver of tender ham and putting it in her mouth. But she might have been eating old leather for all the taste it had. They'd seemed so close while they had been putting the house back in order. Even when they hadn't worked in the same room, there had been the feeling of a shared goal holding them together.

But it had taken only a few days to straighten up the mess. Now they were back to exchanging polite conversation over the dinner table. It wasn't fair to complain, she told herself firmly. They'd come so far in a relatively short period of time. Two years of hurt and misunderstanding couldn't be wiped out in one night of talking or a few days spent cleaning house.

Intellectually she understood that, but emotionally she was impatient and anxious to get on with their lives. She found a piece of Muenster and chewed it absently. If Chase could only trust her enough to share his feelings a bit. Whenever she asked him how he felt or how things were going at work, he answered with a noncomittal "just fine" and let the subject drop.

"You're supposed to eat the lettuce, too. That's what makes it a chef's *salad*."

She blinked, really focusing on her plate, which she had systematically denuded of cheese, ham, egg, tomato and everything else, until there was nothing left but a pile of rather lonely-looking lettuce. Her eyes came up to meet the amused green of his, and she shrugged sheepishly.

"I guess I wasn't paying much attention."

"I guess not."

The moment of shared amusement seemed to relax the faint tension that had gripped him since getting home from work. Gwenn could almost see his muscles unknotting. She wanted to offer to massage the last of the tightness from his neck, but they weren't quite to that point.

She dug her fork into the pile of lettuce. Patience, she told herself. It was a lot like working a complicated piece of needlepoint. You had to have patience and believe that the finished result was going to be worth the effort you were putting into it. Her marriage was worth any amount of effort it took.

"What would you think if I told you I'm thinking about resigning from the company?"

The question, both its content and the fact that he'd opened to her enough to ask it, stunned Gwenn into silence for a moment.

"Johnson Industries?"

"That's the only company I work for, isn't it? Unless there's something else I've forgotten." He poked moodily at his salad, his eyes on his plate.

"Why? You've been with them since college. I thought you liked working there."

"I did. But I'm not sure it's what I want to do anymore."

Gwenn set down her fork, her meal forgotten. This was the kind of confidence she'd been hoping for, praying for. A pile of lettuce was hardly competition.

"Is this something you've been thinking about since the kidnapping?"

"Yes. But I was thinking about it before then." He pushed his plate away. "I wasn't thinking specifically about quitting, but I knew I wanted a change. I wasn't happy anymore. I knew part of it was because things weren't right between us, but that was only part of it. I don't think I want to be an executive and sit at a desk for the rest of my life." He shrugged self-consciously. "I don't know. Maybe I'm going through a midlife crisis."

"Maybe. But a person's goals can change. Maybe yours have."

"The problem is, I'm not sure I *have* a new goal. I've reached the top where I am. The only step up the ladder is Charles's job, and even if he were to retire tomorrow and I could step into his shoes, I don't think that's what I want. He lives and breathes Johnson Industries. He's sacrificed everything to it. His wife rarely saw him, and his son hardly knows him. He doesn't have any hobbies or interests outside the company. I don't want that."

Gwenn let the silence stretch for a moment, trying to choose just the right words. He'd opened up to her, and she wanted to be absolutely sure that she said the right thing.

"If you're not happy there anymore, then you shouldn't stay," she told him slowly. "But you've been under a lot of strain lately, and I'd hate to see you do something you might regret later."

Chase shook his head sharply. "I'm not planning on doing anything right away. For one thing, until I regain the rest of my memory, I'm under a certain amount of suspicion regarding the schematics. I can't leave until that's all cleared up. Even if that would be straightened out tomorrow, there's still the matter of catching the people behind this mess. I'm not going anywhere until I know who they are."

His eyes settled broodingly on the table. "I don't even know why I brought it up. It's just an idea. Who knows if anything will come of it?"

"Sometimes it helps to talk about something you're not quite sure of," Gwenn said hesitantly. She didn't want to push too hard, too fast.

His gaze lifted to her face, and his mouth twisted in a faint smile. "You always were a good listener."

"Not always. There were times when I didn't want to listen." Her eyes were smoky with regrets. Chase reached across the table and touched the back of her hand lightly.

"There have been faults on both sides. But you can't go back and change things."

"I know. I just hope..." Her voice trailed off. She was afraid to voice her hopes, as if saying them out loud might jinx them.

"I know." His fingers tightened over her hand for a moment, and then the contact was gone, leaving her feeling both warmed by his touch and chilled by its loss.

He picked up his fork again and began to eat. Gwenn followed suit, but she had the feeling that he wasn't tasting his food any more than she was. She cleared her throat, searching for a topic to dispel the charged atmosphere around the table.

"Maggie and Robert want us to have dinner with them tomorrow night."

He nodded, and she had the feeling that he had needed a change of topic as much as she did. "Sounds good to me, as long as neither one of them is cooking."

"That's a terrible thing to say." But the protest was perfunctory, and there was a tinge of amusement behind it.

"It's a matter of survival. I remember your brother's cooking from college and, believe me, I don't remember it with fond nostalgia. It's a wonder we didn't all die of ptomaine poisoning. And the one time Maggie invited us to dinner, she cooked something nouvelle-nouvelle, and I almost starved to death. Three asparagus tips, a teaspoon of goat cheese and an endive, all in raspberry sauce topped with the merest hint of bitter chocolate."

Gwenn giggled, remembering his horrified expression when he'd realized that the meagerly filled plate was all he was going to get. "It was very pretty."

"So is a daffodil, but I wouldn't want to eat one. It was all I could do to keep from nibbling on the sofa."

"And when we got home, you raided the refrigerator and made the world's biggest ham sandwich."

"Which you were more than happy to share," he pointed out.

"I was just keeping you company."

"Sure you were. Is that why you ate the second half of it while I was pouring a glass of milk?"

She laughed. "It wasn't the whole second half. There were only a couple of bites left."

"My sandwich. My bites."

"Your face was hilarious. You looked like someone had taken the last bite of food you'd ever see."

"That's how I felt." His face was alight with humor. "But I got even."

"You tickled me until I was laughing so hard I could hardly breathe."

"Served you right. And then..." He broke off abruptly, his eyes widening as he remembered exactly what had happened then. Gwenn's breath caught, and her gaze locked with his as her memory presented her with vivid images.

Chase's mouth catching the laughter on hers, the warm taste of his tongue. And suddenly there was no laughter. There were just the two of them. The baby was asleep upstairs, the baby-sitter was long gone, and in the brightly lit kitchen, passion had flared as quickly as it ever had in the darkness of their bedroom.

His hands were impatient with her clothes; her blouse was torn open, her skirt pushed roughly up, and her panties were dragged carelessly downward. She was delirious with the sudden explosion of passion. There was the chill of the counter against her bare bottom and then the heated pressure of his hands as he slid her forward, his hips arching up until they were joined.

A pin dropping would have sounded like an explosion in the sudden quiet. The memories were as vivid as if it had happened only yesterday. Gwenn's skin felt flushed, and a warm pressure settled deep in her belly. Chase's breathing was a little too quick. He lifted his hand as if to touch her face, and Gwenn leaned forward, as eager for his touch as she had been on that years-ago night.

Then the phone rang.

The sound was as startling as an elephant's trumpet at a wedding. Chase jerked his hand back, knocking over a bottle of salad dressing. Gwenn jumped to her feet, tipping her chair over in the process. The sound of it hitting the floor was still echoing in the room as she snatched the phone off the hook and muttered an incoherent greeting into the receiver.

It was a woman trying to get her to take a subscription to one of several magazines, none of which she wanted. By the time she hung up the phone, her breathing had steadied, and she was able to turn and give Chase a calm, if distracted smile.

"Just someone peddling subscriptions." She moved back to the table and set her chair to rights before picking up her half-eaten salad. "Shall I tell Robert that we'll meet them for dinner?" She scraped the plate into the sink, wondering how she could sound so calm when her stomach was still quivering like unset Jell-O.

"Sure." Chase cleared his throat, as if his voice didn't want to work quite right. "We'll meet them at the restaurant. I assume we're going to a restaurant?"

"I don't think either of them is going to try and prepare a meal. They suggested Mexican food, and I told them that sounded fine."

"Fine. Fine." There was a long silence, and then she heard his chair scrape back. "I think I'll go... ah... take a shower, unless you'd like some help with the dishes?"

She shook her head. "You made the salad; I can load the dishwasher. Besides, there's not much here."

"Fine. I'll... ah... see you later."

Gwenn nodded without turning her head and then stood in front of the sink, with the water running uselessly down the drain, straining her ears for the sound of his departure. It was more a sudden feeling of emptiness in the room than an actual sound that told her he had left.

She sagged against the counter, setting the plate down beside the sink and then wiping her hands on a dish towel. Emotions still ran so strongly between them. Desire and need and, she hoped, love. They had to be able to build on what they still had. She couldn't bear it if they couldn't.

If Chase had thought that a few hours away from Gwenn would soften the impact of last night's memories, he was proved wrong the minute he saw her dressed to go out to dinner. After he'd left her in the kitchen the night before, he'd spent more time than he cared to remember standing beneath the cold hard spray of the shower. Then he'd lain awake all night, trying to forget that she was just a few feet away across the hall. All day at work he'd been haunted by the memories of her scent, her taste, her touch.

Now what little distance he'd managed to gain was lost beneath the impact of her beauty. Midnight blue silk swirled around her calves, and narrow straps crossed her shoulders, leaving an enticing amount of skin bare. Her hair was piled on top of her head, leaving a few inviting wisps free to caress her neck.

As she walked down the stairs toward him, he felt like a drowning man going down for the third time. He wanted her so badly. He ached with the wanting. He was sinking in her spell, with no help in sight, and a part of him didn't want to be rescued. He wanted to take her and hold her and never let her go.

Gwenn stopped on the bottom stair, her eyes wide and uncertain as they met her husband's. She couldn't read his expression, and there was something there that she wanted to read. Some change that seemed significant. Before she could decide what it was, he cleared his throat and tore his gaze away from hers, patting self-consciously at his pants pocket.

"I've got the keys. Are you ready to go?"

"Did you let the guard know what's happening?" She picked up a soft cashmere stole she had draped across the banister earlier and settled it around her shoulders. The night air was finally beginning to cool off a bit, though it would be late October before it was likely to get really cold.

"I told him. He'll follow us to the restaurant and try to look inconspicuous."

On the way to the restaurant, Gwenn kept looking at Chase, trying to gauge his mood, trying to decide what it was that made her feel as though something had changed. If he noticed her questioning glance, he didn't acknowledge it. He kept his eyes turned firmly toward the front, guiding the Aston Martin easily through the Friday evening traffic.

The evening was not an unqualified success, but it wasn't exactly a failure, either. The meal was excellent, and as always, Robert and Maggie were wonderful company. Gwenn was delighted with their obvious closeness. She knew from talking to Maggie that the relationship was progressing by leaps and bounds, but this was the first chance she'd had to really see them together. Whether they knew it or not, she didn't have any doubt that they were deeply in love.

She was happy for her brother and best friend, but she couldn't help but feel a twinge of envy as she watched them. She and Chase had once looked much the same. As though all they'd needed was each other, and the rest of the world was superfluous. But the rest of the world had a nasty habit of intruding.

She took a sip of her margarita, resisting the insidious wave of melancholy that threatened to sweep over her. It was sometimes hard to remember all the wonderful times she had shared with Chase. The good memories were so overlaid with the bad.

Across the table, Maggie offered a bite of her meal to Robert, smiling softly as he murmured something for her ears alone. Gwenn lifted her drink, drowning the twinge of pain with the salty-sweet taste.

Her eyes sought Chase. Was he remembering the days when every touch, every glance had been filled with a meaning known only to the two of them? His gaze was also on the couple across from them, and his expression was brooding. Gwenn said nothing, but he seemed to sense her eyes on him, and he looked at her.

There was so much in his eyes, so many things she couldn't interpret: pain, memories, loneliness, need. It was like seeing to the center of his soul, and Gwenn shut her eyes, unable to bear the impact of so many emotions. When she opened them again, he was still looking at her, but his gaze had left her face to skim over the silky skin of her shoulders.

She nibbled uncertainly on her lower lip. Was there something wrong with her dress? His eyes dropped lower and seemed to dwell for an inordinate amount of time on the shadowy cleavage exposed by the softly draped bodice. When his gaze swept up to meet hers, Gwenn's breath caught at the warm fires that simmered in his eyes.

Her eyes shifted uncertainly, and when they came back to his, he was picking up his fork, his attention apparently all for his meal. Had she imagined that look of desire?

As the meal continued, it became more and more difficult to keep track of the conversation or eat her food, or to do anything except be aware of Chase. The heat of his body next to her in the booth made the jalapeños seem cool in comparison.

If Robert and Maggie hadn't been so absorbed in each other, they might both have wondered what was wrong with the other couple. Chase had little to say, and his eyes had a tendency to settle broodingly on his wife. Gwenn alternated between talking feverishly and absolute silence.

Once or twice she caught her brother's eyes on her questioningly, and each time she gave him the most reassuring smile she could muster. At another time, it wouldn't have been enough to fool him, but Maggie was a potent distraction, and he had other things on his mind besides the state of his little sister's marriage.

By the time they left the restaurant, Gwenn felt as if she'd been flayed, leaving every nerve ending exposed. Chase's fingers felt like hot coals as he helped her with her shawl. He kept his hands on her shoulders, holding her in front of him as he spoke to Robert. Gwenn was vaguely aware that Robert had suggested they finish off the evening with some dancing and that Chase was politely refusing, but there was a hum in her ears that made it difficult to follow the conversation.

She bid goodbye to Maggie and Robert, and thirty seconds later she had absolutely no idea what she'd said to them. It must have been all the right things, because no one seemed to find her behavior odd.

Chase kept his hand under her elbow until he saw her seated in the car, and Gwenn was torn between feelings of relief and loss when the contact was gone. If only she could read his thoughts. He wanted her, she didn't doubt that. But was it because he loved her or because she was physically desirable?

She huddled deeper into her shawl as she contemplated the sad truth, which was that she'd take Chase however he came to her right now. She was hungry for him, and felt emotionally and physically starved for his touch. If only the physical hunger could be satisfied, she'd settle for that. At least for the present.

It was a short drive home, and all too soon Gwenn was standing in the living room wondering what to do with herself. It seemed too early to go to bed, but it was too late to do anything else. She heard Chase's voice in the hall and knew he was talking into the portable radio Robert had provided, telling the guard that they were in the house and everything was secure.

She heard him enter the room and turned slowly. The one lamp cast deep shadows across his face, picking up the reddish lights in his hair. His eyes were unreadable, shielded by his lashes, and she could only guess at the expression in them as he studied her. She cleared her throat nervously.

"Well, I guess I'll go to bed." She winced inwardly at the falsely bright tone. He stood in front of the doorway, and she moved forward, trying to look as if she hadn't a thought in her mind but sleep. Chase said nothing, and she found herself thinking an incoherent mix of pleas and questions.

Is he going to stop me? Will he say something? Ask me to stay? Tell me he wants me? Oh, please, don't let me walk out. Say something.

She came level with him. One more step, and she'd be out the door, beyond his reach. Alone. She couldn't breathe. He was going to let her go. He didn't want her enough to ask her to stay.

His hand reached out to catch her upper arm.

Gwenn stopped. She didn't turn her head, didn't move.

There was a tension in the air that could almost be seen. Her chest ached. Her vision was blurred. For just an instant, she thought she might faint. It was like starting a fall down a steep hill and having someone snatch her back at the last moment.

She slowly turned her head until she could look up into his eyes. He said nothing, only continued to look at her as he lowered his head. Their eyes were locked, and every movement seemed to slow to half its normal speed. She just had the time to notice the tiny lines beside his eyes, the shadow of a day's growth of beard on his cheeks.

A kiss, she told herself, that's all it is. Just a kiss. She could smell the woodsy fragrance of his cologne, and a faint, indefinable scent that was only his. If she never saw him again, she'd still be able to close her eyes and remember that scent, and Chase would be as clear as if he stood right in front of her.

His eyes were endless green pools that beckoned her to fall deeper and deeper into his spell. A kiss. Just a kiss. But it was becoming difficult to think coherently. She could feel his breath on her mouth. He was only a fraction of an inch away, and she'd die if he didn't touch her soon.

Then his mouth touched hers, and the world exploded into a thousand spinning pieces.

Her lids fell shut as he used his hold on her arm to tug her off balance until she fell into his arms. Gwenn came up on her toes, burying her hands in his hair, molding her body to every hard inch of his.

His hands caught in her hair, tugging the pins loose until it cascaded through his fingers in a silvery blond fall. Her mouth opened, giving access to the marauding thrust of his tongue. His hands slid down her back, his fingers kneading her buttocks, pulling her into the rigid strength of his thighs.

Gwenn moaned, feeling him pressed against the heart of her need. Wanting him. Needing him. He dragged his mouth from hers, and his lips slid down the taut length of her throat, his teeth nibbling the sensitive skin as his fingers came up to tug at the straps of her gown.

She felt the straps give and whimpered with satisfaction as the bodice dropped to her waist and his lips closed hungrily over one swollen nipple. There was an instant where that was enough. The eager tug of his mouth at her breast gave her a moment's satisfaction. But it was only a moment, and then the throbbing demand that burned low in her belly demanded satisfaction.

Chase's hands were rough with the fragile silk, and she heard the harsh sound of seams giving way. But she didn't care. All that mattered was that he have access to her body and she to his. Buttons and zippers frustrated her fumbling fingers, adding to the trembling urgency of the moment.

She had to have him. Had to have him now! And suddenly the last barriers fell aside, and they were touching. Masculine hardness against her feminine softness. Flat planes against inviting curves.

She was delirious with the feel of him, steeped in the warmth and scent of him until she was aware of nothing else in the world. Nothing mattered but this moment. The two of them. Together.

Chase sank to his knees, taking her to the floor. The pile of clothing cushioned them as he rolled to put her on top of him. His fingers were almost bruising on her hips as he lifted her, positioned her and then lowered her.

A low wail broke from Gwenn as the emptiness was filled. Her moist sheath enclosed the heaviness of him as if made for him alone. She arched, her hair tumbling down her back as her nails dug into the furred surface of his chest.

She felt his fingers at her breasts, kneading, stroking. He thrust once, twice, and the world shattered around her. She gasped, her breath caught in her lungs. Her knees tightened against him; her body tightened around him. As if from a great distance, she heard a low guttural moan, and then his body surged upward, exploding within her, filling her.

For a long moment they were frozen, a still-life portrait of lovers at the moment of satisfaction, and then Gwenn slowly slumped foreward, her breath leaving her in a long sigh.

Chase brought his arms up to circle her back, holding her against his chest, burying his face in her hair. They lay that way, their clothes a tangled heap beneath them until at last he shifted. Gwenn moaned a protest as he moved her to the side and stood up. She was too limp to move, too exhausted to worry about the discomfort of the floor beneath her.

Before she could force herself into a productive movement, Chase bent and lifted her in his arms, and she snuggled against his chest. He carried her up the stairs and into the bedroom that once had been theirs. She'd turned the covers down earlier, and he laid her on the crisp sheets.

"Don't go." They were the first words either of them had spoken. Gwenn's fingers caught his when he would have straightened away from the bed. She didn't care that she was pleading with him. She didn't care about anything except that he stay with her.

"I'm just going to shut out the light," he told her huskily.

"Leave it." The invitation was unmistakable, and she read his response in the flare of his eyes. She tugged on his hand, pulling him down onto the bed. Her body, which had been so satiated a moment ago, was tingling again.

It didn't seem possible, but the second time was even more satisfying. Perhaps because some of the urgency had been dulled, leaving them time to make it a long, slow climb. Time to explore every nuance of their coming together.

Afterward, lying close against his side, listening to his breathing slowly steady, Gwenn let her fingers slide through the crisp hair on his chest. She wanted to know what tonight had meant to him. Did he love her or only want her?

"Chase, do you..."

He pressed his fingers gently over her mouth, and she tilted her head until she could see his face.

"Don't, Gwenn. Not now. Give it time. Give us both time. Don't ask too much too soon." She read the uncertainty in his eyes and knew that he was as uncertain of his feelings as she was of hers.

She let her lashes fall, concealing her disappointment. They were working on the rest of their lives together. She'd give him the time he'd asked for.

Chapter 14

Though nothing was said, as the days went by Gwenn became convinced that Chase didn't want to give up on their marriage any more than she did. There was a new warmth in his glances, an intimacy in his touch that she hadn't seen in years.

If they were taking tentative steps toward putting their marriage back together on a mental level, there was nothing tentative about its physical health. It was as if they'd been lost in the desert without a drop of water and were suddenly offered a chance to bathe in an exquisite pool.

Each night they slept cuddled together in the bed that had been Gwenn's alone for the past two years. They made love, rediscovering the intense physical compatibility that had once been such a part of their relationship. Each touch was intensified by the long drought that had gone before. Each sensation was magnified by the memories of two years of loneliness.

But as satisfying as their lovemaking was, the nights Gwenn treasured most were the nights when they didn't make love at all. The nights when Chase simply held her in his arms and they enjoyed just being close. Those were the times that gave her hope for their future together.

Though the police continued to guard Chase wherever he went, there was no sign of the kidnappers. Their identity and affiliations were still a matter of pure speculation, and unless the missing pieces of Chase's memory fell into place, it looked as if things would stay as they were. The company was slowly piecing the information contained in the missing documents back together. A few more weeks, and they'd be able to go on from where they'd been before the papers disappeared.

That was hardly consolation for Chase. As far as he was concerned, the bottom line was that *he* had taken the plans for reasons he couldn't even remember, and therefore he was responsible for the holdup in delivering a product to the customer.

He also wanted the people responsible for his kidnapping. Though the physical signs of his captivity had disappeared, he felt that the mental scars wouldn't be healed until the last of his memory returned and he would know who had tortured him.

He needed to be able to put faces to the nameless horrors that still caused him to wake in a cold sweat. Until then, he wouldn't be able to let go of the rage that simmered deep inside.

He had to be able to let go of the past before he could look toward the future. He couldn't ask Gwenn to give their marriage a second try until he felt confident that he knew just who he was. And how could he, when there was a whole chunk of time he couldn't even remember?

Chase pushed open the lobby doors and stepped out into the blazing heat of a September afternoon. He took off his suit jacket and slung it over his shoulder, using one finger as a hook. His eyes narrowed against the bright sunshine.

The more time he spent at work, the less he wanted to stay there. He owed the company his loyalty, at least until the schematics were either found or replaced, but he didn't think he'd be staying long once that happened. He tugged his tie loose and unbuttoned the collar of his shirt. Smog and all, it felt good to be outside instead of sitting behind a desk.

He scanned the parking lot, looking for the bright red of the Aston Martin, but the only red cars in sight were two Volkswagens and a Honda. He glanced at his watch automatically, but he knew he was early. Gwenn wasn't supposed to pick him up for another ten minutes. With the Porsche in the shop, she'd given him a ride this morning, taking his car so that she would have transportation to a meeting she had scheduled.

He could have gone back into the air-conditioned building to wait, but he didn't even consider that option. Once he was out of there, he wasn't going back in for anything short of a tornado. He lifted his hand to the guard who sat patiently behind the wheel of his dark sedan. The man had followed him to work this morning, and then, assured that Chase wouldn't be leaving the building, he'd left for the day, and returned when Chase was due to leave.

A boring life, Chase decided as he crossed the parking lot to the wide strip of grass and trees that provided welcome relief from the endless expanse of concrete. If he'd thought of it, he could have caught a ride home with the guard. He was becoming so accustomed to the silent shadows that he was inclined to forget they existed.

He set his briefcase down and dropped his jacket on top of it. Standing beneath the shade of a huge elm, he felt at least ten degrees cooler and a hundred times more relaxed. He stretched and loosened two more buttons on his shirt. Except for the fact that he was missing part of his past and was uncertain of the direction his future would take, he could have said his life was perfect.

"Chase!"

For a moment he couldn't move, couldn't even breathe. One word. A note of urgency in the voice. The sunny parking lot was suddenly darker, as if twilight had slipped in unnoticed. The name echoed deafeningly in his mind.

"Chase!"

The word reverberated as though it had come down a long, long tunnel. Distorted. Like a voice from a nightmare. He turned and it was as if he stood outside his body, watching the actions unfolding but not really connected to what was happening.

There was a blond man running across the parking lot toward him. Doug. Some fraction of his mind provided the name. The other man ran up to the Chase Buchanon who stood frozen. His face was flushed, and he was slightly breathless.

"Chase. Thank heavens I caught you."

From a long way away, Chase could feel his hand balling into a fist, could feel each nail bite into his palm. And then, the fist was moving. Lifting. And it smashed into Doug's chin. Doug's eyes widened in the millisecond before his head was jerked back with the force of the blow. He staggered, catching his heel on a sprinkler. And then he was lying on the lush grass, looking up at Chase.

And suddenly, it was all there. The missing weeks, the missing information. Chase had it all.

"My God. It was you."

He stared down at the man he'd known since childhood, feeling the barriers in his mind dissolve like mist before a brisk wind. Breaking away gently. No pain this time. The final pieces fell softly into place, leaving him complete. Whole.

"It was you."

"Have you gone nuts, Chase! Why did you hit me? If it's my cologne, I'll change it." But Doug's laugh cracked in the middle, and panic began to flicker in his pale eyes.

Out of the corner of his eye, Chase saw the guard running across the parking lot, his hand resting on the butt of his gun. Without taking his eyes off Doug, Chase gestured sharply, and the guard stopped at the edge of the grass strip, still alert and ready to defend his charge but waiting to see what would happen.

"What's going on, Chase?" Doug tried to sound belligerent, but he got to his feet very slowly, keeping a wary eye on Chase's hands.

"Why?" In some distant corner of his mind, Chase knew he should be angry, knew he *would* be angry. But his major emotion at the moment was bewilderment. And betrayal.

"Why what? You're not making any sense." Doug rubbed at his swelling jaw.

"Why did you set me up? Why did you try and sell out your own company?"

"My company? Don't you mean my father's most precious companion?" He broke off abruptly, as if aware of how much his bitter words revealed. He gave a strained laugh. "Besides, I don't know what you're talking about. You went through a lot, Chase. Maybe you haven't recovered as much as you thought."

"Shut up." The words were gritted between his teeth. Beneath the hurt, anger was beginning to boil up, and Chase found that it was all he could do to keep his hands off the other man. Once he would reach for him he knew he wouldn't be able to stop.

"Lieutenant Lawford is here, Mr. Buchanon," said the guard, moving closer to him.

Chase dragged his eyes away from Doug in time to see Robert's bright green Fiat turn into the parking lot at a speed that almost lifted the two left wheels off the pavement. A second later the little car squealed to a halt next to the three men, and Robert stepped out.

"What's going on?" He snapped the question out as he joined the small group.

"It was Doug," Chase told him flatly.

Robert's gaze swiveled to Doug, and the bigger man seemed to shrink, his massive shoulders hunching inside the tailored linen of his jacket.

"I don't know what the hell he's talking about. I came out to give him a message, and he punched me and now he just keeps saying that I've done something."

"Doug's the one who set me up." Chase kept his voice clipped and dispassionate. Cold rage burned in his eyes, making them an icy green.

"What do you remember?"

"Everything. I knew something was going on, and I suspected Doug was right in the middle of it. I'd decided not to say anything to anybody until I knew exactly what he was up to. There'd been a trickle of information turning up in the wrong places. Nothing major. Just bits and pieces. We've been working on a pretty revolutionary new radar system for the navy. It would have been devastating if some of the documentation was lost."

"This is ridiculous. You can't expect me to stand here and listen to this. He obviously needs a doctor." Doug started to turn, and Chase lunged forward, his hand coming out to catch Doug's wrist in a seemingly gentle grip.

"Take another step, and I'll break your arm."

Doug froze, feeling the power in those long fingers and a pressure that stopped just short of being painful. He turned slowly, his eyes meeting the arctic chill of Chase's before turning to Robert in a desperate plea.

"This is ridiculous. Surely you can see that he's had some kind of a relapse."

Robert studied him coolly for a moment. "Let go of him Chase." Doug started to relax, only to freeze as Robert continued, "Marco, if Mr. Johnson moves, I want you to shoot him. Don't kill him, but make sure he won't be going anywhere."

"Yes, sir."

The officer drew his gun and pointed it at Doug. Robert gave Doug a friendly smile as Chase eased his hand away. "Marco ranks as a Distinguished Expert with guns. He won't miss."

Doug turned pale, his eyes glued to the .38. "This is ridiculous." But all the bluster was gone from his voice. He was beaten and he knew it.

"Go on, Chase."

"I knew Doug was selling the information, and I had a feeling he was working his way up to bigger game. That last day I searched his office and got the last of the proof I needed. I went to engineering and took the documents and hid them."

He ran his fingers through his hair. "Stupid of me. I should have just called security, but I had this idea that maybe if I talked to Doug, I could get him to see the error of his ways. I wasn't thinking too clearly."

He rubbed the bridge of his nose, remembering the way everything had seemed almost surreal. The realization that a man whom he'd know since childhood, a man who'd been almost a brother to him, was quite probably a traitor had triggered a shutdown in his mind. He hadn't been thinking clearly, hadn't been able to reason things out very well.

"I knew it would just about kill Charles if he found out. I don't know how I expected to keep the knowledge from him. I took the papers and then called Doug to meet me. We were going to meet in the parking lot. I was standing by my car when I heard him call my name, and I turned around, and he was running toward me. I heard a noise behind me, and then it felt like my skull exploded."

He stopped, remembering what had come afterward. The questions. The demands. The pain. The details were blurry, and he suspected they always would be. Perhaps that was his mind's way of protecting him.

"You set me up."

Doug seemed to wilt, all the bravado going out of him. "They didn't tell me that they were going to hurt you. They were just supposed to keep you out of the way while I got hold of the papers. Only you'd already taken them."

"Doug, I have to tell you that you have the right to remain silent. If you give up..."

Doug gestured sharply, cutting Robert off. "To hell with that crap. You've got enough to hang me on his testimony alone. Besides, my father can afford the best lawyers. I'll probably get off with nothing more than a slap on the wrist."

Robert shrugged. "It's your choice."

"What the hell were you thinking of?"

Doug's eyes skimmed to Chase and then away. "I had some gambling debts. Dad had already told me that he wasn't going to pay any more, and they were threatening to start breaking fingers." His eyes dropped to Chase's hand, where the skin still showed traces of new skin, and the little finger was still slightly stiff. He flushed.

When he continued, his voice was sullen, like a little boy who'd been caught in a misdemeanor and resented being caught.

"I was sick of going to Dad for every penny. It's all going to be mine when he goes. Why should I have to beg for money? The guys I owed suggested that I could pay my debt with information. So I did.

"Everything had been going smoothly until you started snooping around. I could tell by the way you looked at me that you suspected something. The others were getting real nervous about you, but I convinced them to leave you alone. And then you searched my office, and I knew you must have found proof."

"It was pretty stupid to keep documentation of your dealings," Chase told him wearily.

"That was my insurance. They knew I had enough to put them away. When you called and said we had to talk, I knew the game was up."

"So you called your friends and set me up."

"They were just going to keep you out of the way for a while. And then, when we realized you'd hidden the papers, they said they'd persuade you to tell them where they were. They never said anything about torture."

"What the hell did you think they were going to do? Politely ask me to give them the papers? Did you think I'd just graciously hand them over? And then what?

"I knew you were involved. I knew all their faces. Did you think they'd just let me walk out?"

"They wouldn't have had to get nasty if you hadn't been so stubborn."

"Get nasty? That's a pretty weak term for what they did to me."

"Chase." Robert's hand closed over the bunched muscles in his friend's forearm. "Calm down. We've got him. And we've got other things to worry about."

With a conscious effort Chase relaxed, taking a step back, as if only by putting some distance between himself and Doug could he be sure he wouldn't go for the other's throat.

"What have we got to worry about?"

"Was Gwenn driving your car today?"

"What's happened? An accident? Is she all right?"

"It doesn't look like an accident. We found your car parked alongside the 210 Freeway. And we have a woman who called in and said she saw a black van force a red sports car off onto the shoulder of the road."

"Gwenn?" Chase could hardly get the name out.

Robert shook his head. "There's no sign of her. I think maybe Doug's partners have her."

Gwenn wondered if there were any documented cases of a person actually dying of fright. If not, she just might become the first. She took a deep breath, trying to slow the rapid pace of her heart.

From the first moment when she'd realized that she was being forced off the road, her heart had been beating double time. It was beginning to feel almost normal. Now she was sitting on the edge of a scuffed vinyl chair in a motel room that had definitely seen better days, and her pulse was finally beginning to slow. Not because she wasn't still frightened, but because the rush of adrenaline had eased.

She kept her eyes on the floor. She'd tried asking questions, and that had gotten her absolutely nothing. All she wanted to do now was to avoid drawing attention to herself. If she didn't look at her companions, maybe they'd forget that she was there. She didn't have to look at them to know what they looked like. One was tall with wavy blond hair and chiseled features. The other was short and dark. And there was a third outside, but she'd caught only a glimpse of him.

The room was motel-beige. The only spark of color was a rather bilious floral print that hung crookedly next to the door. The two men talked between themselves, unconcerned with the fact that she could hear every word they said.

"How long do you think it will take?"

"Johnson said to give him a couple of hours. He's got to get in touch with Buchanon and set the whole thing up."

"Can we trust him?"

"He's too far in to pull out now. We can trust him. All he wants is enough money to live in high style in Rio, and Buchanon can provide that."

Doug. Gwenn shivered. Doug had set this whole thing up. He'd apparently been behind Chase's kidnapping. She wrapped her hands around her upper arms, hugging herself. All the years she'd known him, and she'd never realized he was capable of something like this.

These men wanted the documents Chase had hidden. Doug wanted money, and they were going to use her as a bargaining chip. They must have been watching the house for weeks. They'd known that she had Chase's car. They'd picked a section of the freeway that was relatively empty to force her onto the shoulder. And even if there had been witnesses, by the time somebody could get off the road and get to a phone and call the police, they had been long gone.

They weren't making any effort to conceal their faces, and they must know that she could hear the names they were mentioning. They didn't care how much she knew, which either meant that they figured they could all get out of the country before the police could catch them or they didn't plan on her being alive to hand out descriptions.

She shivered again and took a quick breath to control the wave of panic that washed over her. She couldn't let this situation get the better of her. She had to hang on to her self-control and to the thought that Chase would be here soon.

She'd have to wait for him and hope that he had a way out. She'd already decided that there was not a whole lot she could do on her own. Even if she were an expert at some nice, lethal form of self-defense, she was dealing with three men with guns.

She'd make it through this, she told herself. She and Chase would both make it through this. And if she got out of this alive, she was going to tell Chase how much she loved him. It had come to her that she hadn't told him that yet. There was a part of her that hung back, afraid to risk that vulnerability, wanting him to take the first step.

Now all she wanted was a chance to tell him she loved him. A chance to feel his arms around her. And she was going to get that chance, she promised herself. She would come out of this alive.

For now, all she could do was wait for Chase.

Chase shut the door of the Aston Martin and stood beside the car for a moment. In his right hand he held a leather portfolio. The fingers of his left hand traced the deep gouges in the bright red paint. Robert said that it didn't look as though Gwenn had been hurt. Maybe she hadn't been hurt, but she must have been badly frightened.

He looked at the unprepossessing building in front of him. Gwenn was in there. His fingers tightened on the portfolio, and he had to make a conscious effort to relax them. Control. That was what would help Gwenn. He took a deep breath and snugged the belt that circled the waist of his jeans. A heavily embossed silver buckle clasped the dark leather. Not his style, he decided, but the men waiting for him probably wouldn't know that. And the transmitter that was hidden in the buckle made the ornate style necessary.

His eyes skimmed the cracked parking lot. There was a man standing beneath some unhappy bushes that bordered one edge of the building. Chase let his gaze skim over him, as if not seeing him. He dropped the portfolio, and as he bent to pick it up, he muttered the man's location, hoping that Robert was right about the power of the transmitter.

He couldn't afford to worry about that. The guard was Robert's problem. He had to think about Gwenn. He had to be sure she came through this unharmed, and God help them if she was hurt.

He started across the parking lot, keeping his pace easy. He needed to take all the time he could. The more time he could give Robert, the better. From the moment he entered that motel room, things would have to be played by ear because he had no idea what he was going to find. He didn't even know that Gwenn was here, though he'd specified that as part of the deal.

He stopped outside the door and drew a deep breath before lifting his hand and rapping briskly on the peeling paint. There was a brief pause, and then the door opened a crack. Chase kept his face expressionless while the man on the other side examined him. After a moment, the door opened just wide enough for him to slip through and then shut behind him.

The first thing he saw was Gwenn. She was seated in a chair next to the bed.

"Chase." She whispered his name and moved as if to get up. A sharp gesture from one of her captors kept her where she was, but nothing could dim the flare of hope that lit her eyes. Chase only prayed that he could fulfill that hope.

A quick glance was enough to tell him that she was unharmed although shaken up and probably scared half out of her wits. And she was in control of herself. He might need that.

The second thing he saw was the .45 automatic one of the men held with an ease that spoke of familiarity. He held his hands out from his side in obedience to a sharp gesture with the gun's muzzle, and the other man came forward and searched for weapons. Chase noticed that he was careful to stay out of his partner's line of fire.

Once assured that Chase was unarmed, the gun was lowered, but it wasn't put away. They weren't taking any chances. Chase was playing this one by Robert's rules, and he sure as hell hoped that he knew what he was doing.

"Is that the documents?" It was the tall blond man who spoke as he lowered his gun, and Chase nodded.

"They're here." He handed the portfolio over and then gestured to Gwenn. "I've kept my end of the bargain. Now I want my wife."

"All in good time, Mr. Buchanon. First, Julian will check to make sure that the documents are the correct ones." The shorter, dark-haired man moved to stand beside the blonde, taking the portfolio from him and unzipping it.

"So, Doug's guess was right. Your memory made a miraculous recovery when you knew your wife was in danger. He thought that might be just the incentive you needed to remember where you'd put the plans. I hope he made it clear that it would be a very foolish mistake to call your wife's brother."

"He made it clear." Chase hooked his thumbs in his pockets, careful to keep his hands well clear of the belt buckle. Gwenn hadn't said anything since she'd whispered his name. Her wide gray eyes hadn't left him since he'd walked in the room, and it was all he could do to keep from running over to her and taking her in his arms. He had to play this cool and easy. Both their lives depended on him banking down his rage. He had to give Robert time to take care of the guard outside, and he had to find some way to distract these two long enough for him to get to Gwenn.

"What would you have done if I hadn't regained my memory? Seems like quite a long shot to kidnap my wife."

"If your memory had remained stubborn, then we would still have had your wife as a bargaining chip. Just out of curiosity, where did you hide the papers?"

"They were in the spare tire on my car."

Anger flared briefly in the man's eyes. "So we had them in our hands today when we stopped your wife."

Chase nodded coolly, and after a moment the other man shrugged. *"C'est la guerre."*

The dark man was still poring over the papers in the portfolio, and Chase hoped they looked right to him. Would he be able to tell that there were pieces missing, things skewed slightly?

"You don't mind if I smoke, do you?" The blonde had used his left hand to pull a pack of cigarettes out of his shirt pocket, and tapped the pack on the gun barrel until one slid out.

Chase felt cold sweat break out along his forehead. Goose bumps came up across his shoulders as he watched the flame catch on the tip of the tobacco. Nausea churned in his stomach, and it was only sheer willpower that kept him from throwing up. He dragged his gaze from the glowing tip of the cigarette to meet the malicious amusement in the chill blue eyes behind it.

"More memories?" he inquired politely.

The cool contempt in the question made it possible for Chase to shake off the recollection of those eyes laughing at him while the stench of his own singed flesh had made him retch.

"Nothing important."

The discreet electronic beep seemed unnaturally loud in the small room and the blonde's fingers tightened around the gun, lifting the muzzle slightly. Trying to look unconcerned, Chase lifted his wrist to look at his watch.

"The alarm on this thing always has had a mind of its own," he remarked casually. Out of the corner of his eye, he saw Gwenn frown in confusion, and he held his breath, waiting for her to say that his watch didn't have an alarm. But she said nothing, and he gradually relaxed.

Robert had the guard. Now all he had to do was figure a way to get these two goons off their guard and get Gwenn to some position of relative safety.

"This is all your fault, you realize."

Gwenn's eyes widened in stunned surprise. He hadn't spoken to her since he'd entered the room, which she'd understood. But she hadn't expected his first words to be a reproach. "My fault?" Her voice came out in a croak.

"I told you not to take my car this morning. Maggie could have taken you to work."

"But..." What was he talking about? It had been his suggestion that she take the Aston Martin.

"If you'd done as I asked, you wouldn't have gotten yourself into this damn stupid position."

"Stupid?" That was exactly how she felt. She must be delirious, or maybe she was unconscious, and this was all some kind of bizarre nightmare. She closed her eyes, hoping to get a grip on reality. But when she opened them again, she was still sitting in the same room with the same three people, and Chase was still glaring at her.

But there was something in his eyes. Something beneath the apparent irritation. A plea?

"Stupid?" She could only repeat the word while she struggled to come to terms with this apparent insanity.

"Stupid. I told you I didn't want you taking my car, but you threw such a fit about it."

"A fit?"

"Do you have any idea what it's going to cost to get the dents out of the driver's side?"

"You can't blame me for those. *I* didn't hit the ear." This whole thing didn't make any sense. Everything was turned around, and yet she knew instinctively that the only thing to do was to go along with this madness.

"But if you hadn't taken the car, there wouldn't have been any scratches on it." Chase saw that both men were watching the confrontation. The blonde's eyes were amused. The dark man seemed indifferent. Chase moved a step closer to Gwenn. "This is the last time you borrow my car."

"You don't have to get so nasty about it." It wasn't hard to call up a hint of tears. Hysteria was only moments away.

"Nasty! I think I'm being fairly restrained, considering what this is costing me." He took another step. Just a little closer. "The car is the least of my worries. Do you have any idea how important those documents are? Do you know what this is going to do to my career? Did you think Charles would just blithely hand them over and tell me to use them to save your life?"

Another step.

That was exactly what Gwenn did think Charles would do, but that obviously wasn't the answer Chase was looking for. She shook her head silently, biting down on her lower lip to keep from screaming at the total madness of this whole situation.

"When these things turn up on the market, he's going to realize that I sold the company out. I'll be lucky if I don't end up in prison for the next forty years."

Another step. He was within range now. *Stand up, Gwenn.*

As if hearing his unspoken plea, she shot to her feet. Tears streamed down her cheeks, and her eyes were wild and unfocused. "I don't care about your job, and I don't care about those stupid papers, and most of all, I don't care about your damn car!"

"I might have expected that."

Yes, he had their full attention. The gun was dangling loosely. They weren't worried about what their captives were doing. They were enjoying the show. He inched forward another few inches. Gwenn had put her hands to her face and was trying to choke back sobs, but he couldn't worry about that right now.

"You never have cared about the consequences of your actions." He was only half aware of what he was saying. Blondie first. He had the only visible weapon. "Robert raised you to be a spoiled brat." Robert would know that it was almost time. He had to make this work. There wouldn't be another chance.

"Now!"

His foot caught the fair-haired man in the stomach, shoving him into the other man, knocking them both off balance. He didn't wait to see what would happen from there. He spun around and lunged for Gwenn, who was staring wide-eyed. He heard her breath whoosh out as he caught her around the waist and hurtled her onto the bed, rolling across the sagging surface until they both fell off the other side, twisting so that his body sheltered Gwenn.

There was an ugly splat of sound above their heads, and little bits of plaster rained down on top of them. A crash was heard as the door exploded inward, and then the wonderful sound of Robert's voice.

"Hold it! Drop the gun!"

There was an instant of silence so intense that Chase could hear his own blood rushing through his veins. Beneath him, Gwenn was so still that she hardly seemed to be breathing.

And then came the muffled thud of a gun hitting the carpet.

"Smart move." All the tension was gone from Robert's voice, and suddenly it was all right to breathe again.

Chase lifted his head to look down at Gwenn and thought he had never seen a more beautiful sight than her tear-stained face.

"Are you all right?"

She nodded dazedly. "I think so. Is that Robert?"

"Cavalry to the rescue." He laughed shakily and dipped his head to kiss her on the nose. "Have I told you that I love you very much?"

Gwenn blinked up at him. Had she just heard what she thought she'd heard? Had he told her that he loved her?

"What?"

"I love you." His mouth skimmed over her damp cheeks. "I've been so stupid. Holding back all this time. I should have admitted it weeks ago."

In the background, Gwenn could vaguely hear her brother's voice reading her former captors their rights, but it seemed so far away. It didn't really seem relevant to her in any way.

Chase's mouth found hers, and she responded automatically to the urgency in his kiss. She wiggled her arms free of his weight and threw them around his neck, holding him tight. She was safe. They were both safe. That knowledge was only just now beginning to sink into her brain.

They were both safe and Chase loved her.

She finally dragged her mouth away from his, drawing in gulping breaths of air. "How... why?" She couldn't seem to put together a coherent sentence. All she could really concentrate on was the warm light in his eyes. A loving light that she'd thought she might never see again.

"I'll tell you everything you want to know later. Now all that matters is that I love you."

"I love you, Chase. I never stopped loving you, even though it may have seemed like I did for a while."

This time their kiss was slow and tender, a loving affirmation of what they felt for each other. A renewal of their wedding vows. A promise for the future.

"Excuse me. I hate to break up this tender moment, but this doesn't seem like exactly the right time or place for this kind of thing."

Chase dragged his mouth away from Gwenn's and rolled onto his back. Robert leaned against the end of the bed, a study in indolent ease. Only the broad grin on his face spoiled his casual pose.

"You always have had a lousy sense of timing," Chase complained. He got to his feet and reached down to help Gwenn up, throwing his arm around her shoulders to hold her close to his side.

Robert shrugged. "Sorry." He looked from one to the other, his gaze bright with questions. "It's pretty obvious that neither of you is hurt. Can I take it that you've straightened things out between you?"

"You can take it any way you like." But Gwenn's smile was all the answer her brother needed.

"Well, if you two are through, I don't see any reason to stay here any longer." He stepped back, gesturing them through the door ahead of him.

As Gwenn stepped out into the warm dusk, she felt as if she was leaving all the bad memories behind and walking into a bright new future. She looked up at Chase, her smile wide. "It will feel good to get home."

His arm tightened around her. "I think I'll carry you over the threshold." And she knew that he felt the same way she did.

She took a deep breath. The whole future was laid out before them, and this time they knew how easily their love could be lost. They wouldn't make the same mistake again.

Epilogue

I thought Maggie was the most beautiful bride I've ever seen." Gwenn's voice was wistful, as she remembered how exquisite her friend had looked as she walked down the aisle.

"You were much more beautiful." She flushed with pleasure and leaned her head back against her husband's arm until she could look up into his face. "Do you really think so?"

"Definitely." He brushed his mouth across hers and then settled her more firmly against his stomach. They were sitting in front of the fireplace in their living room. A small fire crackled on the hearth, casting the only light in the shadowy room. Outside, rain fell in a soft curtain, blocking off the rest of the world. It wasn't really cold enough for a fire; March was the beginning of the Southern California spring, but the cozy atmosphere was worth the mild overheating.

Besides, Chase had come up with a delightful way to stay cool. Gwenn snuggled back against his chest, enjoying the feel of him against the skin of her back. Wearing nothing but a pale lilac teddy, she was comfortable.

"Do you think they'll be as happy as we are?"

"Nobody could possibly be that happy," he murmured against her ear. "When you come close to losing something, it makes it even more precious than it was before."

She giggled as his teeth nibbled on the lobe of her ear. There were a few moments where the only sounds to compete with the fire were soft sighs, and then Gwenn dragged her mouth away from his and stared back into the heart of the fire.

"How's Doug?" The muscles in Chase's arms tightened and then relaxed. Gwenn sat up straight as he moved to fuss unnecessarily with the fire. For a moment she thought he wasn't going to answer her question.

"Charles says he's doing as well as can be expected. He's not really set up to cope with prison, but he's more of a survivor than any of us could have guessed."

"How's Charles holding up? He seemed to have aged so much when he came to dinner last week."

Chase shrugged. "It's not easy knowing that his son was prepared to sell out the company. Doug didn't really care where the information went—he just wanted the money. All in all, I think Charles is doing remarkably well.

"Johnson Industries has always been his first love. He's throwing himself into the job of salvaging our reputation, putting the company back on a premier level. I don't doubt that he'll manage it."

"Was he upset when you told him you wanted a leave of absence?"

He turned to look at her, his smile rueful. "Not at all. He said he didn't want to see me make the same mistakes he'd make when he was my age. Said that I should take my beautiful wife on a long trip."

"I'm glad. I know you were worried about hurting him."

"That's why I waited as long as I did to tell him what I wanted. If I still want out of the company when we get back, I don't think Charles will fight me."

"Good."

He set down the tongs and moved back into his old position, with his back against the sofa, his wife snuggled in his arms. "Are you sure you don't mind leaving the shop for a few months? You've worked very hard for that place. I don't want you to feel like you have to sacrifice it just because your husband is having a midlife crisis."

"You're not having a midlife crisis. You're just taking time out to make sure you've got the right goals. And the shop will be just fine. Robert and Maggie will be back from their honeymoon in two weeks, and then Maggie will be able to run the place very competently. As my new partner, she has just as much of a stake in the place as I do."

He nuzzled her hair for a moment and then leaned his cheek against the top of her head, savoring the feeling of her in his arms. They sat that way for a long time, neither of them speaking. It was Gwenn who finally broke the cozy silence.

"Maggie says that she and Robert have decided that they want a child right away." She felt the sudden tension in his arms and swallowed hard. She'd been trying to find the courage for this for weeks. Tomorrow morning they were leaving for a lengthy driving tour of the country, and she wanted this issue out of the way before they left.

She drew a deep breath. "I was thinking that maybe we might want to consider the same thing ourselves." She rushed the sentence out.

Chase's arms tightened around her until she could hardly draw a breath and then they relaxed suddenly. His hands moved to her shoulders, turning her until she faced him. Her eyes flickered over his face, but the uncertain light of the fire made it impossible to read his expression.

"Gwenn, is this what you want?"

She nodded.

"Really, truly what you want? You're not just saying this because you think it will make me happy?"

"This is really, truly what I want, Chase. For a long time after Livvie was killed, all I remembered was the hurt. But then I started to remember how much she gave us. She was such a happy child, and we're richer for having known her. But that isn't enough anymore."

"Be very sure, Gwenn. We can't get Livvie back. I'd give anything in the world if we could, but we can't. A new baby isn't going to be like having Livvie again."

"I know. I want a baby, Chase." She took his hand and pressed against her stomach. "I want to carry your child, and I want to see your face when you feel it move for the first time. I want to feel your son or daughter nursing at my breast and know that it's a living, breathing creation of our love."

Chase's palm cupped her breast, his thumb brushing across her nipple. Gwenn was mesmerized by the look in his eyes. She'd never felt so beautiful, so desirable, so loved.

"Maybe we can work on this while we're on our trip." He let his hand slide around her back, easing her down onto the rug. His fingers nimbly worked the tiny buttons that held the teddy together, spreading the fragile silk open to bare the softness of her breasts.

Gwenn moaned as his tongue flicked lightly against her nipple, teasing it into a taut bud. Her fingers delved into the thickness of his hair. "Maybe we could start working on it tonight," she whispered breathlessly.

"Maybe we could. But most of all, tonight I want to work on showing you just how much I love you."